I0691272

# THE CURVE
# OF THE LAND

## DIANA DURHAM

SKYLIGHT
PRESS

© Diana Durham, 2015

First published in Great Britain in 2015 by Skylight Press,
210 Brooklyn Road, Cheltenham, Glos GL51 8EA

All rights reserved. Except for the quotation of short passages for the purposes of criticism and review, no part of this publication may be reproduced, stored in a retrieval system or transmitted, in any form or by any means, electronic, mechanical, photocopying, recording or otherwise, without the prior consent of the copyright holder and publisher.

Diana Durham has asserted her right to be identified as the author of this work.

Designed and typeset by Rebsie Fairholm
Publisher: Daniel Staniforth
Cover photos of Chûn Quoit by Jonathan Guilbert. Background texture by Sascha Duensing.

**www.skylightpress.co.uk**

Printed and bound in Great Britain by Lightning Source, Milton Keynes.
Typeset in Adobe Caslon Pro.

British Library Cataloguing in Publication Data:
A catalogue record for this book is available from the British Library.

ISBN 978-1-908011-92-3

# ✿ PROLOGUE

Aʟʟ down the western flank of Britain, where the land branches and frays out into the sea as if trying to blend with the salty waves, are found large numbers of ancient megaliths. In the Highlands and Lake District, down the rocky backbone of the Pennines, across the Border Country, Wales and the south west peninsula, standing stones, stone circles and dolmen survive from a time before record. Though the grandest structures of Stonehenge, Avebury, the Rollrights are found in the plains and meadow lands of the west country, nowhere is there a greater concentration or variety of megaliths than in the furthest western tip of Cornwall.

The winds blow almost constantly over this small curve of land that forms the top half of England's claw-foot. The winds come out of the west, very often bringing rain that sheets horizontally across the land for months on end in winter, sometimes bringing storms that boil up the seas to thrash against the dark cliff heads. These violent, rearing cliffs support the hard, high granite plateau that forms this land, almost an island, joined to the rest of Cornwall by a strip of marsh only four miles wide between Hayle on the north coast and Marazion on the south. From this eastern border to the point of Land's End is about ten miles, and nowhere is more than three or four miles from the sea.

The southern part of this area is softer and more lush than the north, sheltered from the first strike of the winds and seas. Early vegetables are grown in its protected coves and valleys, cream tea served to summer visitors. In the more desolate north, the sea winds have sculpted the land to their own shape, and it rises in a series of smooth curves of moorland, floating like broad backed waves under the sky. What few trees survive are bent permanently over into the curve of the land. If you drive along the north coast, or cut down along the small roads that traverse these moors, it is easy to see where the sculptor Barbara Hepworth, who lived close by in St Ives, drew her inspiration from. The terrain is echoed in many of her sculptures: smooth, rounded shapes, staked out by telegraph poles, chimneys of old mines and by the plentiful tors and standing stones. In the villages the grey stone houses huddle together, enduring the winters of rain, the storms, the hard times – but nothing has endured longer than the ancient stones.

St Ives, on the north coast, and Penzance, in the south, are both fair sized towns, brimming with tourists in the summer; yet despite their proximity, and despite the smallness of the area, it is possible to experience an extreme remoteness in the district of Land's End, formerly known as

Bolerian or Bellarian, and now as West Penwith. The remoteness is due to depth of antiquity, not distance in miles. This accumulation of time passed, of century layered upon century, is embodied in the stones and rendered into a touchable continuity by their presence.

Legends and rumours about these megaliths are as plentiful as the stones themselves. The giants built them, some of the stone circles are maidens turned to stone for dancing on a Sunday, many sites are entrances to the underworld, they are the haunt of spirits or ghosts or worse, lights can often be seen around them, from the faery folk, or the dead. Most of these stories are embedded in the distorting amber of folklore. Any strange encounters or experiences at these places are ephemeral – they exist only as one person's story, non-verifiable, non-recordable. Occasionally an account is collected in a book, even reported in a local newspaper, especially if the eye-witness is deemed reliable.

This was how the larger world, to the extent that it took any notice, was informed of one such event. A reporter from the *Penzance Gazette* was drinking a last beer with some of the locals in a pub at Morvah when in walked a pale and wide-eyed farmhand, Eric Morsby. He was shaken up, yet, after a beer and a whisky chaser, happy enough to have an audience for his amazing tale.

Chûn Quoit is a massive stone dolmen set on lonely moorland above the cliffs of West Penwith's wild north coast. A huge, curved granite capstone is supported by four upright slabs that lean inwards as if forming the stem of a giant mushroom. The area around the monument contains many remains of ancient settlements, and the Quoit itself stands slightly downhill from a stone enclosure known as Chûn Castle. Eric Morsby was standing on the seaward part of the slight slope that led down from this 'castle' to the Quoit. He was staring out into the twilight, trying to make out the pale shape of a sheep that had strayed from its safe field. The Quoit was crouched and dark against the pale sky. To Eric Moresby its rounded granite mass was as familiar as any other part of the landscape and he paid it no special attention, until, that is, he saw a ball of white light suddenly burst out of its capstone. At the same time there was a loud violent noise, like a gun retort or a thunderclap, that reverberated out over moorland and sea. Forgetting about the lost sheep, he turned and ran back along the path as fast as he could, jumped into his dilapidated van and accelerated off down the bumpy lane.

The reporter, who knew Eric as a steady, unimaginative type, was impressed and thought his story worth at least a picture of the Quoit and a longish caption. And unusually, one of the nationals, it being a slow news day, reprinted the story, minus picture, in a small slot on one of its inside pages.

# ℘ CHAPTER ONE

Jᴇssɪᴄᴀ could not take her eyes off the goddess. She had not expected this from a workshop, even one entitled 'Descent to the Goddess: Shamanism for Women'. The bare wooden floor of the Hampstead church hall was draughty but Jessica, clad in leotard and track suit pants, did not notice. She had never seen such a metamorphosis. Jessica did not consider herself much of a workshop enthusiast: her normal reluctance was due not so much to conservatism as to a horror of pretence. One or two previous experiences had made her very wary of workshop leaders and attendees who seemed content to wax lyrically effusive about faked experience. What Jessica craved was authenticity, and here it was staring her in the face. The woman was in her late 40s, with cropped white hair, strong, dark eyebrows and a large mouth. Her eyes were closed in concentration, her mouth open as she inhaled and exhaled, making a terrifying noise like the death rattle. Dressed in a black leotard and loose skirt, she was kneeling on the floor, her arms back supporting her leaning body. She was a big woman, tall, full-bodied yet graceful. Slowly, as if no longer under her control, the woman's neck arched back and up, her head dropped, her legs moved sinuously under her and she gradually twisted over and around onto her front. All the time uttering the strange breathing noises. She had embodied the dark goddess: not good, not bad, not lovely, not ugly, just completely disruptive.

The atmosphere in the dimly lit hall was charged. An extreme discomfort had taken hold of the half dozen or so other women who were watching along with Jessica. To witness such complete abandon seemed taboo, as if one were present at the Eleusinian mysteries themselves. Yet it was impossible not to look, and in watching, to be drawn deeper into the necessity of participating, because to observe and not to be immersed oneself would indeed be a profanity. However, the growing realization that they were soon going to be asked to do the same was an appalling thought. The movements, the sound were so 'other', they fitted into no familiar context. Jessica had done exercise routines before – aerobics, pilates, yoga – but it had all been from the mind, controlled. This was all or nothing, it could not be faked, came from another place altogether, one that had been banished a long time ago. As they sat there transfixed and helpless, flashes of differing emotions shot through the group, from incredulity to anger.

After what seemed an age, the woman stopped her strange breathing, opened her eyes and slowly untangled herself from the position she had landed up in.

'Phew.' She shook her head, rubbed her eyes and smiled at her motionless students. 'That's what I call the dark goddess energy. We need to contact that.' Cora was hugely impressive, Jessica realized, not only because of her ability to move as she had, but also in the way she could nullify the reactions that smouldered like lit fuses in her workshop participants. 'Come on, you start moving, listen to your blood stream, listen to your neurons – they want to do new things.' She spoke with a Californian accent. This was no English woman. Awkwardly, the others tried to do the same. They were self-conscious, frightened even. 'Close your eyes, don't worry about anyone else – we're all here in love, we're all here to become naked…'

Jessica closed her eyes and leaned back. The doubts and inhibitions that would normally have filled her seemed to have been moved out away from her, as if the goddess had been able to blast a clearing within her psyche. The woman was moving slowly, still half-dancing round the room, touching the others here and there, guiding, encouraging.

'Let go here – that's it. Suzanne, you're doing it but you're not really doing it are you?' She put her hand on the pelvis of a woman with dark glossy hair cut into an immaculate bob and a frown on her face.

'Cora, I'm not sure I've got this right,' said a red-haired woman in her early 40s, who also sounded American. Cora walked over. 'There's no wrong or right, just relax, think of your breath as a wind, blowing through the cave of your mouth, your body, shaping stone. We're talking micro-movements, letting your body move. You can't do it wrong.'

The sound of breathing intensified. Cora turned the lights down and put on some music. She continued to move round the room, talking, almost chanting. 'We are descending down into the realm of Ereshkigal. We are Inanna, all the loveliness of earth, of light, of woman, going down into the darkness, through stone and earth, before time, deep into the body of the mother; stripped down, facing the eyes of death, hung on a meat hook to rot.'

Jessica was only half listening. In the dim light, with her eyes shut and her body on the cool bare floor, she lay peaceful, still. She wanted to stay like that, a secret pool of water unrippled; but obediently, if reluctantly, she tried allowing her abdomen to move in little, fluttering spasms. She dropped her jaw and let out air, a gasping, rattling breath against her throat, she inhaled deeply, and let the air out again.

'We must die to ourselves. This death is deep healing, it goes beyond all those things that fracture us into pieces – time, schedules, housework, relationships, our jobs, our names, where we came from – all these things are meaningless in this realm...'

Jessica allowed her arms to slide out to the side and over her head. She tried her thigh, the thigh bone and the buttock, letting them arch and roll over. Her breathing became more rhythmic; the room was full with the sound of hoarse breathing and bodies slithering in slow motion across the floor.

'This is what we must look at, this is what we must reconnect with, that invisible and dark flow of ourselves, our source of being, the great mother energy, the mystery of earth and birth, from where we had our beginnings. We must face Ereshkigal's wrath for our forgetfulness, we must own her again, include her, love the side of ourselves that is always her. And this is how we regain our power...'

Her eyes now fast closed, Jessica felt as if she were being pressed through stone, claustrophobically crushed into small passageways. She began to be frightened that her breath would have no more room to move and she would die but then the pressure eased and she was suspended in black space, sprinkled with tiny points of flashing light, the energy nuclei of her body. A black streaming wind pushed through gently across her chest, a silver breeze fanned down through her face and neck, a small eddy formed in her stomach. She had no idea how or how long she had been moving when Cora's voice was heard over the swishing and gasping sounds.

'OK, when you feel ready, open your eyes, and come to a sitting position. Slowly, slowly, take your time.' The music faded and was cut.

Jessica opened her eyes. She felt wonderful, renewed. Cora came and sat with them, folding her long, big legs under her. She smiled: 'Any words?'

But there weren't many.

'Few words, but we had an experience?' They all nodded.

'Very good, well thank you, dear ones, perhaps it's time.'

Their clothes were strewn on the chairs that lined the old church hall. As they got dressed Jessica approached Cora. 'Cora, that was great, I've never done anything like that before.'

'Well, it's not something that I bring in immediately.'

'I had an amazing experience. I was surprised, I thought I'd have to have done it for longer or something. How many more sessions will you be able to give?'

'I need to get my dates sorted out, I think my tour starts in a few weeks – isn't that right girls?' Cora looked over at the other American woman, who Jessica now realized was one of a pair, both overweight, both red-haired, both wearing turquoise T-shirts. They nodded in unison.

'Yes, so we've got some more time yet.'

'Oh good.' Jessica looked across at the dark-haired girl who'd been frowning. 'She's going on an amazing tour – of ancient sites, isn't it Cora? With some guy who lectures about them and strange lights and things?'

'Earth lights, yes.'

'Oh?' Suzanne did not seem very enthusiastic. Watching her, Jessica suddenly had an idea. 'I know Cora, you must come to dinner when Paul gets back. Suzanne and Steve are coming and you can tell us about it then.'

Jessica and Suzanne walked down the traffic-choked Hampstead Hill to the tube station.

'What d'you think of it?' asked Suzanne. 'I mean I'm not sure how much is imagination.' Jessica tilted her head to hear against the noise of engines running in neutral.

'I think it's very subtle, but if you get it, it's really releasing.'

At the kiosk outside the tube station Suzanne bought some chewing gum while Jessica hesitated over a glossy magazine and bought a newspaper instead. The lift arrived while they were buying their tickets and they ran through the barrier as the doors were just starting to close. There was no one else down on the dimly-lit, stuffy platform and their words echoed in whispers through the curved space.

'So how long's Paul been away now?' asked Suzanne.

'God, it seems like ages, six weeks. I'm feeling quite odd about it really,' Jessica replied.

'About what?'

'Seeing him again.' Jessica was aware that her brief phrases reflected her reluctance to examine more closely the multiple issues which had arisen in her while Paul had been away. But she also realized that Paul's imminent arrival would soon force her to confront both him and her complex feelings.

The electronic notice board blinked the yellow message that a train was approaching.

'He's due back soon?'

'The end of this week, that's what I heard last anyway.'

The train pulled into the station and they moved towards the nearest set of opening doors. The carriage was full, and they had to stand, hanging on from the handcords.

'How often have you heard from him?' Suzanne went on. Jessica found her unusually persistent. Jealous of her own privacy, Suzanne rarely pried into others' lives.

'Well, when he's in a town, he phones quite often, but out in the more remote areas, you know, it's difficult.'

'So you have been in touch.'

'Oh yeah, he rings me to find out if his car is OK.'

'Oh come on –'

'I'm serious, he does.'

'You mean that's all he asks about, he isn't interested in how you are?'

'No, but he does always ask me about the bloody car.'

Suzanne giggled delightedly. 'But you have missed him?'

'At first I did a lot.'

'But then it feels good to be on your own again, I understand that.'

Suzanne had to change at Camden Town. She started to fight her way out of the carriage. 'See you soon.'

'OK, bye.'

Just how good it had felt to be on her own was in fact a source of some anxiety to Jessica. It was true that she had missed Paul, but only for the first two days. After that, she had experienced a growing exhilaration at a newly claimed – or reclaimed, she wasn't sure which – sense of freedom. She felt parts of herself spring back into shape, parts she did not realize she had pressed out of her shape. She began to discover ways in which she had allowed herself to grow dependent on Paul by suppressing sides of herself that subconsciously she did not think he would recognize or understand. It was a subtle form of self-censorship, but potent for being so subtle. She had tried to mould herself into his world, with his values, and neglected her own.

Paul's immaculate, poppy-scarlet, fuel-injected Golf GTI, reluctantly left in Jessica's care while he was away, now symbolized for her the conflict between them. For Jessica, learning to drive had been an important achievement. Tasks that grounded her in the physical world were both assuring and challenging. Driving never became second nature for her, it was always exciting, and a bit frightening. She had been dismayed to discover how much better she drove when Paul was not in the car with her, tense with apprehension, barking out abrupt commands and criticisms. When he was there, her confidence ebbed away, she became infected by his anxiety and unable to think clearly or respond competently. On her own she drove faster, reversed accurately into tight spaces, not out of skill so much as intuition, and felt sharply aware of everything around her on the road as she played Mozart's operas (which she could not play when Paul was in the car as he loathed them) at full blast. She was amazed that she could have been so adversely affected by Paul, and was furious when he phoned from faraway places and asked: Was the paintwork intact? Had she scraped the hub caps?

Now she was starting to feel an almost intoxicating desire to get back to something in herself: an intuitive, mystical hinterland of vision which she had almost ceased to include in her life. As a result she had grown steadily more depressed and dependent on Paul for motivation. While he had been away, she had felt stronger, old vital energies that had been sapped returned. She recognized that none of this was Paul's fault: it had been her own doing. Nevertheless, despite this rational understanding she carried a minor current of resentment towards him and his limitations, which had also become clearer to her. She now felt equivocal about his return. She did not want to go back to her former censored and inert self.

Jessica got out at Kings Cross and walked through the bustling passageways to the Metropolitan line. This time the train was not so crowded and she got a seat. She pulled the newspaper out of her bag and glanced across the headlines. A new report on weed-killer in London's drinking water, Chernobyl revisited. The dismal news only returned her thoughts again to the problem of Paul.

When Jessica had first met Paul she had fallen madly in love with him. He was good-looking, dynamic and kind. He was a successful fashion photographer but he also wanted to use his talents to help expose, and prevent, the growing ecological crisis. His concern had grown until it seemed all consuming. He had met Jessica when she was upgrading from a temporary to a full-time job at Friends of the Earth. Jessica knew that if he'd wanted to, Paul could have had a lot of different women in his life, and was flattered that he wanted to be with her. Now she recognized that it was Paul's fastidious nature as much as his fondness for her that kept him monogamous. He did not like messy situations. He did not like hysterical women. He did not like ecological breakdown. He was obsessively meticulous with all his equipment: his camera gear, his car, while at the same time he disliked home-making, and was thoughtlessly untidy in the flat. But the real source of Jessica's new unease with their relationship lay deeper, beyond conscious articulation. She was hungry for something which Paul could not give. She did not want rationality and worthy causes, she wanted poetry; she did not want to be controlled, she did not want mentorship, she wanted soul and ecstasy.

Her thoughts made Jessica frown as she walked unseeing down the car-lined street and up to her massive panelled front door. She walked up the stairs still prickling with anger and turned the key in the lock. A shock went through her: she could hear the TV, and a familiar shabby Billingtons bag lay dumped on the floor, spilling out lens wipes and film canisters onto the newly vacuumed hall carpet. Paul was back, earlier than expected.

'Is that you love?' A fear touched inside her: would he be a stranger now? Her face was quizzical as she pushed her back against the door to close it and put down her bags. He was kind, his smell familiar but newly sensed as he hugged her. He didn't seem to notice her hesitancy; tired and happy he hugged her again. 'How are you then? Have you missed me?'

'I'm fine, I'm fine. Of course, did you miss me? How was your trip?'

'All right I suppose. Tiring, depressing.' She sat down next to him.

'You're back early.'

'Yeah, I've been here a couple of hours, I've even started going through my slides. I've got some great shots for the talk.' Paul was due to give one of a series of lectures on different ecological themes that Jessica was organizing under the banner of Friends of the Earth.

'Great.'

'Yeah.' There was a pause. 'Did you have to work late?'

'No, no it's my workshop night.'

'What workshop's that?'

'I thought I told you about it, it's that one about shamanism.'

'Oh right, dark goddesses and all that. You still enjoying it?'

'Yes, it's amazing.'

'So how are you Jessie, it's good to see you, it's good to be back.'

'I'm fine –'

'Is the car OK? I couldn't see where it was parked.'

'The car is fine too. I had to park it round the corner. Hey why don't I run you a hot bath and make you a whisky and lemon.'

'That sounds great.' Paul stretched out and looked at his watch. 'Let me just watch the news.'

'I'll go start the bath –'

'No, stay for a minute.' Paul put his arms round her and pulled her into him. Jessica felt more reassured. The sweet warmth of their closeness allayed her fears. Perhaps it would be OK after all between them. She stayed for a moment in this thought, then realized she was uninterested in the news as she had heard most of it already. She undid Paul's fingers and got up.

'I've seen this, I'll go start the bath.' She went into the bathroom, rinsed out the bath tub and turned on the hot-water tap. In the kitchen she filled the kettle and started squeezing lemons.

Paul lowered himself into the steaming water while Jessica, wrapped up in a large yellow towelling robe, sprinkled in essential oil of sandalwood. She handed him a glass of hot whisky and lemon and sat down in the white Lloyd Loom chair which she had so gleefully snapped up from the second hand furniture shop on the corner by the main street. She loved their bathroom precisely because it had just enough room for a chair. She also liked its plain tiled whiteness, now smudged by the steam.

'Aren't you coming in?'

'You enjoy it on your own for a bit.'

11

Paul lay staring at his glass, his face suddenly lined with fatigue. Jessica looked at him with a half-smile.

'Is that nice?' She liked indulging him in the pleasures she enjoyed herself.

'It's great. It's the first bath I've had in six weeks.'

'Oh no, really?'

Paul took another sip of his drink. His eyelids were almost closing. Jessica put her empty glass down on the window ledge. The alcohol, the hot steam, Paul's drowsiness all helped calm her. She took off her robe and stepped into the tap end of the bath.

'You're falling asleep.'

'Yeah,' said Paul, moving his legs apart to give her shorter ones room. 'Is it nice to have me back?' he said sleepily.

'Of course,' said Jessica.

Paul was still asleep when Jessica got up the next morning, but her patter from bedroom to bathroom to kitchen and back again, switching lights on, running taps, gradually woke him. He lay in the half-light, watching Jessica in her robe, in underwear, in clothes, opening drawers, examining her face, brushing her hair. A cloud of depression seemed to have invaded him on waking up. It hadn't been there in his dreams, coloured fragments of which were rapidly receding from recall.

'Do I smell coffee?' he mumbled. Jessica turned to look at him.

'You 'wake? Yes, d'you want some?'

'Mm.'

She brought two mugs in and sat down on the edge of the bed, angled towards him. 'How are you feeling?'

'Not too bad.'

'Did you wonder where you were?'

'No – no I don't think so.'

Jessica looked anxiously at Paul.

'By the way,' he said, rubbing his eyes, 'I talked to Steve yesterday. He and Suzanne are coming over on Saturday.'

'Oh yes, I want Cora to come as well.'

'Cora?'

'The workshop leader –'

'Why?'

'Why not? She's great, and I think Steve will find her very interesting –'

'I don't want a bloody dark goddess coming to dinner.'

'Well, it's too late now, I've asked her.'

'Why the hell didn't you ask me first?'

'She's my friend, I don't have to ask permission do I?' Jessica's voice was no longer soft.

'I'd just like a quiet evening, I don't want to have to deal with some maniacal Californian woman –'

'God, why are you always so negative?' Stung into anger by Paul's ill temper, Jessica was now almost shouting. 'Why can't you be a little bit more open? I'll tell you, I haven't missed you – I've found it very freeing to operate on my own, not to be undermined all the time –'

'Don't be so dramatic.'

'I'm not being dramatic, I'm being realistic. This is what I experience from you. I've realized a lot of things while you've been gone. The way you censor things, pour cold water on everything, never really talk about what's going on in you –'

'Oh God, here we go.'

'Yes, and there you go. Suppressing things again, ridiculing me. You want me to keep a certain shape so that you don't get impinged upon, threatened –'

'I suppose this is what you call a warm home-coming, lecturing me on all my vices –'

'Don't you try that, emotional blackmail. Anyway I think you've been more concerned about your bloody car than me, that's all you ever seemed to ask about on those expensive long distance calls.'

'What's your problem Jessica?'

'I've started to see that I've been undervaluing a whole side of myself by being with you, and that's not healthy –'

'Well no one's forcing you to stay here – if this Cora woman has shown you just how badly done by you are –'

'Don't patronize me. The fact is Cora is a friend and she's not frightened of her emotions. She doesn't suppress what she's feeling like you do. I can talk to her, which is just as well because I can't talk to you!'

Fury and a sense of failure stung tears into Jessica's eyes as her voice got higher and more out of control. She slammed out of the room feeling exhausted and unwilling to pick up the pieces.

Paul heard the front door slam and the flat fall silent. Jessica's anger had taken him aback, but he knew his mood had infected the situation and he dismissed what she'd said as part of a new fad. He lay inert in the bed, no longer able to sleep. The thought of getting up and doing things – unpacking, sorting through and sending off his slides, making phone calls – seemed to loom above him like a great mountain peak of effort, impossible to reach. He tried to find a little chink of pleasure in the day ahead to motivate him. The enjoyment he used to have from looking through his pictures was marred now by the pain of their content. It was irritating to him that Jessica seemed so uninterested in his trip. He wondered if she wasn't rather selfish: caught up in her own projects, forgetting about him and his world. These thoughts wandered through his mind in a familiar order. He wasn't sure about them. Without realizing it, he was still registering the impact of what he had seen on his trip. The enormity of the destruction, the horror of it. Up until now, his exposure had been in small doses. Jessica's apparent disinterest in his work stirred more than just irritation: it was somehow threatening, as if it undermined the partnership they shared in such important work. How could he do it all on his own? Paul leaned forward and pulled at the corner of the curtain, drawing out a thin rectangle of light. He lay back again, staring up at a pale grey sky, bright above rooftops. A few birds swooped past in formation. A jet droned across in the opposite direction, slow and clumsy on its long descent into Heathrow. Paul curled over on his side, blinked his eyes a few times and then closed them.

Distracted by their row and the image of Paul's face that she carried with her down the stairs, Jessica was unable to make up her mind whether to take her bike or go by underground to work. She preferred to ride and it was quicker; what's more, she hadn't ridden yesterday because of the workshop, but the sky threatened rain, and even though by now she was pressed for time, she felt the need to just sit impassively on the tube and recollect herself. After fifteen minutes or so, and several stops, of rather fruitless and blank thought, she decided she ought to read the newspaper she had bought the evening before. Dutifully she ran her eyes over the centre page feature on the long-term damage of Chernobyl, with pictures of desperate peasant women, maps and graphs showing the extent of radiation. In the bottom corner of an inside page a small square of print caught her eye with the title '"Close Encounter" Lights Frighten Farmhand'. It was a report of a sighting of a strange white light over a dolmen near a farm in the Lands End region of Cornwall. Jessica struggled to find a pen in the far corner of her bag and ringed the article. I must remember to show Cora, she thought.

Delays on the journey meant that she reached her destination awash with the gritty discomfort of being late. She couldn't find her ticket, dropped the paper that she had held but not read and debated in a manic way as she emerged at last into daylight whether she really had time to buy a coffee. She nevertheless hurried over to the narrow Italian sandwich bar, the sole redeeming feature of the traffic-washed wastes of Old Street. Inside, the gurgling roar of the large espresso machine dominated like a comforting promise, vindicating her decision. The father and son team processed the queue's requests with a speed born of expertise and enthusiasm and she was soon walking swiftly back along the street clutching a white paper bag and a polystyrene cup. She felt uneasy about the cup though, made as it was by one of the most polluting methods of production, and from one of the most difficult to break down materials. Many within FOE argued that take-away food of any kind was unacceptable. There were different levels of extremists, some were vegans and disapproved of leather shoes and belts.

Buffeted by the onslaught of heavy traffic on City Road, it seemed to take an age to reach Shepherdess Walk and its equally inaptly named tributaries, Nile and Underwood Streets. These were both very narrow and overhung by old, mainly empty warehouses of dirty, grey-blue bricks and stained, opaque windows. The mustard yellow corner building with its tree green door and plant-filled window stood out from the general gloom. She pulled open the large door and slotted the 'In' sign next to her name on the notice board, then ran up the three flights of stairs to her office. Like the rest of the building, the walls and surfaces of her office were painted a now grubby white. A few FOE posters adorned the walls, and there were one or two pot plants on desks and window sills, but the overall effect was strictly utilitarian.

The desk opposite was empty.

'Is Bill still away?' Jessica asked. A girl in trainers and leggings who was photocopying in the corner looked up and glanced at the polystyrene cup. 'Yes' she said. Bill was the Researcher for their campaign. He was one of the vegans. He was also a Buddhist and spent his weekends and most of his evenings running workshops and retreats. So busy had he been that he had requested sick leave due to stress.

'God, how much longer is he away for?'

'Don't know,' said the girl whose name was Tracey. She was American, a temporary Campaign Assistant, who regarded Jessica, the Assistant Campaigner, as jaded and unprofessional. Jessica was aware of Tracey's attitude toward her, partly because Tracey did little to hide it. When the girl had first come to work in their department, Jessica had found it unsettling and hurtful to be so readily judged and dismissed. However, latterly she had grown immune to such feelings, realizing that Tracey, filled with the same enthusiasm she herself had begun her job with two years before, was in part right.

Jessica sighed impatiently. She felt scratchy from her row with Paul. Against her better judgment she said out loud 'What's the use of spirituality if you can't cope with your job?'

Tracey didn't answer. Jessica registered irritation. Surely it was more important to turn up for work, albeit late, and drink coffee out of polystyrene cups than to stay pure and not show up at all.

With her thick, honey-coloured hair and soft brown eyes, Jessica was a pretty woman – pretty, and a little self-indulgent. Her sharp, peripheral vision of awareness occasionally glimpsed this weakness and tried to correct it. She wanted to be worthy, to make a contribution to the embattled planet and not simply while away her life in feminine self-absorption, but increasingly she was no longer sure how to do this. She was intrigued by the maxim, first put forward over ten years ago by Theodore Roszak and now seminal to a million self-help and spiritual growth approaches, of personal responsibility, that changes in the world reflect changes in individuals. This idea excited and stirred her. She turned it over in her mind like a smooth, hard pebble in her pocket. Intuitively she felt the rightness of it, but with her customary anxious self-examination, wondered what exactly it meant.

The flyer for Cora's workshop, pinned to the notice board by the tea and coffee urns, had intrigued Jessica when it claimed that deep inner change was its aim. A large number of women who worked at FOE were feminists, and there were many politically slanted lectures or workshops to do with women getting equal, assertive, positive and usually slightly Marxist. To Jessica's mind there was something dirge-like about them, a litany of complaint about women's lot, to which she was not sure she subscribed. But there was another brand of women for whom the Earth was Mother Earth and they were working to save her from the onslaught of the male patriarchy. One of their number, whose opinion Jessica valued, had recommended the workshop to her, so she had gone along, hoping that this might be one way to start finding out how to effect changes in herself, and thus in her world.

The workshop had begun while Paul was away and both it and Paul's absence had heightened her awareness of changes that had already occurred in herself, without, it seemed, any conscious effort. Apart from her other concerns with their relationship, Jessica had realized that without Paul's enthusiasm for her job, she was able to get more in touch with her feelings of exhaustion and futility. Friends of the Earth's campaigns and lobbying tactics seemed to gain inches of ground, while whole continents were going down the drain. Her anger at the destruction had slowly been replaced by a kind of numbed perplexity. Why was the human race so hell bent on laying waste the planet? Sometimes she even started to worry that the more the green movements protested and tried to put the brakes on, the faster the killing machine went. She wasn't sure if her doubts and growing reluctance to throw all her energies into protest were due to a change in attitude in herself or just to the burn-out that most staff experienced after about two or three years of intensive campaigning. Her sense that there must be some strange flaw line running through the human race to cause them to behave, collectively, so irresponsibly, was intensified by the presence of the usual office politics and personality clashes within Friends of the Earth itself, which she found disproportionately distressing. She recognized that this was nothing unusual or outstandingly heinous: human beings everywhere, in large and small groupings, could not get on together. This was obviously not a new or original perception, but nevertheless Jessica's realization, emerging as it did out of incoherent and unprejudiced experience, was painfully new to her. Why were conflict and destruction apparently inevitable? Was it a function of an evolutionary 'law of the jungle', survival of the fittest at the expense of everything else? Was it natural for people to try, with varying degrees of subtlety and grossness, to destroy the environment and one another? Her thoughts trailed off into a mire of speculation. Jessica's mind retreated from the mire, but kept the question 'Why' always on alert, like a pilot light, ready at any flash of new perception to ignite manifold and more powerful jets of thought.

Jessica's annoyance at Bill's absence was tinged with an anxiety to know about the status of a planning application in the southern part of West Penwith in Cornwall where a local businessman was pushing to cut down an ancient piece of woodland, including a large number of centuries old oak trees, in order to develop an out-of-town superstore. The Cornish planning authorities were notoriously weak and ineffective, and the businessman was ambitious and contemptuous of what he saw as sentimental attitudes towards the environment which hampered progress and in particular the progress of his life's achievements. Bill had undertaken to report in detail to her. He was difficult to get hold of by phone, and she could not find any information about it in his files. To phone or write herself ran the risk of covering the same ground and prejudicing the planning authority against FOE. Not even a weak authority likes to feel that it is being pushed around by a third party outside interest.

Jessica had a personal investment in the case: as a child brought up in a suburban enclave of a provincial town, her imagination had been opened up and nourished by holidays in Cornwall. Steeped in vivid memories of what had been literally magical places to her, the seas, cliffs and caves, the moors, with strange craggy stones on them, and the softer southern curves of fields and woodland, Cornwall still felt like sacred ground to her adult consciousness. Through all her growing up, she dreamed of living there, but had to make do with a small semi-wild wooded area not far from her home, where she frequently walked with her parents or played with friends. The trees in this small wood became her friends and her love of nature led much later to a fascination with the Celts and their traditions of magic, and ultimately to a history degree with a thesis on the Celtic reverence for the oak and mistletoe. Evanescent memories, intimations of magic and academic research all now coalesced in the clear conviction that to cut down ancient woodland to build a supermarket was sacrilegious, and must be prevented.

'Tracey, did Bill ... Do you know anything about a planning application in Cornwall – erm, it's a Mr Pascoe ?'

This time Tracey merely shook her head. Jessica glared at her back. She should have done the work herself, she thought, as she rifled helplessly through the papers on Bill's desk.

Jessica gave up on her search and started to go through the post on her desk instead. There were several lengthy, impersonal letters from the Department of the Environment replying to some of her queries. Covering their tracks with long sentences, she thought.

'Is Peter in meetings this morning?' Tracey nodded.

Peter Mason was the Campaigner. He was dedicated and hard working, but unable to deal with people. He would not fire Bill, but hinted that he would like Jessica to do it, and he put up with unco-operative insolence from Tracey. He was zealous however in defending his campaign territory, and as there was considerable overlap with the Water, Wastes and Toxics, Transport and Rainforests campaigns, there was also plenty of confusion and conflict between him and the other Campaigners.

Jessica pushed the letters to one side and applied herself to the report she was writing on the proposed sell off by the Secretary of State for the Environment of key National Nature Reserves, and threats to other wildlife habitats, including ancient woodlands. She was hoping to get it finished in good time before she went away. She and Paul had planned a holiday in Cornwall soon after he had been due to return. Quite apart from her annual longing to return to the sea-drenched peninsula, Jessica now attributed new importance to their plans: hopeful that the time away might give them space to review themselves and their relationship. However her pending absence added to her anxiety about the threatened woodland near Penzance: with Bill away as well, she was worried that any restraining action on the developer would come too late. Furthermore, she would not be able to include any definitive outcome in her report. Jessica emptied her cup. As the dregs of the cappuccino drained across its bottom, they threw into relief a message: 'No CFCs: Ozone Friendly'.

Jessica was swimming into a cloud of bubbles. The swimmer in front of her was not fast enough to put distance between them. There was no room to overtake in the narrow lane in which everyone was instructed to swim in anti-clockwise rectangular circles, and she had to break her pace to stay in the bubble exhaust and not get entangled in the girl's thrashing legs. Strangely enough it was quite enjoyable to be massaged in the stream of bubbling water. She was coming up to her 20th length and could afford to slow down. The pool had been steadily filling up as the number of her lengths mounted, it would be a relief to be finished and no longer have to dodge underwater bodies. When she reached the shallow end again Jessica stood up and pulled off her goggles which stuck so efficiently around her eyes that they left dark circles under them, giving her an owl-like look. She glanced around for Suzanne and saw her still swimming unhurriedly, head floating dry above water, in the 'Any Stroke' slow lane. Jessica waded over, ducking under the dividing ropes. 'I'm finished, see you inside.'

Suzanne smiled and nodded.

The showers were powerful and hot. Jessica revelled in the sensation of the warm water, her mind in abeyance. It always took her ages to rinse the shampoo out of her thick hair, and by the time she was getting dressed, Suzanne had caught up.

'You got time for coffee?' asked Jessica.

'Ooh yeah.'

Suzanne had blow dried her hair back into its perfect bob, and was lining her lips with fuchsia lipstick. She and Jessica met quite regularly after work for a swim and a coffee. Suzanne worked as assistant to the Health and Beauty editor of a woman's magazine and had known Paul before he met Jessica, through photographic commissions he had done for the magazine's fashion pages. Suzanne had met her boyfriend, Steve, at one of Paul's parties. Steve and Paul were old friends from art college. The two men were very different in their make-up, but shared history and a certain ability to be frank – up to a point – kept them in touch. When Jessica and Suzanne grew to enjoy one another's company, this brought the two men together more and bound them all into one of those small and temporary communities that spring up and die down so readily between people who find themselves otherwise strangely isolated by life in a big city.

There was a brasserie around the corner, which, as spring warmed up, had started to open its doors out onto the street. It was early evening, still cool, and the two women sat not quite in and not quite outside the doors, benefiting from the warm air of the café. The traffic outside and the music from the sound system inside made it difficult to talk. They had to shout at each other.

'You're not rushing back home then?' commented Suzanne.

'No, I feel a bit like I used to when I was a teenager, you know? Trapped, nowhere to go.'

'Oh come on, it can't be that bad.'

'It must be, I don't want to go home.'

'Weren't you pleased to see him at all?'

'We rowed.'

'Oh dear.'

'Yeah, almost as soon as he gets back, we row.'

'Well, living with someone isn't easy.'

'How would you know, you don't live with Steve.'

'No, and that's why I don't, because it's a pain.'

'Very wise, very wise.'

'I don't know whether it's because I'm wise or because I'm lazy.'

'You mean you're avoiding something?'

'Yeah.'

'Like all those shirts you don't want to iron.'

'Exactly, exactly.'

Their faces creased into smiles as they giggled like teenagers. Suzanne lived in a light airy studio flat in Kentish Town, and worked in Shoreditch. She had fought her way out of an early marriage to a dashing but claustrophobically possessive young police inspector in her home town of Luton. Her main reason for marrying in the first place was to get out of her stifling suburban home. She came to London and temped. One day a spell with a large magazine publishing company led to a permanent job and eventually her current position. She was studiously glamorous, and thoroughly into all the new beauty products and treatments that it was her job to help cover. Her tiny flat was full of furry animals, with whom she seemed much happier to live than any smooth-skinned men.

Suzanne scraped the last milky foam from her cup. 'So what are you going to do?'

'I have to wait a bit and see. We're planning to go to Cornwall for a few days.

'Oh, how do you feel about that, do you still want to go?

'Oh yes, I do, I love going there so much, it's like I become myself, and that always makes things clearer for me and I think it'll give us some space to see where we are.'

Suzanne nodded. 'We're still coming to dinner though?'

'Oh yes, Cora's coming too.'

'Really?'

'Yes, that's what started the row, Paul didn't want Cora there as well.'

'Well she is a bit weird, Jess.'

'She's not weird, it's just that we're all very straight.'

'That's one way of looking at it I suppose.'

# CHAPTER TWO

PAUL stared with tired eyes at the screen in front of him. It was Saturday morning but he still felt the effects of his trip and a lingering jet lag. He was clicking through slides in quick succession: the green canopy of a huge forest; the same shot with clouds of white smoke billowing up out of the trees; acres of burning tree stumps; the sky in the background streaked blue and pink. There were several shots like this. With a grim expression on his tanned face, he clicked backwards and forwards until he settled on one. He made a note on the desk in front of him.

The pause made him remember something. He felt for his watch in his dressing gown pocket, then picked up the cream telephone at his side and punched out the number scribbled on a yellow Post-It note that was stuck to the phone. He pushed fine fingers through his dark wavy hair and squeezed his blue eyes shut and open, refocusing his gaze for a moment away from the glaring coloured screen to the bare black and white of his studio. Like the rest of his flat, the studio room was small, but high ceilinged, part of the divided attic floor of a large Victorian mansion on the outskirts of Notting Hill. The walls of the studio were white, the windows largely blacked out, the floor stripped and varnished wood.

'Hallo Steve? Hi, it's Paul', he said into the receiver. 'Yeah, I've been back a couple of days … I know, it's earlier than I expected.' Paul smiled into the phone. 'True, I mean you know, this stuff's really taking off now.' He looked up at the screen again, his smile gone. 'I'm actually making some money out of it, yes.'

The man Paul was talking to was sitting in an editing suite in Soho. Steve turned and lounged back in his leather swivel chair, his head outlined against a battery of TV screens from which a brain-numbingly fast and jerky sequence of images hurled themselves: huge mouths, orange-lacquered guitars, legs sprayed with black leather outlined against purple clouds of dry ice, hieroglyphs, pyramids, clouds speeded up. 'Oh it's just a pop video, I'm helping some guy edit it. It's a lot of fun really.' Everything in the editing suite was caramel, cream and pale grey. Venetian blinds veiled the internal glass dividing walls. There were no exterior windows. 'Yeah, make a film about something real.' Steve leaned forward and touched a button. The frenzied attack of images immediately froze. 'The sad fact is, Paul, that there's no way I'd make a film about the rainforest. I'm sick of programmes about the bloody rainforest and so is everyone else.'

Steve was tall and lanky, with blond hair and pale brown eyes. He wore transparent framed glasses and his face had that clear, anonymous look of media people. His impersonal, detached air did not entirely conceal an underlying wary vigilance.

In his studio Paul creased up his eyes again and smiled wryly.

'What can I say, Steve, you're just a jaded old cynic.' Paul raised his voice to drown out Steve's reply, 'Anyway, we're going to be even more sick when we all start choking to death ...'

'And you're sinner turned crusader – they're always the worst. Don't you do any fashion stuff any more?'

'I'll probably still have to.'

'I hope so, it'll help modify your fanaticism.'

Paul laughed. 'Who knows, it could make it worse. Anyway, you guys are coming over tonight?'

'We certainly are, looking forward to it. How is Jessica? Happy that you're back safe and sound?'

'Good. Yes, I think so. I want to show you some of my slides, because Steve, I know you're right, one of the problems with the whole ecological scene is over-exposure, but I've got some ideas about how to do something with another angle on it. I think we've got to find ways to make the crisis seem manageable, focus on what can be done, give people some hope ...'

'Hey, I'm always open to talk ideas, Paul. You do some more thinking, and let's see if there's anything there –'

'Great, OK Steve, seen you then. Oh, em, Jessica's invited someone else along, some woman she's doing a workshop with –'

'Oh yeah, that's right, Suzanne's doing it too.'

'Yeah, I wasn't wild about the idea, but anyway, she'll just have to watch the slides as well ...'

'Sure, that'll work. See you later then.'

Paul put the phone down and went on clicking his slides. Tree stumps in bare, dead land; earth with three-foot-deep zigzag fissures in it where it had dried up; an aerial shot of a small Pacific island with a strange balloon shape attached to it, the top soil washing out into the ocean. Paul had been away for just over six weeks in Brazil and the Cayman Islands on his first major assignment covering ecological issues. The commission was a departure from his work as a celebrity and fashion photographer which he had been lucky enough to break into after leaving art college. The society and fashion world was fun, glamorous and well paid. Paul had flair, was attractively elusive and people, especially women, liked him. He had built enough of a name for himself that he was able to mount one or two successful exhibitions on landscapes, which had always been his enthusiasm. His travel to photograph both fashion and landscapes had alerted him firsthand to the ecological crisis both abroad and at home. He started to find out more. What he discovered made him uncomfortable with his lifestyle. He began to take occasional commissions either for nothing or for a low fee to help out the cause. He had met Jessica just over two years ago while doing one such job for a Friends of the Earth leaflet. The dedication and zeal which had seemed to burn in her with an almost spiritual quality, combined as it was with natural prettiness, affected him deeply. What's more she had an insight and an unsullied, bordering on innocent air, which contrasted refreshingly with many of the women he had known in the fashion world. She came to embody for him his new mission and start in life.

Paul made another note. He was picking slides to illustrate a talk he had volunteered to do for Jessica as part of a series of public lectures she was organizing under the FOE banner. He stared at the image of the island with its balloon of lost soil and registered an odd sequence of emotions. Professional pride and dissatisfaction were mixed with grief and depression. And then the slightly ridiculous perception that aerial shots could turn disaster into pretty but meaningless patterns: an island and its topsoil, its future, its life, became two connecting circles in the blue. Something about the view made him impatient, suggesting as it seemed to that there might be a completely different way of looking at the scene philosophically as well as physically. He decided he was too weary to continue, switched off the projector and the lights and went downstairs to see if Jessica had made any coffee. But she had already gone out shopping. Paul headed for the bathroom.

Jessica disentangled a shopping trolley from the long slotted line of them in the grimy underground carpark. Entering the noisy yellow space of Sainsburys, over-crowded as always on a Saturday morning, the lights made brighter by the gloom outside, she clutched at her shopping list for security, and tried to rationalize the lump of dread in her stomach. She always felt this sense of unease bordering on panic when she came to the giant supermarket. The underlying fear in all the other people there, faced with the rising price of everything and their dependence on this juggernaut food distribution system seemed to wash into her.

Today it was worse because she felt nervous about the dinner party that evening. Instead of relishing the purchase of special items for it, she found herself planning her shopping strategy like a grim terrorist. She dodged manically round the clusters of shoppers and the long, serried rows of goods, registering guilt and disgust. Was it guilt about hurting Paul, about inviting Cora, or guilt about her privileged position in a suffering world, about the mile upon mile of food stuffs, continuously replenished, swaddled in clingfilm, shrink-wrapped, boxed, bottled and tinned that stretched out around her in the glittering palace of plenty where huge lengths of open freezers consumed extra energy to battle with the heating system, while above them thousands of neon tubes glowed with bright, penetrating light.

Organic potatoes and tomatoes, salad, greens, grapefruit, wholewheat pasta, organic coffee, even some organic wine. Recycled loo-paper and kitchen towel, marmalade, chocolates, bottled water. Soon the trolley was looking alarmingly full. 'Can I have some help packing?' she asked the cashier. The woman called out 'Anita!' A plump woman in her thirties came over and looked vaguely at Jessica who was frantically unloading the trolley. She had carefully found two sturdy boxes and placed them at the end of the check out counter, but the blank-eyed Anita started pulling at the wad of coffee-coloured plastic bags.

'No! I don't want any more bags,' snapped Jessica, and started to throw things into the boxes. Anita was extraordinarily slow. Finally everything was out of the trolley and being processed through the laser checking machine. Jessica pulled the empty trolley through the narrow gap, her tension mounting with the pile of goods at the back of the cash desk. Furiously she started to make up for lost time, wedging in cereal packets next to butter, tins in the corners, soft things on top. She realized that Anita was part of Sainsburys' policy of employing people who had developmental problems. She felt ashamed and curbed her irritation.

'Thank you very much,' she said politely when they had finished and she had done the bulk of the packing. Anita just smiled enigmatically without looking at her. She might be slow, but she knew what had happened.

When Jessica got back home, Paul was in the bathroom. A trail of opened envelopes and junk mail littered the hall. She resisted the urge to immediately tidy up, and went into the kitchen to put the food away. It took her about an hour, balancing things precariously in the cramped cupboard space and small fridge of their galley kitchen. By then it was almost time to start cooking. Jessica put the kettle on for coffee, using just enough water, no more. As she was pouring the boiled water over the coffee grains, Paul appeared.

'Hi there,' he said, as if they were the best of friends.

'Hi.'

'Oh great, you making some coffee?'

'Yep, but I haven't made any for you.'

'Yeah, well, we don't want you to work too hard, do we?'

Jessica decided not to answer, bitterness and anger slashed at her insides: he wasn't going to help her, but he would criticize. It was unbearable living in this atmosphere: polluted with sourness. Paul disappeared again. She sat for a while, sipping the coffee, feeling sorry for herself, then started to chop vegetables.

'What are we having then?' Paul came back in and put the kettle on.

'Lasagne.'

'Oh great, my favourite.'

'It's vegetarian lasagne –'

'Oh no, you know Steve hates vegetarian food.'

'Well you shouldn't complain, it's cattle grazing that's helping to destroy the rainforest.'

'Yeah, but you could have got something else, they're not grazing chickens in Brazil.'

Jessica was silent again. Cora was a vegetarian.

'I suppose the goddess doesn't eat meat, is that it?' Paul could often guess what she was thinking.

'Why don't you help, instead of criticizing?'

'Sure, I'll help,' said Paul, picking up the newspaper and turning to go out of the door. 'Tell me what you want me to do.' His voice grew more distant as he went back into the living room and sat down to read.

Jessica felt anxious lest their guests sense the frosty atmosphere in the flat. Usually she would have taken steps to ameliorate the situation, but this time she was determined not to compromise. She wanted to see what would happen if she pushed things to their limit. After all, if she was meant to leave Paul, it was no good just putting off the day. The doorbell rang. Jessica started, and tried to rinse her hands at the tap in time to answer the door, but Paul got there first. She hoped it was Steve and Suzanne. It was Cora. She heard her loud voice from the hallway.

'Hallo, I'm Cora.'

'Hi, come on in, I'm Paul.'

'Where's Jessica?'

'I'm here, in the kitchen,' Jessica called out, and put her head round the door. Cora came in, filling the flat with warmth and life.

'Hi dearest,' she gave Jessica a hug. 'How are things?'

'Great,' said Jessica, her voice shrill.

'Aha,' nodded Cora. 'I smell a divine smell.'

'I'm so glad to see you, look, have some wine.' Jessica gurgled some into a glass. The doorbell rang again. Jessica felt relieved.

After everyone had been introduced and welcomed, Paul ushered them into his studio to show some of his slides, while Jessica finished the last minute details. She and Paul had agreed on this beforehand. Paul particularly wanted Steve to see his pictures, and Jessica thought Cora would find them very interesting. She hoped it would forge a link between Cora and Paul, because Steve, she knew, was not so keen on staring at scenes of ecological disaster.

'The irony is that you've made such a ghastly subject into something beautiful,' said Steve, his feet up on Paul's desk, eyeing the screen warily from above his wine glass. It was one of the slides showing thinned areas of forest, the fires mixing with the glowing light of the sky, banners of pink and blue laced through the broken branches and lone gaunt trunks.

'Yeah right,' agreed Suzanne somewhat unthinkingly.

'Rape is never beautiful,' said Cora emphatically. Suzanne widened her eyes. Paul cringed at what seemed to him a monstrous cliché. To his further disgust, Steve seemed to back Cora up: 'You could be right, you could be right.'

'Why don't you make a film to show just how awful it is, Steve?' Paul was half-serious.

Cora waved her arm in dismissal. 'Films won't do any good.'

Paul switched back on the lights, his blue eyes furious.

'How do you mean?' asked Suzanne.

'We have to take on the karma of our mass actions, we have violated the goddess, and now we have to descend and meet her dark side, we have to be humble, we have to atone.' Cora's words formed a circle of silence charged with Steve and Suzanne's amazement and Paul's irritation. Jessica's voice calling up the stairs 'It's ready everyone!' relieved the tension.

Jessica looked at Paul's closed-in face and her heart sank. She registered a flash of anger herself at Paul for being so stubborn and spoiling her attempts to include him. Now the dinner party would be awkward, just as he had predicted, maybe even wanted it to be. While Jessica ushered people to the table and poured out more wine, it was Steve who took on the role of host, smoothing over the atmosphere with appropriate small talk. Steve considered it an unaffordable luxury not to dissemble one's mood. In fact he had earmarked the need to deliberately develop his own ability to soothe and charm people. To him such social prowess was a sign of professionalism, making it easier to manipulate things to one's own advantage. Getting on in the competitive world of television was a question of the survival of the fittest, which did not necessarily mean the most talented. Altruism could seldom be allowed to motivate at the expense of self-interest. Cora, however, remained unaffected by both natural moodiness and cultivated charm.

'I've told Paul that his pictures are too good, Jessie – soften the impact because they're beautiful to look at – but Cora disagrees with me.' Steve poured himself some more wine.

'Oh,' said Jessica, half listening as she slotted salt, pepper grinder and salad dressing in among candles and dinner mats.

'I don't really think it softens the impact,' said Suzanne, sitting down at the table, and speaking as if she did not expect, or even want, anyone to listen. 'The fact that the sky is pretty or something just seems to make it more awful. I mean, it's so hopeless isn't it? There's nothing you can do – it's really depressing, I think.'

'What's more,' Steve launched in again before Suzanne had finished speaking, so that her last words drifted down and away like falling leaves, 'Cora does agree with me that it's a waste of time to try and make any more films about this sort of stuff – although I think for different reasons?' Steve looked enquiringly at Cora as he went on. 'My reason is that I think people are saturated with it all, that they don't want to hear any more because as Sue says there seems to be nothing they can do about it.'

'But it doesn't have to be that way –' Paul broke in.

'Yeah okay, I know what you're saying,' insisted Steve. 'Obviously you wouldn't have gone on your trip if you thought it wasn't worthwhile – but I want to hear Cora's reasons –'

Everyone was seated now, eating the red, green, white stripes of tomato, avocado and mozzarella starter. Jessica looked at Cora anxiously.

'We have to stop thinking and acting as if we were separate from the Earth,' Cora spoke as if to the world at large. 'Taking pictures – you take moving ones, Steve, and Paul takes still ones – and looking at both pictures are acts of separation and will not change the consciousness that is bringing about the destruction.'

'And – in your work Cora, you feel you are bringing this change about? In … in your workshops?' Steve asked.

Cora nodded. 'I am one of many: many teachers and guides. I work as a psychotherapist, and then I do workshops for women, to encourage them to go deep in themselves, and find the mythic strand inside that is already part of the planet's life. Often we experience this in mythical terms.'

'What about men?' asked Paul.

Cora nodded. 'Yes, it is important for everyone, but this is my work, what I can do. It is particularly important that women re-inherit themselves – they, more than men, carry the Earth Goddess within them, after all …'

Her matter-of-factness seemed to momentarily stymie Steve. Paul just frowned more deeply.

'And these workshops – oh, thank you,' said Steve as Jessica collected his empty plate and added it to the others. 'These workshops are what brought you over here?' Steve went on still in his interviewer mode. Jessica, returning with the heavy wooden salad bowl, was over-hasty to explain on Cora's behalf: 'Partly Steve, but she's mainly here –' she paused in mid-sentence, distracted by trying to find a place near to Suzanne on the crowded table. Cora went on, 'I've come here to tour the megalithic sites.'

'What, you mean just hire a car, and …'

'No – it's much more than that,' interrupted Jessica.

'Yes, it's a bus tour, or, what do you call them, a *coach* tour, that's it.'

'Who's organizing this?' asked Steve.

'A good friend of mine, a man called Richard Lamb.'

'Actually Steve you might find him interesting, he's done this amazing research about lights, from the earth I mean, for a film or something,' Jessica said blithely, ignoring Paul, who sat with his hand on his chin, both sulky and resigned.

'Yeah?' said Steve, puzzled but interested.

'Earth lights,' said Cora. 'They appear where there's geological faulting in the earth's surface.'

'But what's that got to do with Stonehenge and all that?' asked Steve, doubtfully.

'Well, that is the great mystery, dear. It's a kind of mystery tour. All the ancient monuments were built close to geological faulting. This magical island has more faulting per square mile than any other part of the world, and a correspondingly high number of ancient sites.'

'How well is this researched?' Steve asked.

'You'll have to ask Richard that. I'm afraid it's all so obvious to me in my sort of naïve way, I don't bother with the statistics.'

'What kind of lights are they?' asked Suzanne.

'All shapes and sizes,' replied Cora.

'I mean, they're not UFOs then?' Suzanne asked again.

'UFOs are unidentified flying objects, love,' said Steve, 'i.e. they're not anything yet.'

'Richard thinks they are UFOs, doesn't he?' said Jessica.

'Is this area also connected with your own work, your interest in deep change – or is it just a hobby?' asked Paul, genuinely puzzled.

'Oh no – yes – it *is* connected,' said Cora emphatically.

'How – what have some ancient monuments got to do with ecology?' Paul was looking at her doubtfully.

'Because the ancient ones who built the sites knew this oneness with the Mother, and this knowledge is encoded in the sites both atmospherically and in other ways, possibly including the lights. And these places can act as gateways into that consciousness.'

Paul shook his head. 'I don't get it, I'm afraid. I don't see how going and standing at Stonehenge is a more effective way to halt the burning of the rainforests than *going* out to Brazil, *seeing* for oneself and *bringing* back visual evidence to show others and then *finding practical* ways to avoid further destruction –' Paul punctuated his words with ascerbic, unassailable precision. There was a pause. Jessica was looking down at her plate.

'What about you Jess?' asked Steve. 'What do you think?'

Jessica sighed a little wearily and looked up at Steve without lifting her head. He had, she felt, maliciously uncovered the fulcrum of tension on which their gathering was poised.

'I don't know,' she said.

'Paul frowned, 'What do you mean – you work at FOE after all!'

'Yes I know that,' snapped Jessica, angry scorn in her voice. Suzanne watched, aware of the conflict now publicly exposed. 'I'm just not sure how effective it all is any more.'

'But FOE do a marvellous job – you've done great work there yourself.' There was a hint of entreaty in Paul's voice, bewilderment in his face.

Jessica had been fingering a lock of hair, now she pushed it back behind her ear and gave a mock groan. 'Hm,' she tried to shrug it off, 'I'm probably just approaching burn-out or something.'

Suzanne laughed with her. 'Anyway,' she said, 'I don't see why it has to be one way or the other – can't both approaches be useful?'

Jessica got up and started clearing the dishes.

Steve stretched out his arms. 'That was a great lasagne, thank you my dear,' he said.

Suzanne brought the serving bowls out to the kitchen, both women carefully holding an air of studied normality. By the time dessert was served the conversation had defused itself. Cora asked how they had all got to meet one another, and they in turn found out about how Jessica had gone to Cora's workshop. Then Jessica remembered the newspaper article about the lights frightening a farmhand in Cornwall which she had torn out for Cora.

She got up and rustled in some papers on the floor. 'I thought you'd like to see this, Cora.' She handed it to her. Cora skimmed through it.

'Aha, Cornwall, I'm sure we're going there. Have you seen this, Steve?' Cora handed the article to him.

'And we're going there on holiday,' Jessica said. 'Maybe we'll see some magic lights!' She glanced at Paul who sat aloof from the conversation.

'You know, if you're interested maybe you oughta meet Richard, Steve, he's giving a talk somewhere this week,' said Cora.

'Let's see,' said Steve as he read. 'Where's he talking?'

'I'll get my daytimer, I wrote it down in there.' Cora picked up her large canvas bag and started rummaging through it. She brought out a diary bulging with scraps of paper and business cards. Jessica started clearing dishes again. Suzanne got up to help.

'The Psychical Research Society, it's near South Kensington subway,' announced Cora. Steve wrote down the address as the gathering broke up.

While they were washing up, Jessica asked Paul if Cora had liked his slides.

'Well you heard what she said: she thinks it's all a waste of time,' he answered.

'So you still really dislike her.'

'It's not a matter of whether I like Cora or not, it's a matter of how I wanted to spend the evening. There was no space to discuss my ideas about a film with Steve, instead we spend the whole evening talking about how to save the world through workshops, megaliths and UFOs.'

'They're not UFOs. Anyway, you know Steve isn't interested in making a film about the environment. He's told you.'

Paul banged a saucepan into the wrong cupboard. 'That's not necessarily the case.'

'Paul that saucepan doesn't go in there. Put it down in here.'

'Is that it?' he asked, wiping the counter down and knocking crumbs onto the floor.

'Yeah.'

'Come on then, let's go to bed.' He took her hand. She hesitated, she had been avoiding sex.

Paul pulled her towards him, kissed her on the mouth, stroked her back. She held him, wanting to be still. She felt brittle and tense.

'What's wrong Jess, you got a headache, got to wash your hair?'

'I'm tired.'

'You've been tired ever since I got back.'

She said nothing. She lay inert, trying to connect with depths between them. 'Ow, oh, why can't you just hold me, why can't you be more gentle?'

'I am being gentle.'

'You're not, I'm not just a machine, you know, it's not a matter of just pushing the right button, it's got to do with tuning into something together.'

'Jesus, what's got into you?'

'You don't know how to touch me.'

Paul looked at her in silence.

'Can't you understand that I feel tired and tense and that you can't have rows and expect that to make no difference.' Jessica was becoming slightly hysterical again, her voice shrill and harsh. Paul turned away and pulled a pillow over his head.

Driving back with Steve in the car, Suzanne found herself tired and oddly depressed by the evening. She would have preferred simple frivolity.

Paul's photographs and the currents of their conversation over dinner had sounded darker notes, resonating with the part deep inside herself that felt dark – and empty. Even though she wanted very much to be alone in the cosiness of her little flat, she had agreed to go back to Steve's place initially, because as always when such feelings descended upon her, she was eager for the release that love-making brought, and the feeling, even though temporary, of being filled up.

Steve, yawning as he unlocked his front door, would have preferred to go to sleep and spend time in the morning together. But Suzanne had other ideas. Steve's flat had an unlived-in air to it, more hotel than home, and this impersonal feel was a turn-on for Suzanne. She started to take her clothes off right there in the halogen-lit hallway.

'Come into the bedroom!' said Steve, but she just grinned, standing naked except for her tights, the lights casting a sheen on to her pretty breasts. Steve hesitated: to his own shame-faced amazement he found his thoughts about being tired mixed with concern about the new carpet. Suzanne pulled at his belt and fly, opened his shirt. Half reluctantly Steve embraced her, and they dropped to the beautifully soft, mushroom-coloured carpet and rolled and strained against the wall.

'Come to bed,' groaned Steve afterwards. She followed him into the bedroom, and lay carefully down next to him in the semi-dark. After a while she sat up.

'What's wrong?' mumbled Steve.

She waited until he fell asleep, then made her way back out to the hall, put her clothes on without bothering to wash, and called a taxi. Soon she was back in her tiny flat, soaking in a bubble bath and sipping mineral water. She put on her flannel pyjamas, even though it was barely cool enough anymore to warrant their fleecy softness, and snuggled down into her virginal bed, arranging her stuffed owl, pig, teddy and white baby seal along the wall beside her. She fell asleep wanting nothing more than the soft opiates of material comforts, knowing somewhere that though she might crave deeper comfort, she feared the intimacy and the risk, the confrontation with unbearable dark that marked the way to freedom.

# CHAPTER THREE

THE Psychical Research Society had its headquarters and held its meetings in one of those pre-eminently elegant late Regency terraced houses, white and porticoed, which line some of the better streets opposite the Natural History and Science Museums. The house's proximity to these hallowed halls of rationalism, and the combination of such an unusual organization with so fine a building, represented that uniquely English mixture of the eccentric and the respectable. People took heart as they entered the well-proportioned room, with its voluminous blue curtains and oil paintings of dead founders on the tastefully-decorated walls. Minor establishment figures, who weren't sure whether they should be there at all, felt reassured; while the dedicated enthusiasts were given confidence in their cause.

There was no sign yet of Steve or Suzanne in the gathering audience so Jessica reserved two seats next to her, and sat down to study the programme of events while she waited. There was a plethora of talks and workshops: 'Further Thoughts on Reincarnation' by a well-known author; 'Premonitions – Seeing into the Future' by a university lecturer; 'Advanced Healing Workshops' and 'Workshops for Working Healers'; 'Ritual Magic in the Modern World' by Dorothy Wicks, who, in the small photograph by the side of her name looked like a large and elderly librarian, but was billed as 'the most respectable of contemporary British occultists, the Principal of the Servants of the Light'; 'The Renaissance of Nature', special guest lecture by a scientist whose name Jessica recognized, claimed to show that 'science itself was now transcending the mechanistic view of nature, seeing the universe no longer as a machine running down but more like a developing organism with an inherent meaning.'

'Jessica!' She looked up to see Steve and Suzanne smiling at her.

'Oh hi – here I've saved you seats.' She stood up as they brushed past her. Steve sat down next to her. 'Where's Paul?' he asked as he unzipped his leather jacket.

'Oh, he was too busy to come,' she replied, uncomfortable at Paul's absence and disoriented by a sudden piercing sense of ravishment that had invaded her at Steve's presence.

'You mean he didn't want to come,' said Suzanne in her matter of fact way.

Jessica nodded and smiled, still distracted by the pool of Steve's substance next to her.

A woman walked out into the semi-circle of space at the front of the room, where a table and chair had been placed to one side of a large white screen. She was in her 60s, with silvery white hair, delicate skin and pale blue eyes. Her small figure was neatly dressed in a tailored suit and soft yellow blouse. She smiled at them all, and in a weak, high voice began to introduce both the Society and the speaker. In her well-bred accent, she told them that the Society had been incorporated 105 years ago to investigate psychic phenomena, and she was proud to have been President for the past 15 years. This last with another, modest, smile.

Jessica felt disoriented – she had never been particularly attracted to Steve. Yet it wasn't, she realized, the familiar friend that she sensed now beside her, but that primal, vulnerable presence, not particularly related to the surface personality that is liked or disliked. It was extraordinary, as if she had suddenly fallen into the deep well of Steve, the part that is never shown, which is kept guarded. Jessica stared transfixed at the President of the Psychical Research Society. Standing there before them she seemed to give body to Jessica's half-formulated insight. Her air of English gentility belied the bizarre arena of psychic phenomena over which she had presided for so many years. So too the surface patterns of people's lives belied the deep well that connected them altogether. Here lying just beneath the ordinary world was a promise: that anything was possible, that there existed not far from grasp a root solution to the problems of fragmentation and destruction.

Steve shifted in his seat; she thought she sensed a line of electric awareness between them: but it was so delicate this, like spiritual gossamer. If you thought about it too much, touched it in the wrong way, it would vanish.

'So it is with great pleasure, ladies and gentlemen, that I welcome this evening our speaker Richard Lamb, who as some of you already know, has been doing some very important work on the great megalithic heritage of our country.' The woman smiled and started clapping. The audience joined in, and a man rose up both hesitantly and all in a rush from the end of the front row. He was very tall and his roughly cropped brown hair stood out from his large head. He had welcoming eyes and a wide, fine smile that conveyed an engaging mixture of shyness and childlike joy. In a deep, resonant voice he thanked the President and then, his smile gone, very earnestly thanked the audience for being there, as if by doing so, they were helping with some immense and vital undertaking.

'There is a rumour,' he began, 'that certain prehistoric sites around the world mark places of power, places where contact with supernatural intelligence can be made, where the human mind can enter other space/time modes. The traditional term for that, of course, is enchantment.'

The man spoke with a pleasing mixture of detached authority and controlled passion. The audience started to relax. 'My own research has been mainly to do with the ancient places of North West Europe, and in particular those of the British Isles. We have very little information about the people who built these places. Effectively if we landed on Mars and found these ruins, we'd be in about the same position as we are looking at the ancient megalithic monuments of Europe.'

The enormous mystery of the past welled up in the room. Turning over her new discovery that Steve was a deep well and, by extrapolation, that everyone else was too, Jessica's heart dilated: the universe was suddenly enriched and wonderful again.

Richard nodded and the room went dark. The whirr of a slide projector fan started up and a screen in front of them was illuminated with a large white rectangle. An impressive scene formed out of the whiteness. Under wild skies, a ring of tall, weathered stones. Highlighted in shadow as the rays of the lowering sun hit them from the west, the stones lay upon the ground like an uneven circlet of old gold.

'We have prehistoric earthen mounds, chambered cairns, stone circles and earthen mounds... Some of them date back to a thousand years or more before the Great Pyramid.'

As Richard's rich, measured voice listed the ancient evidence, a charge of excitement shivered through the audience. Now the speaker quickened his pace, as a series of photos clicked into their coloured enlargements.

'The rumour that these are places of power has its origin in several different sources, stories of healing, ghosts and spirits from folklore...' Richard Lamb started to go even faster through his talk and through the slides, as if he had so much to tell them that he had to tear through the material, filling his allotted time full to the brim.

'Then there was the tradition in the early years of this century of psychometrists visiting the sites – these are people who allegedly can pick up information from a place just by being in it. They told us the sites were centres of cosmic and terrestrial energies.' Slides showed sepia tinted photographs of men in high collars and waistcoats standing solemnly around Stonehenge, without the barbed wire barricade of today.

'In the 1930s, French dowsers determined that there were crossing lines of underground water at standing stones. In the last 15 to 20 years the presence of underground water has been a common claim by dowsers at most of the sites, as well as overground energy effects that cannot be identified in the normal ways.'

For Jessica, Richard's words accompanied an avalanche of insights tumbling into her awareness. Underground water, this was really how everyone was: deep wells of mysterious presence, that could interpenetrate one another. She hungered for this undimensional communion, spiritual sex – and avoided it. But it was what everyone hungered for and avoided: by keeping a distance, by categorizing one another in space and time.

'There is also the testimony of the many people who have visited Stonehenge, or Avebury, or the Rollrights in Oxfordshire and had strange experiences at these places. In many cases they have touched a stone and got a shock like static electricity. I've had all sorts of people tell me that, from scientists, archaeologists, retired generals – all the most non-hallucinatory types of people in our society.' Laughter. 'Well, I think they're non-hallucinatory anyway.' More laughter. 'And then in the last ten years or so the rumours have been augmented by results from preliminary scientific experiments where anomalous electromagnetic energy results have been monitored.'

Richard paused, the lights came back on, he took a sip of water from a glass on the table. 'Using the Rollright Stones as our main base, we found – among many other anomalies – unusually high or low readings of radiation; concentric rings of high and low geomagnetism, forming a spiral within the stone circle; and a magnetic pulsing effect in some of the stones ...'

Jessica found her attention wandering. She glanced at Steve and Suzanne. 'Isn't it amazing?'

Suzanne raised her eyebrows and nodded: 'I'm not sure I'm taking it all in though.' Steve pulled down the corners of his mouth but Richard went on before Jessica could ask him what he was thinking.

'There are also many eye-witness accounts of lights appearing close to or in the vicinity of these ancient monuments. Many of the stones used in the megaliths are granite, which contains a high percentage of quartz, or they have quartz veins running through them...'

Richard paused for another sip of water. Jessica looked back and saw Cora's intent face a few rows behind. She smiled at her. She also recognized the two plump red-haired women from the workshop sitting by Cora.

'As we all know from our wrist watches, quartz and energy go together. Granite gives off a high level of radiation. Quartz or crystal is associated with even subtler forms of energy. In one experiment we attached a voltmeter to one of the stones, and a psychic touched the stone. The voltmeter shot up in its reading. We also attached a high impedance meter to a stone, and this was affected when a psychic just visualized touching the stone...'

Jessica looked through the walls of the room to her thoughts. Her eyes rested on a painting of a pastoral woodland scene. A brass picture light was casting a yellow light over the painting. It had been the same in childhood. Places that seemed to merge into light, or air – the way a tree arched and wove its branches into the canopy close to their holiday chalet, a crossroads on the paths that crossed the moors, where bees buzzed over blackberry blossom, the thin strip of sand where the beach ended and the frothing waves and cliff promontory met. Later on, she had felt similar things in the little woodland near to her home, experiences of almost translating herself into the background, into tree, sunlight, earth. She had taken her visionary experiences for granted, until, growing older, she learned that her insights were considered unusual and that it was simpler not to mention them. When she'd been a teenager, all the problems of growing up crowded in and the vividness of her childhood experiences had faded, but she had been left with a sense of puzzlement at the solidity of life in her provincial town, where no aspect of the 'otherworld' was entertained. Always there seemed to exist this sense of disparity between the worlds. It was the source, she saw clearly now, of her frustration with Paul, and she felt new panic and dismay that he had not been there, at the impossibility of conveying it all to him, at the bad omen which his absence now became for their relationship.

The lights went off again and the whirr of the slide carousel started up, pulling her attention back to the speaker and the screen. What she saw startled her: a huge, curved, granite capstone supported by four upright slabs that leaned inwards as if forming the massive stalk of a giant stone mushroom. The megalith seemed massively complete, curled into itself with its own presence and intent. Jessica had never seen anything like it before, so distinctive, enigmatic.

'Another form of energy associated with crystal is light. We're all familiar with the igniters on our gas stoves. Essentially these are small bits of crystal that when squeezed give off an electric spark which ignites the gas. This is a simple piezo-electric effect. On a larger scale, there is the phenomenon of ball lightning, and the more mysterious fugitive light phenomena called earth lights which, although associated with geological faulting in the earth's crust, require a more complex physical explanation than the piezo-electric effect, and also appear to both affect and respond to human consciousness. It is not clear whether it is the strong magnetic fields with which these lights are associated or the frequency of the lights themselves that are the cause of such interactive qualities.'

Still hypnotised by the image of the stones, Jessica began to feel a tingly sensation in her back because she knew what he was going to say.

'A very recent eye-witness account of a light phenomenon occurred at this dolmen, or Quoit, known as Chûn Quoit, one of many different kinds of megalithic structures found in the district of West Penwith, the furthest tip of Cornwall. A farmhand saw a white light appear apparently from out of the structure and heard a loud noise like a clap of thunder. I know of at least one other report of light phenomena associated with this structure.'

Richard allowed a rare pause, then as another shot of the dolmen appeared, this time outlined black against a sunset sky, he went on, speaking more slowly: 'The question is, of course, did the builders of these places know about the unusual qualities of these places and the lights? Was it in fact these special, mind-altering properties that caused our ancestors to build on these sites in the first place? And if so, why were they so important to them, what did they know about this aspect of Mother Earth that we don't? I have become convinced that the megalith builders had a far greater understanding of their environment than we do and that if we are able to open up the secrets of their sites, we will make a significant contribution to the search for an ecological balance in today's society.'

The lights flickered back on, the screen faded, Richard smiled disarmingly and thanked everyone, but his words were drowned out by the applause. A buzz of interest arose in the room as people got up from their seats and pushed forward. A throng collected round him, while others gathered at the table where the books were displayed.

'That was great,' said Steve, turning to the two women with a manufactured expansiveness. 'I think I'll have a word with Richard – if you don't mind waiting, Jessica, we'll take you home?' The well in Steve had closed over, leaving a slight disturbance of the field between them, and a tinge of fugitive confusion in his eyes.

Jessica smiled at him. 'Thank you, that would be kind. Yes, I want to stay on a while.' She watched him edge his way towards Richard. Suzanne was leafing through the books.

Jessica remained in her seat as thought trails and currents of excitement fused in and out of one another inside her. It seemed to her that Richard's talk with all its new ideas and ancient echoes had flowed naturally out of the deep place of connection that had surfaced in her perception while he was being introduced, as if that well had been tapped out of which magic could emerge. Richard's probing of prehistory touched resonances in her own past which rushed up now into piercing memory. Her own fascination with the cultures and magic rituals that emerged out of prehistory; her thesis on the Druidic reverence for the oak and mistletoe, and all the clues she had found that pointed further back. She viewed the megaliths as the awesome remains of unfathomable intelligence. The stones stuck out of the ground and out of the mists of time like tears in the veil, proof of something extraordinary. She had felt that the academics tried to distort by a subtle sleight of hand the full implications

37

of these remains, throwing a cloak of ordinariness over the historical landscape in order to have it satisfactorily reflect their own dullness and escape the challenge of the inexplicable. Was the whole endless tangle of environmental issues not another way to veil over this sense of something deeper, of other possibilities?

'It was a great talk, Paul.'

'Yeah?' said Paul lazily, not taking his eyes away from the TV screen.

'There's a correlation, right, between geological faulting, stone circles and these lights.'

'Really?'

Jessica sat down next to Paul and pulled his head round from the screen: 'Hallo!'

'Hallo,' he said, and kissed her on the forehead. Then his face veered round again to the flickering screen.

'Honestly Paul, can't we just talk for a change? It's impossible with that thing on all the time – or are you just not interested?'

'No, I am, I'm listening. I'm just looking at this at the same time. I'm interested in what's going on, you know, it's the news.'

The newscaster was announcing the government's decision not to shut down the two Magnox nuclear reactors due for closure after their 20 years of service, despite reports of metal fatigue. For a moment Jessica too gazed at the screen, then she went on. 'I wish you'd been there.'

'Yeah, it sounds interesting, I'm glad you enjoyed it.' The news ended and Paul pressed the off-switch on the remote control. 'I've finished my slide selection for the talk, I think it will be very powerful.'

'Oh, good, good. Thank you.' Jessica swallowed her disappointment, but still felt unable to contain her energized intensity in the sleepy front room. She got up abruptly, pulling away from Paul's arm around her.

'What's up?'

'Nothing, I'm going to put the kettle on.'

'I don't know, you tell me off for not listening to you, and when I turn the television off you walk away in a huff.'

'I'm *not* in a huff,' said Jessica, who had just congratulated herself for not reacting to Paul's indifference and creating yet another row.

'Sounds like it to me.'

'Look, I'm *not* in a huff,' she said, putting her head round the door. 'It's just – I've been to a fascinating talk, I'm very excited about it, and you're not interested. But I mean that's OK, you don't have to be.'

'No, that's right, I don't.'

'Sure, but it means that there's less and less that we share, that's all.'

'Just because you go to one talk that I haven't been to, and I want to watch the end of the news, doesn't mean that we no longer share anything.'

Suddenly irritated and tired by their conversation, Jessica said, 'Yeah, yeah, OK – you're right.' There was a pause while she poured out the herb tea. 'I'm thinking of asking him to do a talk for me as well.'

'Who?'

'This guy, Richard Lamb.'

'Why? What've stone circles and strange lights got to do with ecology?'

'Well, that's what so interesting. Richard seems to think that the ancient builders had a much more sophisticated and refined understanding of their environment and that by studying their remains and the light phenomena we might be able to learn something ourselves.'

'That's a bit tenuous though, isn't it? For FOE?'

'Maybe, but why not broaden the context. I think it could be stimulating.'

'Hm.'

'And Steve's interested in him for a film, possibly.'

'Ah-huh,' Paul raised his eyebrows and pressed his lips together and glanced back at the blank TV screen.

'We're going to go and visit him.'

'Why are you going?'

'Because I'm really *interested* in all this. It's rekindling my love of history, well prehistory really. When I did my thesis, the Celts were about as far back as you could go, because nobody knew anything or had any new insights, and because they didn't want to admit that, the megaliths were just ignored.'

Paul swung his legs off the sofa. 'Come and sit here,' he said. Jessica sat down beside him, somewhat reluctantly. She still felt irritated by what she deemed his deliberate indifference, and she was uneasy about physical closeness when she felt so distant at other levels. The fact that this never seemed to worry Paul irritated her again. Paul put his arm around her, heavy and warm, at once comforting and threatening.

They had not made love since Paul's return. Jessica had felt blank and unable to respond. Paul had been bitter and then shrugged it off. Both wondered if it was further evidence of their relationship faltering. Jessica dreaded a repeat of their failure. As they sat together quietly, Jessica became aware of the swirl of thought and doubt in her, like an obscuring haze. As she focussed in on it, the haze began to dissolve, leaving her there in the moment. Paul hugged her more closely, got up without saying anything and went into the bedroom. After a few minutes, Jessica followed him. They were very gentle and careful with one another, avoiding false moves. As a rhythm began to move between them, Jessica became aware of images rising up in her mind's eye: a green lawn by a pond in a friend's garden, a field under oak trees. Each place had to be included by them, they had to be allowed there, and then that was it. The scenes passed more quickly: moorland, a green valley, thickly wooded, cliff heads covered in heather and rough grass and then a mushroom shape, massive stone, outlined against the sky – but it wasn't the image on the screen, they were the other side of the structure – she felt cold alarm, she could not include any more. The current intensified and they were there in the greenness, and they were home in their room in London.

'You were all over the place there, weren't you Jessie,' said Paul, propping himself up on his elbow. Jessica lay in stillness. She felt the curve of his lower arm with her hand, stroked the hairs down towards his wrist. 'You knew,' she said. Then she remembered they had been to the Quoit. She stopped stroking his arm and sat up in bed, unlocking their closeness.

'What's wrong?' yawned Paul.

'Nothing,' said Jessica, frowning in the dark, sleepiness gone.

# CHAPTER FOUR

JESSICA caught the phone as she was about to launch down the stairs. 'Hallo?' She thought it might be Steve to say they were late. A female voice that she knew but could not place said, 'Oh, um, hallo – I was phoning for Paul …'

'He's not here at the moment. Can I take a message?' Jessica looked at her watch. The door bell might ring at any moment.

'Oh, that's strange – he said he was going to be home –'

It dawned on Jessica that the woman thought she was lying. Then she remembered who it was: Caroline, former girlfriend, very beautiful, very smug and rather successful as a freelance journalist specializing in glitzy, clever articles and interviews.

'Yes, he is, he just had to pop out on an errand. I don't think he'll be long.'

'OK – could you tell him –'

'You know what –' Jessica interrupted, 'I'm sorry, I shouldn't really have picked up the phone – my lift is outside and I've got to go –'

'That's fine. I'll phone in again and leave a message.'

'Thanks a lot. Bye.'

Jessica put the phone down and carried on down the stairs. When she got to the door, the phone rang. She stopped and listened to the message: 'Hallo Paul, this is Caroline, wondering where you are! I'm phoning as I said I would to talk about the article, find a time to meet and so on …' The door bell rang: Jessica hovered for the two more seconds it took for the message to end, '…and just looking forward to being back in touch. My number again is 071-370 2734, talk soon. Thanks, bye.' Jessica shut the door thoughtfully behind her as the machine beeped and clicked off.

The black Volvo estate was double parked, engines running. She waved and rushed over to climb in the back seat next to Cora. 'Sorry to keep you waiting.'

'You didn't,' smiled Suzanne.

'Powdering your nose, I know,' said Steve as he eased the car back into the traffic and round the corner onto Kensington Gardens. Steve had arranged a meeting with Richard to discuss a possible film project based on his work. When Richard had asked if he would mind coming out to his home in the Brecon Beacons, Steve had been happy to agree, for he had learned that it was useful to find out as much as possible in advance about prospective film protagonists, and visiting a person's home

41

was always very revealing. Cora and Jessica were keen to be included in his trip, and Suzanne came along for the ride.

The journey gave Jessica plenty of time to contemplate Caroline's phone call. She considered herself to be above jealousy at any time, which she considered an absurd emotion, and given her recent ambivalent feelings toward Paul, to feel jealous would be downright ridiculous. Nevertheless, there was much about the message that puzzled her: was Caroline going to interview Paul? If so, what about, and why would he want to be associated with the kind of lightweight stuff she did – for which he had always professed disdain? All these were questions that could most probably be easily answered, but there were other issues that circled more uncomfortably in half-admitted thoughts. Why hadn't Paul told her? Why was he back in touch with Caroline? Their relationship had spanned Paul's success and early disillusion with his career. It had been turbulent, with many break-ups and re-unions. Caroline could not take seriously Paul's new ecological morality. Had it been ideology in the end and not spent passion that ended the relationship and initiated her own ascendancy? Was Caroline a perennial who would always re-flower in Paul's life? If so, what should be her own stance? Not for the first time Jessica was struck by the suspicion that Paul's attachment to her was tied up with his crusading vision, as if he somehow expected her to carry this for him: a role that she found burdensome in the extreme. There was a sting to the situation, which struck a contradictory note in all her doubts and confusion about Paul and spurred her on to do something about it all, although she wasn't sure what.

'There should be a turning to the right … somewhere, soon,' said Steve. Suzanne consulted the map.

'Erm, yeah, there is, it could be rather narrow, though.'

'He certainly lives out in the wilds, doesn't he?' asked Steve of no-one in particular. Jessica and Cora in the back seat stared out of the window at the rolling countryside of the Brecon Beacons.

'It's so beautiful,' said Cora.

'I know,' agreed Jessica, amazed at how completely London could swallow her up. The countryside always seemed newly created and almost too good to be true.

'Ah-huh, this looks like it.' Steve slowed, signalled and swung the car into a very narrow lane. 'Now, we look for a place standing on its own.'

'This is exciting,' said Cora, 'I've never been to Richard's home before.'

They pulled into a muddy driveway. The house was a converted barn, low-lying and built out of the local dark grey stone, a large-leaved species of ivy growing vigorously up one corner. Its massive exterior was punctuated by a few small windows and a large wooden door. There was no knocker or bell, so Steve banged his fist on the door. Nothing happened. He tried again.

'Oh God, d'you think he's forgotten?' asked Suzanne. Steve shrugged his shoulders. Jessica, still dazed by the countryside, was happy to just stand there feeling the freshness in the air, hearing birdsong. Cora had made her way to the end of the building and disappeared around it.

'Maybe there's another entrance,' said Suzanne, looking after her. Cora reappeared with Richard behind her. He gave them a bashful smile, 'I'm so sorry, I had just gone outside for a moment, I've got this little storage shed – I thought I would hear your car … come in.' He opened the door and they followed him inside.

A step led down from the hallway into the main room, with windowed doors that opened onto the garden. Book shelves lined the whole of one wall, and more books were stacked in piles around the room. One part of another wall had been covered with cork tiles to serve as a noticeboard. It was a mass of photographs, posters and diagrams of megaliths, ancient carvings, stone tablets, cathedrals. On a large desk a thick pile of papers was weighted down by a stone statuette of a goddess.

'I'll put the kettle on,' said Richard and disappeared into the small kitchen on the other side of the hall. Steve picked up one of the books and sat down on the arm of a battered armchair. Jessica wandered over to the noticeboard: some of the images of ancient monuments were immediately recognizable, like Stonehenge, and the Pyramids, some she had never seen before. They all kept their coats on, it was cold in the house.

'I'll go help Richard,' said Cora. She returned in a few moments with newspaper and kindling. 'Steve, there are some logs and more coal outside, can you bring some?'

'Sure.'

Soon the fire was crackling, a glow of warmth built up around it and started to thaw even the cold edges of the room. Richard carried in a tray of assorted mugs of tea and a packet of digestive biscuits.

'Of course it would all make an amazing film,' Richard was saying, 'but I'm so busy with the books, the talks, you know I've had a few people interested, in fact there's a BBC man coming on the tour –'

'Oh? Who?' asked Steve sharply.

'Erm, his name's Peter March, but he's radio, Radio 4, he's quite sympathetic.'

'Oh, fine,' went on Steve. 'So OK, there's all this fascinating stuff – the stones, the lights, the geology etc, but I mean, so what in the end, what's it really about?' asked Steve.

'That's what we've got to find out –'

'We need to understand what ancient man knew,' said Cora.

'What we do know is that these lights are on the increase,' went on Richard.

'There was something in the paper –' said Jessica.

'The Earth is speaking to us, we must learn to listen,' enunciated Cora. Steve looked at Richard.

'I sometimes wonder what it would take now, to be a shaman. I don't know if I would have what it takes …'

'How? How do you mean, I don't understand …' Jessica was frowning, she wanted to understand.

'All that pain.'

'It's going to take women,' said Cora. 'Only women can understand the pain.'

Richard went on. 'The builders of the sites knew about the lights and the geomagnetic fields. I didn't go into this in my talk, but both the geomagnetic fields and the electromagnetic fields of the lights are known to affect consciousness: people have experiences of time loss, memory loss, visions, even abduction scenarios. Ancient man enhanced these fields through the construction methods of the sites, and I believe they also knew how to use them, sometimes in conjunction with the local psychoactive plants, in their shamanic ritual.'

'Magic mushrooms?' asked Steve.

'Yes, or henbane or ergot, whatever was available.'

'You mean these people took drugs?' asked Suzanne.

'In a sense yes, but you can't compare it to what we mean by that today. These plants were considered sacred. They were used with the greatest respect and care.' Richard's intensity lit up the quiet room. Jessica watched him with matching intensity. His long fine hands, his liquid eyes. She felt an empathy with him, and with his passion.

'Together with the enhanced field of the site and the stones, they would help the shaman connect with the planet, with creation. Nowadays we take drugs to escape the pain of isolation, nothing could be more different. We're death-oriented. For centuries we've believed the myth that heaven is where we go when we die, and what is it we celebrate most about the great shaman of our religion? His death, not his resurrection. We see everything from a separatist, death-oriented perspective. That is why archaeologists think many of the ancient sites are burial chambers –'

'Like Simon,' interjected Cora.

'Yes, like Simon, because a few thousand years later some barbaric tribes came along and buried a few rotten ancestral bones in a few of them. Our crude belief system dominates our viewpoint so completely that we can ignore the immensity of these places and their significance …'

'So what were they? And who's Simon?' asked Steve.

'Simon is an archaeologist who's coming on the tour. I've known him a long time, he's very clever and cautious and prevaricates between the possibilities that our research is opening up and endangering his academic career. I mean the point is that I can't prove anything, no-one can. It's too long ago.' There was a pause, as if Richard was debating whether to say any more. The fire crackled and spat out some orange cinders.

'But what do you think?' asked Steve quietly.

'We have nothing comparable today. These places were temples, but not just in a decorative or even symbolic sense. They were points of contact, where the people tuned in, as it were, to frequencies of the Earth's field. Perhaps to get information necessary for survival, or for some collective process of cartharsis or healing …' Richard shrugged and paused for breath.

Jessica stared at him, still frowning. She felt as if her brain was bursting. All the time Richard had been speaking she had been listening as if starving for what he had to say, while at the same time searching for a point of correlation within herself, for a way of meshing in what he was saying with something that she knew was very important but could not find.

'So you mean that if today someone did that –'

Richard shook his head. 'Think of all the time that has passed since this happened. And think of what we have done to the Earth during that time. I mean it almost doesn't bear thinking about, it could even be dangerous.'

Cora's eyes were closed. Steve' eyes behind his glasses were unreadable. Suzanne, sitting on the floor by Steve's armchair, was staring at the fire. The conversation had disturbed her, seeming to demand as it did that she be involved somehow, that she leave her observer role. The flames flickered blue, yellow, red over the coals and logs, like a wordless commentary, a flow of messages, a dance of combustion and transformation. She felt a sudden unaccountable sadness, and a strong desire to leave. The still silence of the countryside that circled out for miles outside the barn weighed in upon her. Its unbroken immensity stirred and changed only by their own thoughts and words, by the flickering of that small but generic fire. She shifted her weight from one leg to the other, fiddled with her hair and looked round anxiously at Steve. How much longer would he want to stay?

To her relief the conversation seemed to be completing itself. Steve agreed with Richard that the film could use the coach trip as a framework for presenting both Richard himself and his work. Steve would work up an initial treatment to be agreed with Richard. He would have to work fast, as the tour started soon, but if he was able to get a commission, a film could still work even if it only included part of the tour.

Jessica found herself once more almost overwhelmed with swirling threads of connection and excitement. The presence of Steve, the empathy with Richard, the excitement of what he was saying – and, oh yes, she must remember to ask him if he would give a talk as part of her series. Yes she would do that. Meanwhile the elusive connection was tugging at her mind. What had he meant by the shaman, and the pain, what did Cora mean? She must sort it all out. She must remember to think about it. Everyone was getting up to leave. She started up too, and with a flash of urgency approached Richard. As she came up to him, he reached out his hands for hers. He immediately agreed, with great enthusiasm and warmth, to give a talk. For a moment more she stood there, holding his hands with hers, looking into his smiling face: she felt an unspoken connection between them, a deep understanding. She forgot to ask him about the pain.

It never occurred to Steve that the content of his films might be as or more important than the process of making them itself. His ambition netted other people's lives and projects voraciously but remained undiminished by them. As a result, unhampered by any hint of emotional investment, he usually did well when selling his ideas. Commissioning editors, programme executives relaxed when they heard his even tones: here was a man they could work with, someone who wouldn't make too much fuss if they wanted him to compromise a little, allow them some control. Somewhat to his surprise, Steve had managed to get a meeting with one of the BBC's Science and Features producers. Knowing how deeply conservative the BBC still was, he was not pinning too many hopes on it. As one of his friends had quipped, the BBC's science department had only just heard of Newton.

Kensington House, near Shepherds Bush, was an unprepossessing 1960s building, incongruously squashed in next to a row of red brick Victorian terraces and looking, in comparison, decidedly shabby. Steve was given a visitor's label and directed through the warren of flimsy-walled corridors. The man who greeted him was of medium height, with curly brown hair, touched with grey, above a neat featured face, with sharp brown eyes and a thin, rather mean looking mouth. He reminded Steve of a well-worn brown nut: condensed and difficult to crack. He was dressed in an old pullover and non-descript, grey trousers. Steve immediately classified him as typical of long serving, fully paid up BBC apparatchiks. A studied dowdiness, an intense, closed-in expression so characteristic of the slightly paranoid yet club-like atmosphere of the institution. Quite why so many BBC men were of the same physical type baffled Steve, but he knew that all over the sprawling empire of Television Centre, White

City, not to mention the Regions, there were these little brown men beavering away at their projects, forcing immense aspirations through the fine sieve of the system, their ruthlessness and self-interest veiled by their clipped cultured accents and informal, gentlemanly manner.

'Good morning, how are you doing,' said Steve in his slightly mid-Atlantic style. Ignoring the social pleasantry the man just said rather curtly: 'Hallo Steve, have a seat.'

'Thanks, I appreciate your making the time to see me.'

'Yes, I don't have very long I'm afraid ...'

'Right, OK, I have a treatment with me, which I can leave with you, but basically the idea ...' Steve launched into a neat summary of the main themes of his film.

'Mm,' said the BBC producer at the end, looking at his fingertips.

'And as far as finance goes,' Steve decided to carry on, 'my information indicates that a co-production deal with the States is a good possibility. This kind of subject matter is a growth area now, it's just taking this country a little longer to catch up, which means that this could be a first for you of course. Just some examples of what I mean: the Time/Life book series on ancient sites sold a record-breaking 500,000 copies through mail order alone, over a period of just two months in only two states; last year a similar kind of series on one of the major networks received an average of a ten rating, making it one of the top 20 of 400 syndicated programmes for that year; 400 million dollars worth of audio/visual tapes on similar topics were sold – people are hungry for this subject matter ...'

'Mm, or is it hunger for sensationalism? We have to be very careful here in Science Features, as you know, that we do not commission programmes on their commercial appeal alone.'

'Of course not, no, I realize this, but quite apart from its popularity, this subject has excellent scientific integrity as well. I think that makes a winning combination.'

'Well – good. Thank you very much for coming to see me, it is a very interesting idea. Let me read the proposal and I will get in touch with you.'

Steve knew when there was nothing further to be done.

'Fine, great, thanks again for your time, I look forward to hearing from you.' They shook hands and Steve left. He had been there for about 20 minutes. It had been a fishing exercise, a meeting just to see what other proposals might be floating around, so that the insiders could figure out in advance how to protect their own projects.

About a week later Steve got a letter. Its five lines read: "The phenomenon of Earth Lights seems well-established and not in doubt, but the suggestion that these phenomena might reveal more about ourselves and our relationship with the geological properties of the earth, is not in any way proven. It is a theory, but there seems no real evidence to support it."

Steve chuckled to himself. No programme had yet established the existence of earth lights, that in itself made exciting television. As for the other comment, every science programme he had ever watched was a mixture of provable fact and speculation based upon that fact. He knew that the subject was too close to UFOs and the lunatic fringe for the BBC to take a risk on. Moreover, as he had often thought, many at the BBC were intent on making programmes for their peers, other programme-makers, rather than for the general public and what they might be interested in. He wasn't too worried. He was already in discussion with Channel 4 who took a much livelier, lighter attitude towards ideas. They were also much more interested in the commercial possibilities of the project.

Jessica was hanging upside down from the seat of a chair. It was a stacking chair, made of gloss brown metal tubing with a canvas seat and back. Her legs were pushed through the back of the chair, toes pointing at the ceiling, her hair was brushing the floor. Blood rushed to her head. Several other women were in similar positions on the same kind of chair.

'OK, now, how about lunging over the side – like this.' Cora grabbed an empty chair and lay down sideways across it, her hands grasping the leg and back rest, her legs high in the air. Then, lowering her legs and easing her grip, she let her legs hang down the side of the chair, her head still dangling from the other. The women followed her example.

'Fun, isn't it? New things to do with a chair – yes! That's good. OK, OK, yes a few more – good, good.'

It did feel good. Jessica experienced an unexpected sense of liberation in exploring such an everyday object in this bizarre way.

'OK, let's get upright again.' Cora was frowning slightly. She narrowed her eyes for a moment and then, 'Yes, and a little bit of hyper,' she started clapping her hands and stamping her feet. 'Run, children, move round and round, stamp your feet. Fast as you can, faster, faster.' Cora put on the Ride of the Valkyries. It was difficult to run fast and stamp their feet. The women felt clumsy. 'Yes I know it's not easy, but never mind, come on now.' Cora stood slowly turning in the middle of their moving circle, clapping her hands. Then she changed the rhythm, going even faster. 'Now, stop running and start – spinning! Find your own space. I want you to spin fast, like you did when you were a kid – faster, faster, and now the other way, fast, fast. Yes, and back the other way again – quick, quick. We're going to evaporate – yes, disappear into thin air – and now back the other way again – yes, OK, OK, and now collapse, be dead, hit the floor.' Gasping, the women staggered to a halt and gratefully folded themselves down onto the floor.

'Lie on your backs, arms and legs spread out. You're in a circle. Breathe, yes, deep breaths, close your eyes. We've been manic, now we're going to go into our quietness, our blankness. Feel those circles still spinning round your heads. That's good, let them spin your normal selves away, your normal thoughts away.'

Jessica thought about her day at the office, about the steam baths where she was going with Suzanne afterwards. She let them go. She thought about Paul, about Richard, about Steve, about Caroline. Small pangs of worry and excitement accompanied each. They too span away. The music had been turned off.

'Here there is peace, or the deadening weight of inertia.' Cora was still standing in the middle of the room. Her voice near and faint like an audio lighthouse beam as she slowly turned round and round. 'A blankness of despair or completion. A bleak nothingness or a light emptiness. Let your breath move in and out. Become still like a rock. You are a rock, a stone, the earth itself. You are the cavern. Water flows through you, winds blow cool on your forehead.'

Jessica's body felt heavy and separate from her. Her forehead was cool.

'Still, still, listening to your blood stream, to the lymph; listen to the heartbeat, to the musical symphony of the hormones. What do you find there?'

Jessica was not part of the cosmos this time. She wasn't sure what was happening – was anything happening? Futility, a river like snakes, black encoiled meshes, of unfinished ends, dilemmas and events that made no sense.

'Don't judge what you find there. Don't try to change it. Just look at it, learn to be dispassionate. Look with the eyes of death.'

Jessica felt dismayed. She could not find the strength to be dispassionate, she felt in danger of being overwhelmed by exhaustion, coming to the end of her reserves. Her bright hope-and-scheme-filled world all shrunk down to a small bundle of grey rags, proven to be nothing. Fear that she really wasn't anything, could achieve nothing, curled inside her.

'OK, now go further, go further down. What's at the core? What's at the core of the earth, of the sun? No one knows, no one has proven anything. It is a great silence – but you go there, and find out!'

Jessica was falling, falling through darkness. This was better than being squashed in the small, mean space. She had no feelings, nothing, not good, not bad. This was a new freedom. And then she felt flushed, something was travelling from the inside out, breaking like a wave over her skin. Fire, fusion at the core. Suddenly she had to move, to roll slightly from side to side, otherwise she might burn up. She needed to find the cool winds again. She pictured the ocean, all around the island of Britain, grey choppy waves, huge green rollers, estuary currents, different kinds of seas lapping at its edges. She felt the wonder of the ocean, of green water and white foam, of earth, of air, the warmth and sweetness of the planet's surface, nourished by fire below and fire above. Then she was on the wooden floor, beginning to feel the draughts, aware of time again; normality returned, and the pleasure of it. The memory of the proposed trip to the Turkish baths with Suzanne rushed back in and filled her with uncomplicated happiness.

Jessica pulled on her track suit in a relaxed daze. 'Oh Suzanne, I'm so looking forward to that hot steam. It's perfect that we've planned to go, isn't it.'

'Yeah, I suppose so. I don't know, I'm a bit tired.'

'Don't worry, you'll feel fine when you get there, it'll just really relax you.' Suzanne didn't remonstrate. She lacked the will to try and dissuade Jessica. Perhaps the heat would warm her through, touch her frozen insides. She wasn't sure quite what had happened to her during the session. She always held back anyway, and never expected much to happen, but she had been forced up against a cold, hard edge to her world, a numbed heavy mass weighted against her movement. This metallic density underlay her life, it was her doom, it could never be moved or softened.

The baths were built in a style and on a scale no longer seen, one of the last outpourings of exuberant Edwardian generosity. Heavy mahogany doors with bevelled glass windows led into a large open hall with occasional pillars. The walls were part mulberry-tiled dado, part green swirled plaster, the ceiling vaulted. Cushioned green sunbeds were lined all the way round the hall, interspersed with lockers. The lighting was soft, the noises echoing and muted. Towards the back end of the hall a big, square staircase with massive granite bannisters disappeared into the level below, and something from there was reflected glimmering on the white arched ceiling above. Jessica and Suzanne got undressed, Jessica in great excitement, finding out how the system of lockers and keys worked with the help of a small, middle-aged Greek Cypriot lady in a blue overall with a cigarette held in one hand. She was one of the assistants. In a minced accent she listed the range of treatments available in addition to the five pounds charge, and Jessica booked a body scrub. Then, clutching white towel and cloth wrap, they descended the staircase, feeling the warmer air rise to greet them. To the side of the last stage of the stairway a jade green pool was set into the floor. It had steps leading down to it, and was curved like a snake or hieroglyph. It was the light playing on this green emblem that could be seen on the ceiling above, mistily evoking the pleasures below.

Downstairs the floor was black and white checkerboard, the ceramic walls covered in greyish green, rich textured tiles. There were three large steel shower heads in a row, one with bars curved around it which squirted water horizontally as well as vertically. Opposite was a line of sinks, and through an opening to the side of these were three bare marble slabs, waist high. A woman was laid out on one of them being pummelled and kneaded by a masseur. A sign pointed out the way to the Heat Rooms.

Pushing through a solid mahogany door, the two women found themselves in a generously proportioned room. The tiled walls and floor were white, edged with black, the ornate ceiling painted over with a silver sealant. What looked like a low mahogany table stood in one corner against the wall, and there were about half a dozen oversized deck chairs. The room was warm and dry and empty. A square arch led into another, similar room, which was hotter than the first. They could see that this in turn had an archway leading off into a third room. For now they settled into two of the comfortable deck chairs in the first room. The place was wonderfully silent, with the subdued air of sanctuary, and a notice on the wall requested that people keep quiet.

'This is amazing,' said Jessica in a hushed tone.

'Mm, I've been to places that are cleaner.'

'Oh, Suzanne, the place is *old*.'

'That doesn't mean it has to be dirty.'

'It's not dirt, that's mould up there. Anyway, this place has *soul*.'

They lay in silence for a while, enjoying the heat. Two Arab women came in and went straight into the second room.

'So you find Richard attractive?' asked Jessica.

'Oh yes, he's attractive. Bit mad though.'

'I could do with some of that madness. I sometimes feel a bit tired of sane men.'

'Paul, you mean?'

'Well, don't you ever find Steve that way? Over-controlled, all in the head. No soul – no poetry. Career-minded. I mean Cora's right, that is the rapist mode.'

'You think Richard's not in his head?'

Jessica hesitated. 'No. Not as much anyway.'

'I don't know,' said Suzanne. 'I've never really thought about it.'

More women came into the room while they talked, a small bevy of pink, prim English girls and a tall tanned woman with breasts that stuck down and out like flesh daggers. They decided to go up a few degrees and try the next room. One of the Arab women was stretched out on the wooden table, which they realized was not a table but a reclining bench. Her friend was curled in contented mounds of flesh on a deck chair with her eyes closed.

'I just think,' went on Jessica in a half-whisper. She paused, forming her thoughts, not wanting to say anything too large.

'Yeah?' said Suzanne.

'Well, I don't know. I worry sometimes whether there's some part of me that's getting squashed, by being with Paul.'

'Probably, but would anyone else be any different?'

'Is that how you feel – I mean, with Steve you don't feel that you're just with him, right?' Jessica was shyly curious about Suzanne who, on moving to London, had had a string of affairs and appeared to think it no big deal to sleep with men almost as readily as having a conversation with them. She did so partly in reaction to both Luton and her marriage but also because often the only time she felt real or alive was during sex. She had slept with Steve almost automatically. He liked her apparent coolness and lack of expectation about him and saw more of her. After her marriage, she was not keen to live with anyone, which also suited Steve. At the same time, unless the opportunity presented itself to him in a completely convenient way, he lacked the time or the focus to be much of a philanderer, and, while happy with the arrangement, he felt a little uneasy at the prospect of Suzanne sleeping with others.

Jessica was both nervous of Suzanne's experience, and somewhat in awe of it. She wondered if it was not a really liberated way to approach the world and whether she was missing something by being monogamous. Her past experience had been far more cautious and her liaisons much fewer in number. A relationship at university with a research scientist had in the end made her feel claustrophobic. He was absorbed in his work on superconductors and lived in a world full of machinery she could never understand. She had often longed to break out, to go off with the man whose eyes met hers at a party, to live from passionate impulse. But a mundane sense of loyalty and her inbred conservatism kept her back. What Jessica did not see was the general malaise of disconnectedness and blankness Suzanne was trying to break out of. In her naïve way Jessica attributed her own motivation to her friend. She caught insights at times into the beauty of different men, longed to be released into a medium of divine intimacy, in which any act was sanctioned. Suzanne wasn't conscious of any such possibility. Her affairs reflected her lack of self worth, they rarely brought her much happiness beyond temporary sensation.

'I mean, maybe it is not really natural to be with just one person all the time,' Jessica continued.

'Lots of people are.'

The Arab lady had opened her black eyes and was looking at them. Jessica spoke more softly: 'But you aren't are you?'

Suzanne shrugged. 'I sort of am, at the moment.'

Jessica sighed. It was always difficult to get Suzanne to talk about herself.

Suzanne asked Jessica a question. 'How is it going with you and Paul anyway?'

'It's OK,' said Jessica slowly, unsure of how she really felt, 'and you know we leave for Cornwall in a couple of days, so I feel excited.'

'That's nice.' Suzanne wasn't sure how serious Jessica's feelings of discontent were, she had the feeling that Jessica was much too comfortable to actually leave Paul.

'Shall we see what the next room is like?'

The last Heat Room was very hot, like a dry sauna.

'Gosh, I think I'll burst if I stay here very long.'

'Mm,' agreed Suzanne. The bevy of pink girls appeared and put their heads round the entrance, then came rustling in. After a few moments Jessica said, 'I think I've had enough for now – can we go to the Steam Room?'

'OK.'

They retraced their steps through the Heat Rooms. The Arab ladies were still motionless; the tall, tanned woman had joined them. Two middle-aged women were moving back into Room One, their thighs and buttocks wracked with cellulite. Unashamed of their wrinkled bodies, they settled happily in the deck chairs to chat. The Steam Room was back out near the showers. They pulled open a green steel door and a puff of steam escaped. Inside, the steam was so thick they could hardly see across the room. There were damp slatted wooden benches around the sides. They sat down, almost choking on the white air. Dimly they could just make out other pink forms on the opposite benches. No one spoke. Water dripped continually from the ceiling. Suddenly the door was pulled open and a woman's voice called out, 'Jessica?'

'Yes,' she said, startled.

'Body scrub!'

'Oh right, see you in a minute Sue.'

Jessica followed the woman, who was dressed in shorts and T-shirt, over to the room with the marble slabs. She was asked to lie down on one of them on her front. The woman rubbed her down vigorously with a kind of clay, then even more vigorously with a loofah mit. Next she filled a bowl with warm water and threw it over Jessica. It felt wonderful. The woman finished her off with a quick foot and ankle massage. Jessica paid her with genuine gratefulness. She loved the impersonal touching and the strangeness of being stretched out naked on a cold marble slab like a piece of meat for processing. She went back to the Heat Rooms to wait for Suzanne. When she returned, they decided it was time to try out everything once more and then have fun with the showers. Last of all they wanted to swim through the magical green pool. As Jessica stepped down into its crystal clear greenness she shrieked, 'Oh my God, it's freezing.' She gave a little yelp as she plunged in and swam the two or three icy yards to its curved other end.

'Go on Suzanne, you've got to as well.'

Reluctantly Suzanne lowered herself into the water, and with a softer screech launched across it. Walking up the stairs afterwards they both felt renewed, every part of their bodies tingling and enlivened. The calm echoing atmosphere welcomed them. The Greek Cypriot lady asked them if they wanted anything to eat or drink, and offered a menu. They ordered toasted sandwiches and tea, then lay down on two of the couches, their towels around them.

'Aren't you glad you came? Toasted sandwiches as well, I can't believe this place.'

'Yes, I am.'

The tea came. They relapsed into silence. Jessica picked up one of the magazines lying on the table next to her sunbed. 'Oh God,' she said. It was back issue of one of the colour supplements. Paul's picture of the burning rainforest was on the front cover. 'It's one of Paul's – look.' Suzanne turned to see.

'I've always found Paul very kind,' she said, and looked away again.

Paul was watching the news again. There was a report about the attempt by Nirex to find a disposal site for low-level nuclear waste. He stared at the screen and registered semi-automatically the clearly articulated information and map graphics with pulsing radiation symbols over potential locations in the UK. There was footage of villagers protesting and preventing Nirex officials from gaining access to a pleasant looking field. It was all so familiar. One had been seeing scenes like this now for years, it seemed. Paul was depressed, despite the success of his pictures. In addition to a main feature in the colour supplement that had commissioned him, he had sold many slides to libraries and a range of other publications. But he still felt disembodied, directionless. The front door opened and closed, depositing Jessica. The sudden intrusion startled Paul out of his stupor.

'Hallo!'

'Hallo – ooh that was gorgeous,' said Jessica as she emerged somewhat dazed into the room.

'What was?'

'The steam baths – I told you I was going there.'

'Oh yeah, that's right.'

'Oh Paul, you must go, it's fantastic. They have men's days you know.'

'Oh yeah, sounds a bit dodgy.'

'SStt! It's absolutely wonderful. I love it, it's one of my favourite places of all.'

'Good.' Paul turned back to the TV screen.

'Paul –'

'Yeah.'

'You know Caroline rang the other day –'

'Yeah – so what.'

'Is she doing an interview of you?'

'Yep –'

'What about?'

Paul kept his eyes on the screen. 'Oh, she thinks my defection to serious ecological issues is worth a piece. She reckons she can place it somewhere.'

'I was a bit surprised.'

'Why? The more exposure the better for the cause.'

'But –'

'Sssh,' Paul leant forward to turn the sound up. 'Reports are just coming in of an oil spillage off the Shetland Isles. The extent of the damage is not yet clear but sources say that an oil tanker ran into trouble as it passed through the narrow inlet. There is no indication as to how the accident happened.' The well-groomed woman paused for a moment before continuing with the next item, a state visit by the President of Zambia.

'Christ,' said Paul.

'It's those bloody tankers – they're too big,' said Jessica, turning the volume back down. Paul said nothing. He was frowning.

'Funnily enough the Energy Campaigners have included an analysis of the efficiency of those supertankers in their latest report, they say –' she was interrupted by the phone ringing. Paul answered it.

'Hallo – yeah, it's me ... Right, yes I just heard. Oh really? When? Yeah, OK, I'll do it. Right – I'll get back to you.' He put the phone down.

'What was that?'

'They want me to cover it.'

'What, the spill?' Paul nodded.

'But we're due to go away.'

'Come on Jessica – a tanker's dumped a load of crude which is going to gum up a beautiful area of coastline, and endanger hundreds of species of marine plant and animal life and you're worried about a holiday!'

'It's not just a holiday – it's about our relationship ...'

'Don't give me that – it's about your little schemes getting spoiled. I mean it's typical of you isn't it, you have all these lofty ideas but if anything threatens your little world you don't want to know.' Paul's depression had flashed into disproportionate anger.

'God you can be foul.' Jessica felt stunned and unable to move.

The phone started to ring again. Paul picked it up: 'Hallo? Hi – Yeah! How did you know? … Sure, why not – I've no idea, train probably. Give me a call in the morning and we'll sort something out. Yeah, bye.'

'Who was that?'

'Caroline. She wants to come along, do an interview in action, get some photos.' There was a touch of apology in Paul's voice.

'So – you're going to go away with her!'

'Don't be ridiculous – it's a business trip. You could come too, if you wanted. I can't understand why you're not more supportive of my work.' Paul got up and went out to the hall cupboard where he kept his equipment. He started to carefully wipe down his lenses.

'You don't understand Paul – campaigns and photos aren't enough, they're never going to do it –'

'That's just all that bullshit from Cora,' Paul shouted from the hall, his resentment sparking up again. 'Can't you think for yourself?'

'But you're not thinking for yourself at all,' Jessica's voice was shrill with fury, 'you're only able to take pictures of the earth, and then get paid for feeling all self-righteous. You have no idea what it means to experience the planet as a living entity. You're just a parasite.'

'Oh yeah,' Paul had moved on to polishing filters, 'well, it's my work that supports your fantasy world. Friends of the Earth don't pay you enough to keep you in the style you're accustomed to – it wouldn't even pay for your bloody Shamanism for Women Workshop – you're the real parasite darling!'

Jessica was suddenly taken with an idea. She shouted back: 'Well if you're going away, so am I!'

'Don't be stupid, you don't want to go on your own. This job probably won't take that long –'

Paul did not take Jessica's anger seriously. He'd had his outburst, got his feelings of resentment towards her out of his system, and now, intent on his equipment, he saw no reason for not going on as before.

'I'm not going on my own – I'm going to go away with my friends.'

'You don't mean you're going on that magical mystery tour do you?'

'Yes, that's exactly what I mean. I didn't even consider it before because of our plans, but you obviously don't think they're important, so why should I?'

# CHAPTER FIVE

THE coach that was to carry them on their voyage of discovery was an old-fashioned 1960s model, with a curved front like a stiff, giant-sized insect. Two maroon wings arose from its front window eyes and spread back in two stripes down its body. The rest was cream with plenty of chrome trim. Inside it was fitted out in plastic mock wood and dark red, furry seats with orange and yellow pairs of zig-zags. This was to be their home from home, their ark, during the tour. It stood, temporarily lifeless, with its luggage flaps open on either side engorging suitcases and backpacks while behind it, through tall wrought-iron gates the morning traffic of Hyde Park Corner surged past.

Across the road in the park proper, small fields of spent daffodils bobbed in the breeze and were reflected in the coach windows. Jessica stood looking at the coach, shivering slightly in the early morning, and feeling a shade doubtful about her wrathful impulsiveness. She didn't really like coach tours, and felt alienated from the gathering group of about 25 participants with their expectant and self-conscious air. They were an odd mixture. There were one or two tweed jackets on slightly crumpled looking men, one in his 60s, one in his 40s; a couple who had the unwashed, long hennaed hair look of itinerant new-agers; a young man in tight black bicycle leggings, who, with his long dark wavy hair, looked like a gorgeous young woman. She recognized the two red-haired American women from Cora's workshop, but was disinclined to break out of her bubble of retreat to talk to them.

A voice behind her said: 'Oh, I'm so glad you're coming, my love.' She turned and gave Cora a hug, but, as if sensing Jessica's self-imposed exile, Cora moved on through the crowd without staying to chat. Richard's face appeared amid the throng; intent on welcoming others he did not see her at first. She felt suddenly shy, like an adolescent overcome with a crush; and then, to her great surprise, she saw the slim, elegant figure of Suzanne walking swiftly up from the tube station. Jessica waved and ran up to her, pleased and excited like a schoolgirl.

'Suzanne! What are you doing here?'

'Didn't you hear about the film?'

'No!'

'Steve's got the go-ahead from Channel 4. He's going to set things up and join the tour later on, so he wanted me to come along and sort of keep an eye out. I already had the holiday booked, just in case. But what about you, what are *you* doing here? I thought you were going away with Paul.'

Jessica shook her head. 'Not any more.'

'Oh dear, another argument.'

'Paul insisted on chasing after an oil slick instead of going away together – and …'

'Gosh,' said Suzanne, looking round distractedly. Jessica shut up, she didn't really want to mention Caroline anyway.

The group had now lost its self-conscious air and ripples of animated conversation flowed amongst the forming clumps of friends of friends. The door of the coach opened. Richard climbed onto the steps and called out for people's attention. His rich voice carried easily above the hum of conversation.

'I think we're nearly all here now, and I just want to welcome you all very warmly, and also introduce a very important part of our enterprise, Pete Drummond, our driver.' A man with a reddened nose (he was a keen beer drinker, but never when driving), roughly shaven cheeks and deadened grey/brown eyes nodded his head curtly at the crowd. Pete was a local from Richard's part of the world, and ran the coach as a private business. Richard continued, 'As you can probably tell, from its pristine condition, this coach is Pete's pride and joy – as well as his meal ticket – and I know we'll respect that. The tour, as many of you know, has been put together on something of a wing and a prayer. I don't have a beautiful glossy brochure ready for you, with all the stopping places, but don't worry, literature will be available at most of the sites we'll be visiting, and of course,' he coughed, 'my books also contain any background information you may need and I do have some with me for sale. So at this juncture I will just say that we intend to steam up the motorway to our furthest and most northerly point and return roughly along the western side of the country, taking a more scenic route. So thank you in advance for your interest and co-operation, and I think we can now get on board and make a start.'

Jessica saw Cora, who was standing at the bottom of the steps, reach up and say something to Richard, who blinked and nodded and said, 'Oh yes, one last thing, it might be of interest for some of you to know that, hopefully anyway, on the latter part of our journey we will be joined by a film crew. A good friend, Steve Glass, is to make a film about Earth Lights and my work. In fact his partner,' Richard looked around and, ignoring or not noticing Suzanne's embarrassed glance, gestured towards her, 'another good friend Suzanne, is already with us on the tour.'

Richard smiled generally at the two of them. Some of the grouping turned to look curiously at the 'film' people Jessica and Suzanne, who tried to shrink away. In a sudden flash of irritation, Jessica recognized Bill the Buddhist from work. She pretended she hadn't seen him.

By now the bus was vibrating with the noise of its diesel engine, everyone climbed hastily aboard as if it were about to leave without them and with much shuddering and revving they finally pulled out into Park Lane only to become more or less instantly immured in the misnamed rush-hour traffic. Slowly they inched up to Marble Arch, where the flow eased a little as they headed down Bayswater. It took a good three quarters of an hour though before they had left the last of the jams behind and the A40 widened into the M40 just past Beconsfield. As the speed picked up, people's conversation dropped off, leaving many staring out of the windows, comfortably stationary as the landscape moved past and their thoughts moved with it. Motorway flyovers, fields, an airfield with huts, a bridge, a very ugly modern hotel on the corner of two major roads called The Rest House, more fields, cows, an artificial ski-slope, a housing estate.

Suzanne had the window seat to begin with, she and Jessica would take it in turns to sit there. Suzanne did not consciously notice that she felt unusually happy. Everything around her was revealed to be beautiful in the most profound way. Even odd, miscellaneous things, like the artificial ski-run or an articulated lorry. It was as if the curse of judgment had been lifted from her and without its blinkered assessment she was aware of possibilities that were hidden before. What may have seemed gross blots of existence were now seen as minor flaws, transitory and ultimately harmless. As for the forms of nature, the trees, the thick hedgerows, the way tall vigorous green weeds with pink flower heads grew up gladly in the middle of the safety barriers, these were exquisite beyond expression. Everything was tinged with a glow and a softness, as in some primordial creation. She was unconcerned with past or present, content and filled out in the present. Things had slowed down, magnified themselves. The iron bar of herself might still exist somewhere, with all the general ills, but right now there was a baby smiling from the back of a car as they overtook, and small white clouds dashing across the sun.

Jessica was leaning back in her seat with her eyes closed. After the adrenalin of decision and departure she felt drained and tired. She supposed her relationship with Paul was now over. Nothing seemed to have resolved as she had sensed it might, and after the tour she would have to start all the cumbersome machinery of separation: finding a place, moving her stuff, thinking about what was next. To her disappointment, she seemed to feel nothing: neither sadness nor excitement at the prospect of being on her own again, and free. A pang of self-pity went through her. Suzanne did not want to hear about it – Suzanne never wanted to get involved – and Cora was still floating close to Richard, concerned with the larger whole of the group.

Jessica sighed and opened her eyes. Richard was making his way down the aisle, talking to each person individually, a brief hallo, how are you, or answering questions. He came to Suzanne and Jessica's seat, beamed widely and squatted down to be nearer their height. 'Hallo you two, I'm sorry I haven't said hallo properly before –'

'Oh that's fine,' protested Jessica.

'Well – I've been busy, but also I feel that you both – well, I know I don't have to worry about you.'

'How are *you* doing?' said Jessica pointedly.

He gave a big sigh. 'Okay, okay, I think. I'm really glad to have you along though, it feels very supportive.' He clasped Jessica's hands in his for a moment.

'You're looking particularly well, Suzanne.'

'Thanks,' she smiled.

'Great, I'll continue on my rounds – talk to you later.' With a final squeeze he let go of Jessica's hands, stood up and carried on down the coach.

'I think he likes you,' said Suzanne, unhelpfully. Jessica decided to ignore her.

They were now looking out at deep countryside. The buzz of conversation had risen again as people got used to being under way. Cora came and squatted beside them. 'Isn't it beautiful? I so love this country you know. There's some sort of marriage that I always experience inside me when I'm here.'

'It is beautiful,' agreed Suzanne, gazing out at the soft green fields. 'But you know, I don't recognize this – is this a new route or something?'

'Yep,' said Jessica gloomily. 'This is the new motorway that after years and years of protest the government finally succeeded in bulldozing through pristine Oxfordshire countryside.'

'Ah, so in seeing its beauty we spoil it forever.'

'God knows why they have to do it,' said Jessica as an old farmhouse, once remote, flashed past.

By noon they had joined the M6 and were skirting round and over the vast suburban sprawl that Birmingham deteriorates into. Jessica stared out in fascinated disbelief as tower block after tower block panned out in grim formation on either side around them, joined by smaller lego-like wafers of maisonettes, walkways, roads and very occasional scrappy bits of grass. Gradually the buildings turned industrial, and closed in on the motorway as it narrowed and ran on stilts through the conurbation. Warehouses, their rows of windows smeared yellow ochre with age and dirt, factories with strange protuberances of pipes and air ducts, old, smoke-blackened brick chimneys. The traffic had grown heavier, moving in thundering rows along the lanes, with no room for overtaking. Lorries, tankers and car transporters were as plentiful as ordinary cars. Everything was coated in grey dirt and blended with the grey exhaust air and tarmac.

Once past Birmingham, the long, uncurving ribbon of the motorway widened out on its journey north, but the traffic remained relentlessly heavy. Green banks on either side prevented any views of the countryside. Signs for road turn-offs and motorway services were the only distinguishing features.

At one of these signs their coach turned in. It was time for lunch at The Country Table. Pete Drummond pulled up outside a flat-roofed, rectangular brick building with large windows down one side of it. The bus disgorged its passengers, then moved on to the petrol pumps. The Country Table turned out to be a huge cluster of wooden veneered stands and counters, alternately laden with snacks and drinks or cash registers, and adorned with large electric brass 'oil' lamps and miniature lamp posts.

'Jessica?' said a voice behind her in the queue. She turned round and with a shock of displeasure saw the close-cropped head and pink features of Bill. 'Jessica, I'm sorry, I've only just noticed you. I'd have said hallo earlier.'

'Hi Bill, I thought you were due back at work.'

'I asked for another extension. But between you and me, I'm not sure if I'm going to return at all –'

Wouldn't make much difference, thought Jessica.

'Oh?' she said, leaning forward to extract an egg mayonnaise sandwich from under the clear plastic flap of the counter shelves.

'Yes, I've been trying to perceive the right direction for me, and I think I'm coming to the conclusion that protest is incompatible with the spiritual path.'

'Protest,' said Jessica flatly, adding a strawberry yoghurt to her tray. 'You mean the campaigns and things.'

'Yes – you see acceptance is the Buddhist way.'

'Accepting that the earth is going down the drain?' Jessica glanced at Bill's empty tray. 'Can't you eat any of this?'

'I'm going to ask if there's butter in the croissants. Accepting that it is not my way, perhaps.'

'Yes, well, it's probably a good idea to make up your mind. I think FOE would appreciate it.'

'Beans on toast please,' said Bill to the red-faced woman behind the hot food counter. Jessica took some coffee and made her way to one of the cash tills, hoping she would lose Bill, whose total self-absorption exhausted her. She was looking round for Suzanne, who had gone to the loo. She was right at the end of the queue. Bill caught her up. 'I never realized you were interested in this kind of thing, Jessica.'

'No – well, I don't know that much about it.'

'I feel this is a much more appropriate way to heal our planet home than through anger and blame.'

'Mm,' Jessica was irritated at hearing her own half-articulated thoughts paralleled, and in the process exposed as naïve, even ridiculous. She looked round for a seat. The Country Tables were crowded. She saw a place near the window and headed over. To her dismay Bill followed. The round wooden laminated table was littered with the previous occupants' debris – triangular plastic sandwich containers, coffee filters, screwed up paper napkins. Jessica pushed the rubbish onto her tray and placed it on the window ledge. Bill fixed his large, round grey/brown eyes on hers.

'"Love your enemies", that's the western text; the Buddha teaches non-attachment which is the same kind of thing.'

'What?' said Jessica distractedly, trying to pull open the plastic corner of her sandwich holder.

'Are these seats free?' A woman with a face rather like a lioness, tanned skin, strong almost masculine features and a thick mane of golden brown hair was staring at them. She was dressed mainly in purple, with leopard skin print leggings.

'Yes, yes,' said Jessica in relief, moving her yoghurt carton closer to her sandwich.

'Thanks,' the woman sat down next to Bill. 'You're on the tour aren't you?' she asked them both. Jessica nodded.

'Over here, Ronald,' the woman called out in a loud, ringing voice. A tall young man with chin length hair came over and joined them. They all introduced themselves. Ronald was a surveyor, and also the local Earth Mysteries Group co-ordinator for North Gloucestershire. The woman's name was Helen, she was a psychic, based in Glastonbury, and ran workshops to encourage others to develop their own psychic abilities. She was also working on a book on the same subject.

'We know each other from FOE,' Bill said, 'but I was just saying that protest is not necessarily the way to save the planet. I feel we have to work on ourselves first.'

Ronald pushed back his mop of hair, and nodded as he took a large bite out of a ham roll.

'I don't know,' said Helen, 'I think the Mother needs all the help she can get. Do FOE sell solar-powered fridges? I've been trying to get one for ages.'

Jessica shook her head. 'I don't think so, it's mainly smaller, personal items like T-shirts and earrings. But I should think the magazine staff could tell you where to go for one.'

'You don't know then?'

'No, no I don't.'

Helen looked at her with disapproval.

'There's no point, you know, in getting rid of appliances and things that we already have, and which are quite functional – that causes pollution too.'

'I've managed without any fridge until now.'

Jessica nodded again, mildly impatient with the woman's combative approach at such an early stage of acquaintance, and distracted by lines of conversation that were drifting across from the next table. She glanced over.

'It's always easy to make extravagant claims about the distant past.' The speaker was a man of about 40, dressed in new jeans with a white line pressed into them and a tweed jacket in an American-style check. He had chubby features that gave the impression of carrying a slight smirk under a thick blond/grey thatch of tightly curled hair. As he spoke he was carefully alternating white and brown sachets of sugar in a bowl on the table, or playing a form of minimized chess with the salt and pepper pots.

'But archaeologists have been just as guilty of that as anyone else.'

'We have made claims about the past, yes – but they have been sensible, moderate, realistic claims, based on logical surmise and whatever facts were available –'

'I'm not sure I agree with that. The idea of thousands of slaves dragging huge slabs of rock for hundreds of miles across the countryside seems just as fantastic as telekinesis – and less interesting! What's worse, it poses as rational thought while being just as unsound as some of the wildest new age claims. For one thing, where is the evidence for the huge population needed to supply that many slaves?'

The other man was slight and dark, dressed in worn and shapeless corduroy trousers and a faded blue jumper. He kept pushing his hand through his straight, black, slightly oily hair, that fell obstinately back again over his forehead.

'You're not telling me, Peter, that you, the serious-minded, sober, experienced Radio 4 reporter believe in telekinesis?'

The dark haired man pushed back his hair again in exasperation. 'What I'm trying to say is that no one knows how these places were built and whatever we do we need to keep an open mind.' He seemed to feel Jessica's attention on him and looking round nervously, flickering his gaze across her face without registering either hostility or friendliness. 'If you're so disparaging of any other ideas Simon, I wonder why you've come on this trip.'

'I'm keeping an open mind of course – anyway, it's fascinating, there's such a crazy array of people here, I think it'll be amazing.'

Jessica felt her anger rise at the arrogance of the man. She turned back to her table. Bill was explaining in great detail to Ronald and the lioness Helen what he did, what he believed in and why he was probably going to leave FOE. Helen was chewing her food in silence, giving him a look every now and then as if she were deciding whether or not he would taste good if she ate him. Ronald had a polite expression on his face, blinking as he strained to catch the flood of information that he wasn't really interested in and which was difficult to hear in the loud echoing cafeteria and tried to eat his lunch at the same time.

Jessica finished her coffee and got up from the table 'See you later,' she said. Helen and Ronald looked up, but Bill carried on unabated. His behaviour made Paul's dismissive attitude towards the tour and her interest in it seem justified. This uncomfortable thought, with its echo in the archaeologist's comments, increased her impatience with the talkative Buddhist. She went outside to the carpark and met Richard about to come in through the glass doors.

'Will we get to Castlerigg in time to visit the stones?' Jessica asked him.

'I hope so,' he smiled, and his large energy bubbled over her. She felt childishly excited. 'Oh great!'

The coach pulled up outside the Old Bell Hotel in the small town of Keswick at around mid afternoon. The tour members quickly divided into those who craved rest and afternoon tea, and those who could not wait to find themselves in the presence of the stones – whether through genuine excitement or a desire to get their money's worth, or perhaps a mixture of both. Eventually a compromise was reached: and approximately one hour later a straggling line of people wound its way slowly up the hillside. The remains of spring were still evident in this more northerly clime. Fields of luminous green grass turned to moorland where moss and heather dominated; the tall mature oaks and horsechestnut trees of the valleys gave way to wild cherry and hawthorn, their gnarled limbs still smothered with creamy pink blossom. The sun on her forehead, the breeze circling round her shoulders, the sickly sweet smell of blossom, the innocent smell of grass, the intent staccato chant of bees as they moved in and out of flowerheads, and the rhythm of her walking body after the long journey all lulled Jessica into a trance of simple happiness. She no longer cared why they were there, in fact if anything she began to experience the aims of the tour and the presence of the other people as interfering in her communion with mother earth. She slowed her pace, dropping back behind the main cluster of walkers, hoping to avoid any interruption of her reveries. Cora was striding ahead, talking to the pretty young man with long hair; Richard was at the front of the group, deep in conversation with several disciples; Suzanne was walking slowly on her own, head down.

The mountains of the Lake District surrounded the Castlerigg circle in rows of green waves, growing fainter like diluted washes of watercolour in the further distance. Yet, despite its magnificent setting, at first sight the circle itself was disappointing. In the bright, matter-of-fact daylight, the stones looked like – well, like what they were – uncut slabs of rock, crudely positioned in an uneven circle. Richard gave people time to rest or explore after their trek up the hillside. Jessica walked slowly round and in and out of the circle of stones, alternately gazingly intently at their craggy surfaces to see if she noticed anything special about them, and allowing her gaze to travel out into the surrounding vistas. Perhaps the best way to visit these places was on one's own, certainly the odd assortment of people standing around the site detracted further from any residual atmosphere there might have been.

Richard cupped his hands to his mouth and called the group over. Jessica, resisting an impulse to go running off into the green distances on her own, obeyed the summons and gathered with the rest just inside the circle. Richard was sitting against one of the fallen stones, one long leg stretched straight out, the other bent in to his body; his arms rested on his knee, or gestured as he spoke:

'Archaeologists tentatively associate Castlerigg with a number of other circles in the northwest of England, and it may date from around 2000 BC. They have, of course, no idea why these places were built.' Some of the group sniggered, Peter March, the Radio 4 man Jessica had overheard, stood solemn as ever pushing back his hair, while his conversation partner Simon Greaves betrayed no expression on his face other than its apparently permanent smirk.

'These places are of course literally megalithic, but they are also subtle. Notice, for instance, how some of the top edges of the stones echo the shapes of the hills behind them. If you come over here –' Richard stood up and ambled over to a stone that had a flattened top, 'you won't all be able to see this at once, but if you crouch down behind this stone,' with some difficulty Richard folded his long form up behind the stone, 'you'll see the most complex example of what I mean.' The breeze blew some of Richard's words away, and the group clustered closer around him.

'This is the view across to the south of the circle: those three stones directly opposite us echo the shapes of the three intersecting hills behind them, the point where those hills intersect is also the point where this stone,' Richard tapped the stone he was crouching behind, 'and the one opposite intersect, and this marks the exact spot of the most southerly rising moon at Castlerigg, an event that occurs as part of a lunar cycle that takes 18½ years to complete.' Richard eased himself back up. One of the red-haired women knelt down in his place.

'Yes, come on, a few of you have a look now, and maybe the rest later on: it doesn't have to be one at a time – yes, several of you – OK – and another lot? Good: OK.' Jessica joined Cora and the young man, Adam, behind the stone. Sure enough, the effect was just as Richard had described. A small, squat stone with a wave-shaped top mirrored the roll of hills behind; a taller stone pointed on one side repeated the angle of a steeper hill in its backdrop, and a third stone, not quite as tall as the middle one, with a slightly rounded top, outlined the round rise of a third hill. The middle of the flattened foreground stone's top intersected with the point where the hills crossed over in the view.

'So that's the moon's dance,' Richard continued, 'but over here,' he walked swiftly over to the tallest stone in the circle, 'as the midsummer sun sets in the northwest, this stone throws a shadow path that extends all across the valley and aligns with that notch in the far mountains which marks the Candlemas rising sun.' Heads turned as Richard pointed across to the far mountains. 'These two alignments, one lunar, one solar, formed the two foundational axes for this circle; using these axes, the ancient builders generated interlocking circles, and from them derived the rest of the groundplan geometry. In other words,' Richard slowed his speech and increased the volume, 'we are looking here at a grand marriage: the marriage between the sun and the moon, between Father God and the Earth Mother, ensuring fertility and life to men and the land.'

Jessica smiled with pleasure at Richard: he had wrought magic out of what had seemed unshapen lumps. She touched the rough quartz surface of the stone in front of her. It was patterned with pale jade green and vivid ochre lichen. The breeze was growing stronger, the afternoon's warmth cooling into early evening. The group shifted and stirred as the wind made it harder to catch Richard's words and goose bumps began to spread down bare arms. Richard was turning in a slow circle as he spoke, articulating with his fine hands.

'Two interlocking circles, as many of you probably know, form that archetypal shape of sacred geometry known as the vesica piscis. This is a symbol of symbols – it can signify Christ, sexuality and it is also a symbol of the Grail: the union of all dualities – inner and outer, sun and moon, male and female, God and man, etc, signifying the state of completion that the Grail brings.' He paused to draw breath. A hawk tipped from side to side high on the air streams, the grass rustled around them. What was she touching? A megalith, neolithic culture, a vibration?

'So you see, this circle leads in many directions, including to the Grail

Castle itself! But may I suggest that now we follow this alignment,' he pointed back down the hill, 'and return to the hotel and supper!'

An uncertain rattle of applause and some laughter ran through the group. Some people were distracted by the chill in the air, by the beauty of the view, by hunger. Others were giddy from all the information that tantalized with possibilities yet eluded comprehension. Jessica felt a moment's confusion – were they going so soon? How could they experience the marriage then?

A tall, elderly man with silver hair spoke up from the back, his voice fragile with the first quaver of age: 'Are we talking about something purely symbolic here, Richard? Or was there some more literal way in which this place, or others like it, were used to create this marriage?' The rest of the group stirred, people wanted to go.

'That's a huge question, Terence, and an important one, but my sensing is that we should start back and discuss things further over supper.' There was a rumour of agreement, then that was it, and people started to drift away. Jessica lingered on; if she could be the last to leave, she might be able to experience the spirit of place without the distracting presence of the others.

'Are you going to stay here my love?' Cora asked her as if it was quite a normal thing to do.

'No, I just want to see what it feels like on my own.' Cora nodded and waved. Jessica watched her and the rest of the group meander down the hillside and over the first stile. She only had a few moments, because she wasn't sure she could find her way down on her own. She stood in the middle of the circle and surveyed it, then walked outside the stones to quite a distance on their far side. The sky was still bright with the first tinge of golden evening light, the breeze brushed softly through the grass. The stones stood stolidly, darkly, a sheep ba-aed. Jessica struggled with her own self-consciousness: could she feel something or not? She glanced over at the gap in the hedge through which the last straggler had disappeared. Time was short, getting shorter. There was the hawk again. The circle of people had broken up, leaving the circle of stones to evening, soon to moonlight. She thought of the sun's rising and setting, the tides of the moon, she had a sense of great heavenly arcs spinning and intersecting, right here in the ground, beneath her feet, fixed and vibrating in the stone patterns around her, and then she knew that she did not want to be there alone any more and started to walk past the stones and down the slope. Once over the stile she broke into a run, telling herself that she needed to catch up with the rest. Eventually she saw Cora's back ahead of her, the last in the group.

# CHAPTER SIX

THE dining room echoed with excited conversation and the occasional ripple of laughter as dinner was served and hungrily consumed. The walk up the mountains to the circle of stones had metamorphosed the disparate collection of individuals into an enlivened body of people. The physical exertion had eased people's numbness from the long coachride; the stones and Richard's comments had engaged them on their quest, and the chance to rest and freshen up on their return had completed the revival. Now instead of guarding mutual reservations they were starting to relish each other's colour and essence and to become fascinated by the dynamics of their interaction.

Suzanne was sitting at one of the small corner tables with a young man in a silvery-grey jumper, and a round-faced, middle-aged German woman. Tired after the climb to the circle, she now found herself too hungry to contribute much to the conversation of their small group. Uta, the German woman, spoke fluent and perfectly articulated English.

'Really, I think this tour is going to be wonderful, I am very glad I came. Usually, you know, I visit the coast when I come here –'

'By here, do you mean England?' asked Gabriel, who spoke quietly.

'Britain,' Uta replied with a smile, 'yes, yes, I *love* to come here. You know I would live here if I could.'

'Why, why do you love it so much?' asked Suzanne. The woman shook her head.

'The atmosphere, you know is very special here, all these monuments, they are a part of that – but I think a lot of it has to do with the sea. Britain has so much coastline because it is an island. Germany is a much bigger country, but we only have a small amount of coastline. And I think this accounts for the great flexibility in the British character.'

'That's an interesting thought,' said Gabriel. Uta paused and looked at him with a shy smile of delight. He seemed to radiate a spacious, attentive presence; every time he spoke, the corners of his mouth looked as if he was about to break into a smile.

'Having to contend always with that force of the sea,' Uta went on, 'larger and stronger than oneself – it teaches you that you have to go with life, that there is a force beyond your own human will ...'

Her appetite now satisfied, Suzanne found Uta's deep voice soothing, with its earnest, melancholic accent. As she spoke about the coastline Suzanne pictured the island kingdom from above, saw the marsh lands, the industrial ports, the grey waves of the North Sea, rolling green surf of the Atlantic. The atonal sibilance of the collective dinner time conversation was the sound of the water as it washed against the coast.

'So people who live inland – are they more intractable?' asked Gabriel.

'I think so – dangerous ideas take hold – like Nazism of course, and Communism. Both of these took hold on continents where the sea is very far away.'

'A conservative or 'red neck' kind of attitude, you mean, exists in the middle of the land mass and gets modified as it moves out to the coast?'

Uta laughed. 'Well, perhaps. I have not thought all about it, but yes, I think the sea is very important. It is like a spiritual force in our lives, and this island is very special, this is what all these wonderful monuments that we are travelling to see are about ...'

Suzanne glanced across at Jessica. She could see her in profile sitting at Richard's table, the centre of the hubbub.

Looking round the table, Jessica suddenly realized that seated at it were mostly women. The only man other than Richard was Terence, who had asked the unanswered question at the stones. The two red-haired American women were sat next to each other, a woman who called herself Bahira was next to Jessica, and Helen, tonight wearing paisley leggings, was next to Richard. For most of the meal their conversation centred on answering Terence.

The American women felt that the ancient priests who designed the sites were initiates of the great mystery traditions and knew how to use the places they had built to tune in to higher astral realms to receive guidance. Helen had said that her psychic perception registered something funereal there – she felt it was all about death ceremonies, probably for important members of the tribe. Terence himself felt that the site was both symbolic of a cosmic order and served as a calendar to help with the cycles of sowing and reaping of crops etc; while Bahira made it clear that the site and the men who built it were carrying on an ancient wisdom brought from Atlantis before its destruction, having to do with unifying the spirit realms with the earth.

Richard listened to it all, nodding his head. He agreed that it was symbolic to an extent, like a Neolithic cathedral, but repeated the ideas Jessica had heard at his home, that experiential rites were carried on, possibly using the qualities of the stones and even hallucinogenic plants to achieve altered states of consciousness.

'And the lights as well?' queried Jessica.

Richard nodded his large head again: 'Yes, I'm aware I haven't spoken about the lights yet.'

Bahira glanced sharply at Jessica, and the swift impression passed through Jessica that the other woman inferred special knowledge on Jessica's part, and resented it.

Richard went on: 'They are an energy form that the earth gives off, the priests may have known how to help create these, summon them up perhaps, even how to 'read' them, like a magnetic tape, to find out about the state of things on the planet. We know the lights carry an electromagnetic field that interacts with consciousness to produce altered states, so that may have been a part of things too.'

By the time the pudding was served, a watery cream caramel, Helen had engrossed Richard in a long duologue about psychic effects at ancient monuments. The red-haired women seemed content to focus on eating their cream caramels, exchanging the occasional quiet remark, while Terence was trying to extract decaffeinated coffee from a stern-mouthed waitress.

Bahira had directed a few definitive comments towards Helen and Richard but, other than a smile from Richard, had achieved no response. She now sat with an air of stiff naturalness that failed to conceal her angered hauteur. In her late 40s, Bahira was perfectly groomed from her well-cut, dark brown hair, streaked with silver, to her shiny court shoes. Diamonds glittered on her manicured hands. Her discreetly made up face was handsome with few smile lines. She was the epitome of the upper-middle class English woman except that her tweed suit was purple and fuchsia, not brown and cream, and instead of pearls she wore a silver chain with an uncut crystal pendant, while her cultured, grating accent clothed phrases like 'special energies' and 'channelled messages' and 'inner child' instead of comments about the weather and the price of houses. The mould was the same but the colours were different: an attempt to make the new age respectable, Jessica supposed.

'What brings you on this tour, Bahira?' She was uncertain how to pronounce the slightly Eastern, slightly futuristic flavoured name, chosen no doubt for its occult properties which her given Christian name, Elizabeth perhaps, or Mary, had been found to lack.

'Well, I helped advertise it through the magazine I edit, and it just sounded so interesting I had to come – which is something I rarely do because we advertise so many different events, that normally, you know, they just sort of pass by without really registering.'

'What is the magazine you edit?'

'It's called *Connections*, it's a magazine to help promote the important work we're all doing, to connect people to one another.' When she spoke Bahira frowned deeply and pushed down the corners of her bottom lip.

'How long have you been doing that?'

'Ooh, a few years. Because I seem to know so many people I was always putting someone in touch with someone about something! And finally my consciousness raised to the point where I realized I needed to start a magazine. I suppose I regard myself as a Professional Networker.'

'So you don't specialize in a particular field, or in Richard's area?'

Bahira shook her head. 'No, no it's true I do not, but I *feel* such empathy with these places, with the people who built them. I just, I don't know, it may sound slightly fantastic, but I feel this is a kind of networking through time, almost as if the builders wanted to leave an important message for us which we would one day be able to read when we had reached the right point in consciousness.' Bahira pressed her lips together and looked at her nails. 'About our spiritual destiny, I suppose.'

Jessica nodded dumbly. She did not volunteer any information about herself, as Bahira did not ask for any. Although she answered readily, with a show of gracious politesse, Bahira's eyes kept flickering towards Richard and Helen. An urgent need to be right seemed to motivate her, edging with ruthlessness her odd combination of upper-class and new age gentility.

The coming of the coffee finally broke up Helen's monopoly on Richard. He smiled out at them all and Jessica could feel Bahira gearing up to take over. Before she could say anything, however, Richard drained his coffee, said how agreeable it had been to dine with them and got up from the table.

Terence asked if anything was planned for the evening.

'No, we thought we would just have a leisurely dinner with a chance for everyone to get to know one another more. I'm sure some will be going back up to the stones, but there's nothing official planned.'

'Oh,' said Bahira, her eyebrows raised a little, but Richard was gone. 'I'd hoped he might be available to answer questions at least.'

'We have to be careful not to overtire him,' said Helen, who also left.

'Well! She's one to talk.' Bahira had been outmanoeuvred, and her composure slipped a little.

After dinner a number of the group sat in the lounge to read or talk, others walked the few yards along the road to the local pub and a secretive few had set off for the stone circle again. Jessica was sure Cora had gone there, to commune with the bright half of the moon before she started to wane. The absence of Adam probably meant he had gone with her. A couple, both with long, hennaed hair, and dressed in faded Indian cottons and jeans, had walked rather self-importantly out of the door carrying bent pieces of wire which she identified as dowsing rods. Jessica wondered what would happen to them all in the moonlight. She felt a certain pull to see the stones herself in the negative of night, yet she had such a clear image of them in her mind's eye that it felt as if she didn't need to go, as if she were still there.

Suzanne came out of the dining room holding a mug in her hand and headed for the stairs.

'Hi there, how're you doing?'

Suzanne gave a sweet smile. 'I'm doing really well, but I'm exhausted.'

'You going to bed?'

Suzanne nodded. 'I'm going to have a long bath first, and then go to bed and read.'

'Sounds wonderful. Are you enjoying this?'

'I'm loving it.'

'Great.'

Suzanne paused on the stairs and looked back. 'What about you?'

'Yeah, I'm glad I came.'

'Are you going to ring Paul?'

Jessica thought for a moment: the idea had not even entered her head. 'No,' she said. 'No I don't think so.'

Suzanne smiled again. 'OK, good night.'

'Good night, sleep well.'

For a moment Jessica hesitated in the hallway. The prospect of a bath and early night also appealed to her, but the evening did not feel quite finished yet. She stepped out of the front door into the night.

The hotel fronted almost directly onto the A-road that passed through Keswick. A path led round the side of the building through the small carpark to some gardens at the back. The air was damp, and Jessica could hear the sound of water: one of the many streams running down from the mountains passed along the edge of the gardens. The half moon in a cloudless sky lit the scene clearly in pale greys and charcoal. An attempt at a formal rose garden with a bird bath was laid out just outside the French windows of the lounge, from which she could still hear a group talking and laughing together; two brick steps led down to an expanse of grass that was more a field than a lawn. High yew hedges divided the grass from the garden above.

Jessica walked along the crazy-paved path by the hedge listening to the heels of her shoes clicking on the stone and debating whether she should fetch her jumper. The hedge curved into an alcove sheltering a bench. The smell of strong tobacco suddenly invaded the cool, fragrant night air and Jessica realized that Richard was sitting in front of her. He was as startled as she.

'Richard! I'm sorry, are you meditating out here –'

'No, it's OK – I just needed a few moments by myself ...'

Jessica nodded. 'I came out to see the moon.'

She made as if to go, but Richard started up, 'No, you're not intruding at all.' He took her hand and sat her down next to him.

A tinge of uneasiness passed through Jessica. Richard's eagerness belied the sensitivity she attributed to him. But he let go of her hand in an easy way and took a long draw on his roll-up.

'So what did you make of your visit to the stones?'

'It was fine, but, well, it's a kind of paradox: if it wasn't for the tour, I wouldn't be there visiting them, but because of the tour – I mean all the people – I found it difficult to really tune in to their atmosphere. It feels as if one should visit there alone, or with a smaller number or something.'

'Mm,' Richard stared up at the moon. 'Yes of course I can understand that, especially if it is the first time someone had been to a site. You didn't want to go up there this evening? I think some have.'

'Yes they have. No, no somehow I didn't feel the need.'

'I find there are ways to be at the sites and cut out the awareness of others. Actually, in today's society we almost have to do that to experience solitude anywhere.'

'Yes, that's true.'

'But also, you know, Jessica dear, sometimes it's best not to go to those places alone. You have to be careful.'

Jessica saw the stones' silvery grey pattern in the night, but no-one else around. She nodded her head. 'Is that what you meant, that time when you talked about what it would mean to be a shaman ...'

Richard took another draw on his roll-up and turned a sudden smile on Jessica.

'I just know that some of my friends have had strange experiences, experimenting, you know, at these places.'

Jessica felt a touch rebuffed. A sting of awkwardness sprang from her but Richard didn't seem to notice. He put his arm around her shoulders.

'Goosebumps! You're cold Jessica, we should go in.'

Half relieved, half disappointed, Jessica agreed. He kept his arm around her till they reached the steps where he turned to bid goodnight to the half moon.

Paul was eating porridge and looking out at a view of cliff tops and shimmering ocean. His bed and breakfast house was situated five miles outside the huddled grey town of Thurso, high up on a narrow cliff road. The brilliant greens and blues of the view formed the only decoration of the dining room, contrasting strangely with the plain brown and beige walls and hearth rug. Two other men, a TV reporter and cameraman, were just finishing their breakfast: the village was full of news crews and journalists. Disasters brought a temporary boom to the local economy in the form of the descending media flock. Paul was uncomfortably aware that, like vultures, he had to be one of the first at the scene to get the best pictures, which was the reason for his swift departure from Jessica.

The two men got up to leave, nodding to Paul with a slightly self-important air. It was eight thirty. Mrs MacNeil, the landlady, came out to clear away their plates. Paul asked if he could have some more coffee and another round of toast. He did not have to rush to the scene: he had gone last evening, as soon as he had arrived, and again at dawn this morning. He had picked his way along beaches coated with oil, seen the sea birds giving their black, heavy plumage a last pathetic ruffle before lying still and hopeless, photographed white surf break over the monstrously long body of the dying ship as more and more black blood poured into the sea. Later in the morning a photographer friend from one of the rich tabloids had got him on a trip in a helicopter, but for the moment he could relax.

For most journalists and news commentators the images of the scene were etched over in their minds with the 'issues': the politics, who was responsible, who should be blamed. Is it the captain of the ship, the practice of licensing ships in countries where nautical standards are low, the agreement by the relevant authorities to let super tankers pass through such dangerous waters? Paul was conversant with how all the arguments ran: he could practically rehearse the newscopy before it was printed. It was too predictable: a rational front for an insane situation. Increasingly it felt to him as if the planet was in the charge of juvenile delinquents.

Mrs MacNeil came back into the room and started to wipe down the other tables with a grim-faced thoroughness. Paul emptied his coffee cup and got up, scraping his chair on the stone floor.

'Thanks, that was a great breakfast.' Mrs MacNeil nodded without looking up.

Paul picked up the payphone in the hall and dialled his home number. It was peak time and he spent nearly three pounds to listen to his own voice on the answer-machine. Jessica must have gone then. Paul still found it difficult to believe that she would go on the trip without him. Ironically, too, Caroline hadn't shown up in the end. He had received a message, no doubt greatly changed in its translation through his landlady, to the effect that something urgent had come up. Urgent, he knew, probably meant someone titled, an invitation from a young Lord or Marquess, their birthday party perhaps, at a country seat suitably encrusted by the rich and famous, past and present. He also couldn't help finding a kind of delighted amusement at the comedy of errors playing itself out: Jessica rushing off to one end of the country, believing he was meanwhile ensconced at the other end with the beautiful Caroline.

The sea out to the horizon was a gently rippling surge of silvery blue, reaching the pale blue haze of the sky in mirroring sweetness. The waves had subsided and the strange carcass of the ship was rocked more gently backwards and forwards over the invisible rocks beneath, slowing the flow of oil. From the air the long black streamer of the slick looked almost pretty on the blue. There it was again, aerial views turning disaster into innocuous patterns, overturning good and bad. The slick was drifting south quite slowly, part of it breaking off with the surf and sticking to the coastline as it went. The clean-up operation was under way, they could see the small ships and the white arcs of the detergent sprays clustered around the worst of the spill.

There was nothing more to be done and Paul hurried to catch the early afternoon boat for the mainland. The train journey from Thurso down to Edinburgh was long but sensationally beautiful. The line zig-zagged across the crags of the Highlands, past silver lochs and green velvet valleys. It was difficult to equate the landscape moving slowly past him with the scene he had just left. All seemed well. The images were serene and lovely as depicted in countless paintings and postcards, but Paul was aware, as he stared out, that like so much of Britain, it was almost impossible to view the land except through the lens of the past. Clichéd images of 19th century travellers in tailored tweeds, steam locomotives chugging through mist, or, further back, Highlanders roaming the tartan landscape, full of the passion of obscure clan feuds. The sight of the supertanker mangled across the coastline was so shocking partly because it belonged to the present: its wreck threatened the ecology of both the land and of history. Yet in prehistory ecological crises on an apocalyptic scale had sculpted the landscape into its present shape as volcanoes had erupted, glaciers gauged out routes through the rock. Paul tried to view the scenery as it was now, without the glaze of the past: a pattern of shapes, an accident of biology, an uninhabited planet.

As if mocking his intention, the train slowed and pulled into one of the small, remote stations en route. Out of the sudden stillness and quiet came a thin reedy sound, which grew and became a band of bagpipers swaying up the road in full battledress. The sound and sight were mesmerising: the music sang the land, the slow creep of people across it, the wars in faraway places, but it did not sing of supertankers.

The train pulled out again, and Paul sat back, savouring what he had seen. Then he realised that Jessica would not be at home and he would not be able to describe the scene to her. A large part of relationship was an accumulation of shared experiences; the larger the accumulation, the more difficult it was to part. The past again: separation meant damaging the fabric of one's past, like tearing hundreds of photographs in half.

At Edinburgh Paul jumped on the small shuttle plane to Heathrow. By late evening he was climbing out of Piccadilly underground station and walking swiftly up Wardour Street to the 24-hour labs who processed most of his work. After dropping off his film he hailed a taxi, and just past midnight opened the door to an empty flat. On the kitchen table was a pile of Richard's books, a basket with two overripe bananas in it and a note from Jessica saying they needed some space from each other. Paul felt his depression close in around him. He decided he was too tired to unpack or bath and went straight to bed after setting his alarm for 6 am.

When the digital beeps penetrated his dreams, realities followed close behind. Jessica had gone, the relationship was officially in trouble and he had no time to think about it. He needed to pick up his slides and get them delivered as soon as he possibly could. In the shower Paul debated whether to take his car. In the early morning it would get him to Soho fast, but he could hit gridlock getting back across town, and parking was always a problem. He decided he'd better not, and ran up the road to the tube.

Paul checked quickly through his slides on the viewing screen. Overall the pictures were good and it was easy to make his selection. Outside again, the traffic was still moving freely down Shaftesbury Avenue, most of it composed of cabs with their yellow lights on. Paul stopped one.

'*The Observer* offices, please.'

The driver hesitated a moment, then nodded: the Fleet Street reshuffle had mixed newspaper offices willynilly through the city, to Kensington, Battersea, Docklands. The cab pulled out into the traffic again: round the Circus, down the Haymarket, along the Strand, back up to Green Park, through Knightsbridge, down Sloane Street, round Sloane Square, down to the Embankment and over Chelsea Bridge to the white and black marble state-of-the-art oblong that had become *The Observer*'s new home. London expanded and contracted according to the amount of traffic flowing through its streets. During the day, it was a huge place: travelling from one part to another took hours, but at night, or in the early morning, everything seemed very close together, like a grandiose village.

Paul's photos were for a special series the magazine was running on ecological controversies. Paul had been commissioned for two other parts and by now his face was known by the picture editor. Paul went over the slides with him, and the assistant typed up notes to accompany them. Then he was free.

It was still only 8 am when Paul stepped back into the day which was already warm and sunny. He felt at a loss: the rush was over, there was nothing he really needed to do. He thought about calling Steve, but it was too early. As the morning was so lovely he decided to walk through it back up to Sloane Square and take the tube from there.

It was a beautiful walk: over the Thames, looking clean and silvery in the early sunlight against the green border of Battersea Park, the Buddhist peace temple suspended like a pendant at its edge; through the Royal Hospital Gardens and some of Chelsea's prettiest and most expensive streets. London was at its best on a morning like this: the day's bustle just beginning, an air of celebration, sun glinting on shop windows, Sloany matrons taking their dogs out, pin-striped businessmen and smartly dressed secretaries clustered at bus stops. Paul felt an elation rise in him as he walked. It was liberating to feel happy in this innocent, spontaneous way, for no particular reason. It exposed and stilled beliefs that happiness was somehow served to him by Jessica, was her department.

He walked through the open door of WHSmith and browsed through the photographic magazines and finally bought one which featured a new Canon lens he was interested in. He hesitated over *Ecology Now*, but decided against it. He crossed over to the tube entrance by the flower stall, but felt reluctant to leave the day, and realizing he was famished, walked past the Royal Court Theatre to the French brasserie on the corner. After scrambled eggs, toast and cappuccino, served by a young waitress who caught his eye and seemed to need to take a long time unloading her tray, Paul was no longer hungry, but began to feel tired. The traffic was now solid round the square, the pavements thick with people. It was hot, and the fumes from the cars were starting to become oppressive. Underground it was even hotter, and Paul was thankful that he did not have long to wait before a train arrived. When he got home, he collapsed on his bed and went straight to sleep.

He was woken several hours later by the phone ringing. The blur of sleepiness was dispelled by a swift rush of expectancy, but when he picked up the receiver, it was Steve's voice on the other end. Paul registered first disappointment, then modified pleasure

'Hey Steve, how you doing?'

'Great, great – you're back then.'

'Yep, feels like it.'

'Do you guys want to have lunch?'

'Er, yeah, that'd be nice. Just me though, Jessica's gone.'

'Oh?'

'On the mystery tour.'

'Oops – do you mind coming here?'

'To Soho? No that's fine – what time is it?'

'Just gone one.'

'I'll be a while, I've got to get up again.'

'Great, OK, see you soon then.'

'Bye.'

Paul lay for a moment in the semi-dark, knowing the bright day glittered outside. He still felt good, his body curled warmly in the neutral room. It was hard to believe that only yesterday he had been flying high above a black oil slick which was ravaging the Scottish coastline: it now seemed remote and long ago. He conjured up Jessica's face in his mind, and tenderness filled him: things would be OK between them, he thought. Then he smiled as he remembered the pretty waitress, very pale with straight wisps of blonde hair, at the brasserie. She had flirted elegantly while serving him breakfast. It had reminded him that women liked him, and that made him feel good too. He splashed his face in cold water and put on a fresh T-shirt, then set off for Soho on the tube for the second time that day.

Steve was in an expansive mode, and insisted on taking Paul to L'Escargot for seafood and wine, instead of Guinness and ham sandwiches at the Red Lion pub.

'So don't tell me Steve, the BBC are going to fully fund this lunch and a 26-part series on *How ESP Built the Pyramids*.'

'Almost right.'

Steve smiled as he poured Paul a glass of Chardonnay. It was by accident rather than personal choice that Steve had achieved a broad specialization in the area of parapsychology. A chance meeting at a party with a hypnotist had led to him making a film as part of a series on alternative healing for one of the BBC's regional programmes. Out of that came a commission to do a short series comparing the more radical aspects of mind-related healing, including depth psychology and the use of hallucinogenic drugs, with the ancient methods of the medicine man and the shaman. The subliminal mind, with its extra-sensory perceptions, is fascinating but very hard to treat visually, and part of Steve's interest in Richard's work had to do with the strong cinematic potential of the ancient sites themselves, so much more compelling than talking heads and computer graphics. Despite his relative success, Steve had been unable to get another commission for over a year. The independent market had become overcrowded with former BBC producers, victims of Thatcher's policy-driven cutbacks. ITV was in the process of re-organization itself and was giving few commissions, and Channel 4 was under financial pressure as it became responsible for selling its own advertising space. The outlets for independent film makers were drying up while their numbers were swelling. So Steve was pleased and relieved at his commission.

'I've got the go-ahead to make a film – about the megaliths and the mind.'

Paul choked on his wine. 'You don't mean all that stuff that –' he coughed again and picked up the water glass.

'Yes, I'm going to use Richard quite a bit, but he won't be the only participant. There are a lot of researchers in this area.'

Paul wiped his eyes on the starched white napkin.

'I'm amazed Steve, but well done, I'm pleased for you –'

'I've got to work really fast, I want to include some of the tour as a way of linking the film.'

Paul raised his hand and wrinkled his forehead in exaggerated astonishment.

'I don't know. The guy's like the bloody pied piper. Jessica, Suzanne and now you!'

'Yeah, but I'm going to make money out of it. Listen, why don't you come?'

Paul looked at Steve in astonishment. Then he laughed out loud.

'You're joking!'

'No I'm not. You've got nothing on right now, have you?'

Paul shook his head, 'Yes, but –'

'And you were meant to go away with Jessica, right?'

Paul nodded.

'So why not come and have a bit of fun for once, and make it up with Jessie. The last part of the tour is in Cornwall, you know, and I think that's when I'm most likely to meet up with them.'

'Why the sudden concern about me and Jess?'

'Well, actually, you could also help me out, I'm going to be really pushed to get this on the road. And you could be my stills photographer too.'

'Oh thanks a lot.'

Despite himself Paul was taken by the idea. It seemed to connect with the feeling of light-hearted well-being that had so inexplicably taken him over. By his third glass of wine he had agreed to go with Steve.

# CHAPTER SEVEN

WHEN Jessica awoke the next morning, sunlight was streaming in through a gap in the flowered curtains and the smell of bacon and toast was wafting up from downstairs. She experienced a moment of childlike happiness: the new day and the tour lay before her, full of fresh pleasures and excitement. Feeling wonderfully hungry, she quickly washed in the small sink in her room and got dressed. The dining room was already filled with most of the tour group. The murmur of conversation and the choppy hard sounds of cups on saucers, cutlery on plates echoed through the room with its old-fashioned parquet floor and panelled walls. Wishing to preserve her crystalline mood, Jessica, smiling but not looking directly at anyone, found her way to an empty table in the corner. The waitress dutifully took her order and poured her coffee from a battered silver pot. Jessica took a sip; it was surprisingly good, strong and recently brewed. She savoured the flavour and her new, clean sense of freedom. She had been right to come away on her own: it would give her time out from her job as well as from Paul, space to discover who she was again.

She took another sip of coffee and looked out of the window. The sky was still colourless, neither grey nor blue; drops of dew shone in the grass. She found herself picturing the argument with Paul the night before he left for the Shetland Isles. She recognized that the scene had been a repetition of many before it. No matter how many times she had tried to evoke for Paul her intuitive grasp of the world, her words never elicited any answering response. Her anguish over his lack of comprehension would flash into anger when it occurred to her that it was really stubbornness on his part, a refusal to take her seriously; and she would start all over again, insisting that he was not really *listening* to her, until both of them felt stale and exhausted.

Jessica frowned. She would have liked to prolong the pristine early morning. She wanted to rein in her thoughts, stop them spilling out into past or future, to remain poised within the simple containers of her momentary experience: her coffee cup and saucer, the white painted windowsill, the feel of the mahogany table beneath her fingers. Perhaps she had been trying to grow within too restricted a container: she rebelled against Paul's relentless, blunt masculinity, it drove her nearly insane. She hated his insistent rationalism, that forced her to stay on a narrow, straight spectrum, never allowing for that space into which she could drift and bring back illogical but true connections. A woman like her shouldn't have to deal with this. There were qualities she needed from a man that Paul just did not have: empathy, intuition, a certain kind of sensibility. She knew it when she came across it in other men.

A voice interrupted her thoughts.

'Ah, now it's me invading your solitude – do you mind if we join you?' Jessica looked up into Richard's face and answered his smile of inquiry with her own of startled recognition.

'Can't see any other tables …' Helen and Gabriel were with Richard.

'No, of course not.' Jessica felt shy, yet now genuinely happy to have her reverie dispelled by company. At the same moment, her breakfast arrived.

'Good morning everyone,' said Helen, looking disapprovingly at Jessica's bacon. Gabriel smiled at Jessica as he sat down beside her.

'Have you two met?' asked Richard. 'Jessica this is Gabriel, a good friend and spiritual ally, and Gabriel, this is Jessica who is being very supportive of my work.'

'Nice to meet you,' Gabriel said quietly. Jessica nodded. She found him difficult to place. He seemed oddly angelic, his smile too readily displayed.

'Please forgive us Jessica,' Richard continued as they gave their orders to the waitress, 'if we talk business a bit.'

'That's fine, I'm still in my early morning haze, I'm happy to just sit here.'

'So Gabriel, Helen is very keen that we visit your wonderful community as part of our tour.'

'Yes, I am, I think it's important for us to visit some modern sacred sites as well as ancient ones.'

Gabriel smiled and nodded.

'How would that work for you, Gabriel? Can you put us all up? I mean, that's what we're talking about really, isn't it? An overnight with you instead of another pub or hotel, just for something different.'

'Oh absolutely,' agreed Gabriel matter-of-factly. 'We can accommodate about half, if some people don't mind sharing rooms; and the rest can stay in Bed and Breakfasts in the village, all of which are very nice and friendly and have a good relationship with us.'

'That could be fun, break into smaller groups, see inside the locals' homes.'

'And what I also thought,' went on Gabriel, 'is that we could prepare a really special meal for the whole group, and then, if you are agreeable Richard, we could organize a talk for you in the evening, with the rest of the community, and also put the word out in the surrounding area.'

'Hmm, I'm not sure, to be honest, that I'd want to give a talk, I'll have been doing a lot of that.'

Gabriel smiled and nodded. 'Of course, I understand that.'

'Maybe we could have a dance – or ceremony, create a ritual space, and let others on the tour speak about their experience,' said Helen.

Richard looked doubtful. Gabriel had a neutral expression. 'I think we'll have to feel it out at the time. By then people may well just want to relax and visit the local pubs for the evening – I assume there are some?'

'Oh yes, some really good ones. I think you're right, let's wait and see what fits.'

Richard nodded and glanced at Jessica, 'What do you think?'

She shook her head. 'I think it all sounds wonderfully intriguing. I'd certainly like to stay there, whatever this community is.'

'Good,' smiled Gabriel.

When everyone was packed back into the coach Richard got up to address them, raising his voice above the drumming of the engine.

'Good morning everyone,' he smiled his wide smile, 'and welcome to our second day of the tour. I hope you all slept well and are as excited as I am to be setting off on our quest together. Just before we get on our way there is a piece of admin I need to sort out. Five days from now we are due to visit Bath, Avebury and Stonehenge, and at the moment we are booked into a local hotel pub in the vicinity. However, with your agreement, it is my proposal that we take up the kind invitation of our friend Gabriel and stay instead in the small village of Dayton with the Dayton Community. Some of us would stay in the community home itself, and some in village Bed and Breakfasts, but we would all eat our evening meal in the community and in the evening we could meet there, or we could have an equally spiritually uplifting time in the local pubs which Gabriel assures me are excellent!' There was a ripple of laughter.

'The Dayton Community, as I think some of you already know, is an intentional, spiritual community of some 40 to 50 people, which for over ten years has been a point of light and encouragement for many of us. So, if I have your permission, I will go ahead and cancel the other booking and alert Dayton to our arrival. Are there any comments or objections? Please feel free to say if there are any.'

A few people in the group shook their heads; most seemed to have no feelings one way or the other.

'Very well then, that's great, we'll make the arrangements, and if anyone has a preference for staying in a B&B or in the community please let me or Gabriel know.' Richard glanced at the taciturn Pete in his place by the wheel. 'So let's get going. All that remains is for me to tell you where we're headed today.'

The juddering of the coach intensified as Pete swung it out of the small car park and onto the narrow road.

'We're going first to Ilkley Moor, erm, there's a couple of features – out of *many* – there to look at, then after lunch, onto Llandrillo in North Wales, and the Moel Ty Uchaf circle and Dyffryn Ardudwy Cairn, with our overnight in Shrewsbury.'

People's attention was wandering, to the view speeding past outside the coach windows, to their inner thoughts.

'We're going to take a slightly longer way round to Ilkley,' Richard persisted, the PA system fighting to keep his voice audible above the churning diesel. 'As you can see we're heading north-east when we should really be travelling the other way, but we're going to join the coast road at Whitehaven, and then head south. This will take us past the notorious Sellafield Nuclear Reprocessing Plant which, I don't know, we just thought, it somehow felt appropriate to do this, to contrast modern and ancient technologies, to feel the atmosphere of the place, to bless it – who knows.' Richard shrugged. Helen was nodding vigorously. 'So that's it friends, I'll stop talking now and let you enjoy the beautiful scenery in peace.'

Jessica was sitting next to Cora who had been slowly nodding her head all through Richard's announcement.

'Do you know this Dayton Community, Cora?' she asked.

Cora turned round. 'You know darling, I think I have been there – it's a sweet place.'

'What is it, what do they do there?'

'They're a centre of light, they hold workshops, have speakers and do organic gardening and love one another and go through the shadows together.'

Jessica didn't feel any the wiser, but the prospect of further mysterious and unorthodox worlds opening out before her reinforced the excited anticipation she had felt on waking up that morning.

'You can ask Gabriel more about it, my love, he lives there and he seems like a very nice man, don't you think?'

Jessica laughed. 'Yes, he does, you're right.'

'I think you'll enjoy it.'

Jessica looked back out of the coach window. The rising and falling grey-green hills and valleys slowly processed past them. She thought about the Castlerigg circle again, and the image of the couple leaving after dinner with their dowsing rods. Cora had gone up there too.

'Did you – was it – did anything happen, last night, at the stones? I mean, that you want to tell about ...'

Cora thought for a bit. 'Those other two were there, for a while.'

'The hairy sandal couple?'

'Yes, Stuart and Hazel, and they wanted to measure things with their coat hangers.'

'Their dowsing rods, yes, I saw them leave.'

'But when they'd gone – we did a dance.'

'You and –'

'Adam. We wove in and out of the stones, very slowly, sometimes holding hands, sometimes apart.' As she spoke, a sudden vivid image formed in Jessica's mind's eye of Cora and Adam in the moonlight, moving to the stones' stillness, the quiet mountains beyond; and as swiftly a wave of erotic energy moved through her.

'Adam wanted very much to make love – the stones can do that of course,' Cora looked at Jessica, 'intensify the current. But,' she shook her head, 'sometimes it just connects you with the wrong level of things, and it doesn't lead anywhere.'

'You mean it should lead somewhere?'

'Love-making can change things, yes, it can be – an act of magic. Or it can be, well it can be a lot of things of course, and Adam is young and I didn't feel I had the goddess's blessing, so we just danced with the stones.'

'God, Cora, you make me feel, so, I don't know, so conservative I suppose. You know I take sleeping with someone really seriously, or maybe I'm just shy or inhibited or something, but Suzanne, she's the same, it's no big deal to her –'

'I take it seriously too my love, but we're all different. Sometimes it's because of a need, sometimes it's because it is right.' Cora's face broke into a smile. 'Good morning my love, how are you?' Jessica had not noticed Richard's approach down the aisle of the coach.

'Good morning, good morning, I'm feeling good, we're on our way, and all is well, and with you ladies I hope.' He looked at Jessica.

'Yes, thanks.'

'What town is this Richard?' Cora asked.

'This has to be Cockermouth,' Richard bent down and peered out of the window, hovering close to Jessica's head. 'Yep, we're out of the mountains now and very soon we'll be on the coast road.' He straightened up and brushed his fine hand very lightly across Jessica's shoulder as he moved off down the coach.

'Cora, why doesn't Richard have a girlfriend, or a wife – or does he?'

'Oh yes, he has a wife, but they're separated. Not that long ago.'

'What happened?'

'She wasn't really interested in his work, and for him it's all-consuming, it's his life. So there was this split between them, and then – it kept getting wider – other people, you know – until that was it, things just weren't going to work for them.'

'I see,' said Jessica uncertainly, looking out at the scenery again.

Pete swung the wheel over as they turned left onto the coast road. The day was turning bright but hazy and the sea stretched out in broad, flat satin quiet, the waves curling slowly as if enfolded in self-contemplation. The road was busy with the first holiday traffic of the season: caravans, campers and cars with bicycles strapped to their roof racks or towing trailers. The occasional sandstone and slate farmstead crouched against the hills, sheep cropped the smooth grass and the ubiquitous straight lines of the dry-stone walls bore witness to the indefatigable efforts of their long dead builders. Round one of the headlands they could start to make out the pale grey, alien shapes of the notorious reprocessing plant. A tower with a bulb-shaped dome, large box-like buildings, and, as they drew closer, row upon row of cylindrical containers, tanks and pipework that corkscrewed over everything. The plant was set well back from the road in a huge area enclosed with high barbed wire fences. Uta, the German lady, was sitting next to Suzanne. She shook her head.

'Ah, it makes me so sad that this terrible place is here, in such a beautiful part of England, and on this wonderful stretch of coastline.'

Suzanne stared dispassionately at the huge complex, which looked oddly familiar, as if it were the generic model for the set of all those low budget science fiction movies that shared the same plot as well and blended vaguely into one another in her memory. This impression of its somehow being a toy helped to diminish the impact of its sinister ugliness. She was able to wrap its raw shapes up in her perception and hold it as a possibility of otherness, of vision for the future, of experiment.

'How could the authorities want to mar such a spot? This was the land Wordsworth made famous. People come here to find transfiguration which he saw and offered – how can all that be ignored so?'

At the mention of Wordsworth Suzanne felt a sudden throb of joy, a sense of resource, of stored richness. She nodded in sympathy with Uta's thoughts:

'I know, but perhaps they really thought it would be OK, perhaps they had a vision and did not think they would harm the land.'

'Oh, but there have been so many accidents here, I know, I am a member of Friends of the Earth, I have followed its history. The sea especially has been badly polluted. No, I think you are naïve a little, I think these men did it all for greed.'

Suzanne pressed her lips together. 'Yes, you may be right.'

The microphone spluttered into life. Richard's voice boomed through it.

'Well folks, I'm sure you don't need me to tell you that we're now passing the Sellafield Nuclear Reprocessing Plant, the largest of its kind in the world. Originally called Windscale, it was re-named to try and eradicate the memory of a bad accident in 1957 …'

'What do you sense darling?' Cora whispered to Jessica.

Jessica thought for a moment. There was that strange hiatus again: did she sense something emanating from the place, or was it just auto-suggestion? Real or imagined, she did register *something*, a force-field, a feeling, a presence. She pursed her lips: 'Fear, I suppose,' she said.

'Radiation,' nodded Cora.

'The irony is,' Simon Greaves was saying to Peter March, 'this place would have been worshipped by our ancient ancestors. In Australia some of the sacred sites are uranium deposits, which we now mine.'

'Well, certain sections of the population and the establishment do worship this place,' Peter replied.

The rest of the journey took them south-east, round the Cumbrian coast, back inland through the Dales, to the small town of Ilkley in the middle of the Pennines. The drive in the old coach round winding roads took most of the morning, and it wasn't till 11.15 or thereabouts that they arrived at the outskirts of the town and could see the moor looming up above it to the south-west. A steep, narrow B-road that circled the lower flanks of the moor led them up to a car park. The coach pulled up, shuddered for a few moments and then went silent. People started to disentangle themselves from their seats, to fold up newspapers, put shoes back on and reach for coats and jackets from the overhead bins.

The long journey threatened to take the shine off Jessica's excitement. She was anxious to get out of the stuffy coach and enter the day. Outside, however, the wind was cold and the journey up into the moor seemed suddenly daunting. A short distance away from where the coach had parked, large, dark grey stone outcrops reared up out of the moorland. Two in particular formed towering cliff-like formations either side of a worn path that led up on to the moor. Richard gestured towards these formations:

'Those are known as the Cow and Calf Rocks: can we all please gather just in front of the largest outcrop, and we'll go on from there.'

Across the road, the large Cow and Calf Hotel was made of the same dark grey green granite and looked, Jessica thought, almost as forbidding as its namesake. The rocks changed the scale of everything, turning Richard's tall figure into a miniature as he stood beneath it, waiting for the group to collect around him.

'Over the years these very familiar landmarks the Cow and Calf Rocks have become almost routinely associated with strange light phenomena. The recess you see over here,' Richard pointed to a cave-like opening in the side of largest rock, 'is called The Fairies Parlour, and it is worth noting that these lights may well have been the origin of the fairies of folklore who were often said to appear at the ancient sites and other locations where faulting occurs.'

The rocks were strangely rounded and holed, as if air bubbles had formed in dough. Jessica noticed initials carved into them, and dated: 1850, 1892. A little escapade on a brief day's outing by young mill-workers, now long dead. The initials seemed to claim the rocks as part of the heavy, well-fingered encumbrances of Victorian England, lending them a counterfeit modernity and disguising their real age – millions of years old. Richard continued.

'OK, let's go on to our main destination now on the moor proper, and I'll say more about the heavily faulted nature of this region.'

There was still a grey haze across the sky which blended in and out of thin clouds to dampen down the blue, and the chill breeze made people walk fast and button up coats and jackets, shivering after the warmth of the coach. For a long while, as they climbed the bare contours of the moor, they could see below them the neat serried rows of the town, but hear only the tramp of feet on the mud and gravel track, the wind in the ferns, the occasional gurgle of a brook alongside the path. In the western sky, the weather was thickening: black bars of cloud frayed into grey fuzziness where rain fell over distant hills, and towering cumulus edged now with silver, now gold, threatened to bear down upon them but never quite arrived. Only after they had walked a long way up onto the curved back of the moor did they lose sight of the town and experience the full remoteness of the spot. The circle stood on what seemed to be the very top of the moor, wide panoramas in all directions, wind-blown, calling some meeting point between bare sky and bare earth. The group gathered round Richard, hair flying, trousers and skirts flapping.

Richard tapped one of the stones. 'This circle is known as the Twelve Apostles, but in fact if you count them, as I'm sure some of you already have, there are thirteen stones, and spaces where several more used to be. The stones and the spaces describe a true circle within a low circular bank. There have been many accounts of shocks received off some of the stones.'

The group stood listening to Richard, touching the stones, staring out at the view. Some sat down tentatively on the lower stones, or leant against them. The stones were all different in shape: some tall and narrow, some short and wide, and they were strangely unworn-looking, with sharp corners and sheer sides, as if the rock was too hard to weather even on that exposed spot.

'The constraints of our schedule mean that we can only visit a very small sampling of the many sites of this area of the Pennines. This circle is one of at least eight circles on this Moor alone. Further south –' Richard pointed into the grey distance, '... on Baildon Moor near Shipley, lie at least two additional circles, and further south still, Bid Moor in Derbyshire has seven stone circles ...'

Jessica stared in the direction Richard had pointed, to where the humped backs of the moors spread out like so many islands of loneliness amid the hidden urban sprawl below them. The Victorian sadness seemed to have soaked into the whole region. The tall red mill chimneys had pointed up out of each ugly little town. People had become enslaved to the crude beginnings of industrialization, the last vestiges of whatever sensibility had existed before vanishing under the materialist, rationalist onslaught. The circles of stone could be forgotten. Their visit now was like picking up a trail that had been left to go cold. Jessica leaned against a stone and shivered, uncertain now whether the morning's promise would be fulfilled.

'That there exists such a concentration of megaliths in this area,' Richard went on, 'comes as no surprise when we recognize that the Pennine area is heavily faulted: for our research shows that the ancient stone sites were all built within half a mile of a fault line. Other phenomena shown to be associated with geological faulting are mysterious light forms of various kinds. Again, research shows a correlation between these lights, faulting and the ancient sites. The Pennine area is well known for its light phenomena. One account, from three members of a Royal Observer Corps team, described a bright white object seen travelling over the moor. It came to these stones, stopped and hovered directly over the circle.' Pausing to draw breath. 'That's about all I can tell you. We'll spend a little more time to get a feel of the site before moving on.' Richard dropped his head as an ending punctuation, and beamed at one of the red-haired American women who immediately went up to consult with him before anyone else did.

Jessica found herself keeping track of Richard. He was currently talking to the quiet woman called Edwina, who dressed in long skirts and earth colours. Next to them Peter March and Simon Greaves were deep in conversation as usual. Peter was touching one of the stones in different places, and seemed to be gesturing to Simon to do the same. Jessica could tell just by the curve of Simon's back and the way his hands fluttered at his hips that he was wrapped in an aloof assurance, his chin jutted forward slightly. Then she watched as he bent stiffly forward to touch the rock. His hand landed in one place, and another, then suddenly he sprang back, the arrogant curve of his body turned to an exclamation mark. Peter looked surprised then laughed. His reaction caused ripples. Richard broke off his conversation to see what had happened, others turned to look. Simon Greaves had received an electric shock.

An hour or so later they were all comfortably ensconced in the neat interior of Betty's Tea Room back down in the town of Ilkley. Waitresses in full black and white uniforms, including little stiff white caps, were serving them excellent Vichyssoise soup, Welsh Rarebit and lines of up-ended dainty triangle sandwiches, sprinkled with the silver and green of fresh mustard and cress. Jessica fought off a compulsion to be next to Richard again and sat at the table behind him instead, where she remained distracted throughout lunch by his table's conversation and the laughter that intermittently engulfed it. Richard and Peter March were quizzing Simon about his experience at the stones, while Edwina was doing her best to empathize.

'I'm sorry to say that our Saul remains unrepentant despite his encounter with the light in the form of an electric discharge,' said Peter.

'Oh ye of little faith,' admonished Richard.

'Oh ye of great gullibility,' Simon replied.

'But what happened, what did it feel like?' asked Edwina.

'It was nothing, like when you get a shock off your car, or a faulty plug or something.'

'You shouldn't incur the wrath of the gods by ignoring their signs, Simon, what *is* it going to take to open your eyes!'

'Good Lord, all this is typical, of course, of the mixed up thinking that so obscures whatever little unworked slivers of real insight there may be in the new age. One minute factoid or phenomenon and you're away – a stone gives off a charge, and the faithful, desperate for a sign, give birth to a whole cosmology.'

'But there are real implications here,' said Peter, a little more seriously.

'Yes, it's interesting, but give me a physicist to discuss it with, not you lot.'

Richard pointed across the room to Terence. 'That's your physicist – not a professor or anything, but Terence taught high school physics for many years. You can talk to him, if you prefer.'

'So what's he doing here?'

'He's open-minded, Simon,' said Peter.

'I think one reason is that he saw "foo-fighters" as a pilot during the war.'

'Saw what?'

'Both allied and German pilots reported contact with a whole range of discoid and spherical flying objects in both the European theatre of war and the Pacific. They were nicknamed "foo-fighters." Some were translucent. Some were very large. There was the usual confusion and speculation later as to their origin – enemy radar decoys, secret weapons, particularly because some pilots reported apparently "intelligent" behaviour, but the lights never harmed anyone and eventually got relegated to the huge miscellaneous file of history.'

'Hm, sounds interesting – I don't know Richard, I think I'm having a conversation about electrical phenomena at stone circles, and end up hearing about the UFO sightings of world war two pilots. You're a magician!'

Edwina, who had been listening with a frown of intense concentration, broke into a smile, and the three men laughed.

Their next destination was another stone circle, this one set amid the north west slopes of Cadair Bronwen just outside the small village of Llandrillo in North Wales. Their route took them first over the moors and through the old mill towns of Hebden Bridge and Todmorden. These were mournful places, tucked claustrophobically between hill and moor, and coloured a drab red brown from the millions of dirty bricks that formed their arched viaducts, deserted factory buildings and tight rows of terraced houses. The industrial remains evoked both the noisy past of desperate working conditions and the present sad quiet of unemployment. Then the Dales were left behind and countryside gave way to conurbation as they took the M6 and circled around Manchester. They headed west to Chester, then further south through Wrexham. Conurbation became suburbs which thinned out into the ancient green curves of the Welsh countryside.

Jessica found herself sitting next to Jonathan, a young man in his mid-twenties with thick cropped brown hair and a ruddy, outdoors complexion. His conversational style was at first staccato and monosyllabic, delivered in a Geordie accent. He described himself as an itinerant cabinet maker, but Jessica was also able to prise out of him that he was an obsessive mountain climber and outdoors enthusiast. In the winter he worked, living in squats or friends' flats in London, and for most of the summer he climbed, sleeping in his tent or under the stars.

'Didn't you stay in the hotel though, last night?' Jessica asked.

'No way, I was in my tent.'

'Whereabouts, by the stones?'

'No, too windy, I came a bit further down the mountain.'

'Too windy, and you a mountaineer!'

'Yeah, but I just needed to get a really good night's sleep. I was tired.'

'So you're not scared of the stones?'

'Oh I've slept in circles and all that before.'

'Have you ever seen anything?'

'What d'you mean?'

'Well, like strange lights.'

'No.'

'What about – I mean, has it ever felt strange to be there?'

'No, well, I sleep too deeply probably to notice anything odd.'

'Why do you sleep there?'

'I don't always. But they're sacred, aren't they? I think it's great, like sleeping in St Paul's Cathedral or something, only you can see falling stars.'

'So you're really interested in Richard's work?'

'I'm interested in the tour, yes, and what he has to say, but I don't hold with that equipment and stuff at the sites. I reckon it's, you know, sacrilegious really.'

'But no-one had any equipment, just a few compasses or divining rods.'

'I know that, but the stuff he has used, the magnetometers, and Geiger counters and all that, I don't hold with that.'

'Do many people feel like that?'

'Aye, there's a number of us. There's us, who'd rather not have any technological stuff at the sites; then there's the real hard-nosed scientists, who aren't interested anyway; and then there's people like Richard, sort of pseudo-scientists I call them. Trying to play both camps, paying lip service to "research" and "scientific" this and that, getting readings here and there, moaning about lack of funding and so on. It's all baloney, I think.'

'What approach would you suggest then?'

'I think we should just trust our own instinct and feelings, and use psychics or something. Whatever these places are, they're all so old that we'll never find out what really went on by so-called scientific methods. Maybe thousands of years ago they did have special properties and so on, but so much would have changed since then, they're probably defunct now anyway.'

'You've given it a lot of thought.'

Jonathan paused. 'Yeah, I s'pose so. If you sleep at these places, you'd be strange if you didn't think about them a bit.'

The hint of patronisation in Jessica's remark dried up the flow of Jonathan's remarks. He went back to staring out of the window. But Jessica persisted.

'And why mountains, what makes you want to climb them?'

Jonathan shrugged, turning his head slowly round again, but looking forwards, not at Jessica. 'I don't know, I've always loved climbing, since I was very young, and I got better and better at it. I think it's the same sort of thing, you know: mountains are sacred too, and they're always far away from our modern civilization which personally I think is crazy.'

'Is that your solution?'

'What d'you mean?'

'Your solution to the problems of society, to experience the sacredness of mountains and the ancient sites?'

'It's not my solution no, it's my way of coping with things. I don't have any solutions.'

Jessica nodded.

'What about you?' he asked.

'Well, I work for FOE, you see, and I suppose I've felt for a while that if we see problems about the way civilization is going, about pollution in particular, we should *do* something about it.'

'Aye, you're probably right.'

'But *what* you do, that I'm not sure about anymore.'

'Hm,' Jonathan said in a tone of non-comprehending agreement. 'Yeah, from what I've heard, that FOE does a good job.'

Their conversation lapsed into an easy silence for most of the remaining journey. Jessica dozed off and on as they drove through the built-up areas, but came alert again once they were into Wales. They stopped for a loo break and the stretch and breath of fresh air helped enliven all of them. As they climbed back aboard, Jessica noticed that Suzanne had sat next to Richard in his usual place at the front of the coach.

About a mile north of Llandrillo itself, the coach took a minor road heading east up into Cadair Bronwen. The road led to a gate, in front of which Pete pulled up and everyone got out. The roadway continued for a while beyond the gate, passing through two more gates before it became a steep, rough track. The Moel Ty Uchaf circle itself did not come into view until they were almost upon it, at the top of the knoll. Then, as at many sites, the view opened up around in broad panoramas: blue mountains in the far distance and hazy green patchwork fields on the softer hills closer by. The stones were chunky and boulder-like, contiguous rather than spaced apart as in the other circles they had visited.

Again Richard gathered them around him.

'Ten years ago the Moel Ty Uchaf circle and the mountain on which it is placed were the centre of a strange phenomenon. A noise like an explosion was heard by people in a wide radius of the mountain; an earth tremor followed, felt up to 60 miles away. Before and after these events, various kinds of aerial lights were seen at all compass points around the North Wales area. The event made headline news: and it was widely assumed that a great meteorite had struck Cadair Bronwen. However, despite searches by police, the RAF and scientists, nothing – no mark – was found.'

The chunky stones stood in wind buffeted silence, as if innocent of the outlandish tales Richard was telling. The group listened doubtfully, looking from Richard to the stones, then gazing out at the quiet view. It was all fascinating, but hard to imagine.

'It's growing late and cold, so we'll let this be a brief visit, and I'll go into more detail about this site after dinner at our hotel.' Richard's tones were soothing. Jessica felt almost petulant. Standing on the wild, wind-shaped Welsh mountainside, she had experienced again a longing to leave the mundane world, and an impatience with the cumbersome linearity of their journey, wanting to step aside from time and normal dimension, to be gathered up somehow into the mystery that these stones seemed witness to.

The rest of the group were glad to get moving again, back down the mountainside to their waiting bus. Soon the mountains turned to border country, and it was not very long before they were entering the suburban outskirts of Shrewsbury where the comforts of hot baths and supper awaited them in their small hotel.

At dinner Jessica found it difficult to tether herself to the conversation at her table. She was sitting with Cora, Adam and Jonathan. Cora was finding out about Jonathan, and Adam was enthusiastic, even passionately supportive of his lifestyle, which he considered totally cool but would in fact rather aspire to than actualize. Having already heard from Jonathan, Jessica felt at least partially excused from participating too much, and found herself glancing across to Richard's table, where he and Suzanne were chatting as if old friends, with occasional input from the two red-haired American women, both of whom, she had learnt from Cora, had degrees in spiritual theology from Matthew Fox's college in California. Jessica sensed, or thought she sensed, that Cora was aware of her distraction, which made her uncomfortable. She found herself worrying lest Cora ask what was going on. She was glad when coffee was served and the group began to reconfigure in the lounge.

Even though it was early summer the evening was cool enough to make a fire welcome, and Jessica, one of the first in the room and craving cosiness, gratefully sat down close to its warmth on a sofa that was angled towards the fireplace. Gradually everyone arranged themselves in armchairs and sofas or on cushions on the floor, forming a semi-circle around the hearth. Richard came and sat next to Jessica, claiming that it was a good spot from which to see everyone. The sofa was small and from time to time their thighs touched.

'So let me begin with a little more detail about the energy phenomenon at Moel Ty Uchaf. The tremor which followed the explosive noise was recorded by the Global Seismology Unit of the British Geological Survey in Edinburgh.'

It seemed to Jessica that a current was building between herself and Richard, keeping her intensely focused on his proximity and all its implications and unable to concentrate very well on what he was saying.

'Strange lights were seen local to Llandrillo and further afield, both before and after the event. Just prior to the explosion villagers in Llandrillo reported seeing red disks of light encircling the mountain and one astronomer saw a blue fireball tracking west. Amateur astronomers reported what they thought to be a meteor travelling south and fireballs were reported over the Irish Sea and the Bristol Channel.'

The burning coals settled and spat in the grate. Jessica stared into their depths, as if watching in miniature the scene Richard was describing.

'After the event, police reported seeing lights in the area and coast guards at Holyhead on Anglesey saw a flaring tadpole-shaped object. There were also reports of 'fires' and descending streaks of light over the mountain at the same time as the explosion.'

The majority of the grouping stared passively and contentedly at Richard, or at the fire, as if they were listening to a bedtime story. Simon Greaves sat in the shadows to one side of the room, listening intently, as if making mental notes; Peter March sipped his coffee and fidgeted, as if he had heard the account before; Bahira, regal in cream velour jumpsuit, gazed in full empathy at Richard, casting the occasional frosty glance over Jessica.

'The following day,' Richard went on, 'police searched the mountainside, the RAF ran flights over the area and scientists were dispatched to scour the area – all found nothing. One of the Edinburgh Seismic Unit team of scientists was sure the tremor had not been caused by a meteorite, pointing out that if it had been it would have had to weigh several tons and the huge scar such an object would make on the landscape could not have been missed by anyone.'

He paused and half turned towards Jessica with a smile. Then looking back out at his main audience again, 'So there you have it, the extraordinary tale of the magic mountain.'

'Do you mean to say,' asked Terence, 'that there was nothing at all found, no further studies carried out – ?'

Richard shook his head. 'Well, as I said, there were various studies made immediately following the event. One group with a Geiger counter obtained extraordinarily high readings of radiation, but that was about it. It gradually fell out of the news because nothing else could be found.'

'I remember the incident being reported,' said Simon Greaves.

'It's easy to see why so many magical stories and legends have grown up around these places,' said Edwina timidly.

'The trouble is,' said Helen, 'that the word 'magic' has come to mean unreal, like those other words: myth, legend, story – when maybe there's something real, i.e. a real phenomenon that is magic and which these sites are in tune with.'

Jessica warmed towards Helen. A lot of the group nodded. The older of the red-haired American women spoke:

'It's the same with so-called religious or spiritual experiences: seeing visions, being 'transported', having some kind of peak or near death experience – none of these phenomena can be physically documented, but they are real to the people they happen to.'

'The question *is* what *is* real?' stated Bahira, emphatically.

'Absolutely,' Peter March agreed. 'We all know that those huge megaliths we see are real enough; many of them weigh several tons. If they fell on top of us they would crush us. Yet we also know that at the subatomic level they are only energy, held together by the spinning force fields of tiny particles, which themselves are found to be simple but unpredictable patterns of vibration. Physical reality no longer really exists, but you wouldn't know it from the way we still picture the world.'

'Isn't it true to say, Richard' said Gabriel quietly, 'that in shamanism there is no objective world. Material or objective reality is an agreement made out of our deeply held beliefs.'

Richard nodded his head in pleasured agreement: 'Believing is seeing, not seeing is believing,' he said. Simon Greaves looked on askance.

Gabriel smiled: 'And to say that something is real or imagined has no meaning, because imagination means the process of creating images, which everyone does, whether a child or a nuclear physicist. It is not to do with whether something is real or unreal; the reality that most people subscribe to is *already* imagination.' There were murmurs of agreement.

'Yes, but you are over simplifying things horribly,' broke in Simon. 'We *find out* things about the world and that affects what we image. A toddler bumps into one of those megaliths and finds out that it hurts. No one told the toddler that rock is harder than flesh, the toddler experiences it in the physical world. Now that is not a shared belief, it is a shared experience.'

'But there are those stories, you know what I mean,' Adam was frowning trying to remember a specific example, 'of people in emergencies being able to do superhuman things, like lifting a car that has fallen onto someone –'

'And sometimes toddlers don't hurt themselves when we all think they are going to, or they hurt themselves a good deal more when around adults that are worried about all the dangers surrounding them.' It was the younger red-haired American woman, who spoke sternly, avoiding Simon's eyes. Bill opened his mouth to say something about the power of meditation. The group conversation had taken hold like a well made fire and burnt steadily for a little longer, dying away gradually as people broke away, some to the bar, some to bed, some for a night walk before sleep.

Richard seemed to merge himself deeper into the sofa, stretching slightly and rubbing his eyes. 'Mm, it's good to feel the group coming together,' he said, his voice made sonorous by a half-yawn.

'Yes, it must be,' said Jessica, suddenly earnest and serious as she had found herself in past situations, a defence against the outright admission of flirtation and desire.

'Ooh you know, I think I fancy a beer – can I get you something?'

'Erm, yes, thank you, that's kind – I'll have half a Guinness please.'

Jessica sat nervously while Richard went to get the drinks. She felt both apprehension and fascination at the thought of being unfaithful to Paul. She wanted to fling herself off the cliff of her caution and loyalty, but at the same time was desperately uncertain about it all. She half wished she had asked for a full pint of Guinness, she could let the alcohol overrun her fears. Richard was back, handing her her glass with a hint of formality, as if aware of her concerns and not sure which message she wanted him to receive. Again, there was a macro-second of awkward pause: the worry that words would dry up and there would be nothing to say, that they would be left frozen and complicit in the stare of mutual sexual assessment.

'It sounded amazing – all those things that happened in Wales,' Jessica said, drinking deep of the thick, black liquid. 'I mean it's really strange that it's all not better known about or researched or something.'

Richard nodded and sighed, but his answer sounded automatic, as if going through the motions. 'Oh I know, it's crazy.'

'You know what I *love* about all this,' continued Jessica, suddenly tapping a richer vein of conviction and throwing it open to share, 'is that it, well, it takes magic and legend and so on *seriously* and, is ... taking steps to not just *explain* it scientifically, but kind of put magic and science on the same footing ...'

Richard nodded, and again his response had the ring of a stock phrase: 'It's good of you to say so, it's certainly one of my aims.'

Jessica felt a shade of confusion pass over her and took another sip of beer.

'Richard, have you ever experienced, you know, the kinds of things we're talking about: altered states, the presence of ... of another dimension?'

Richard rubbed fine fingers over his face and scratched his eyebrow. 'I've seen lights on ... two occasions, I think. I have to admit to having sometimes felt fear at some of these places – not for quite a while now though. Otherwise, I have only sensed other dimensions under the influence, I'm afraid, I've experimented to some degree with one or two of the mind-altering plants that the shamans used, or still use . I've never spontaneously come to the threshold of the faerie world.'

'When I was a child, sometimes on holidays in Cornwall, or in a wood near where I used to live, I'd sort of go into a different state.'

'Really?'

'Yes, it's hard to remember it now, it's all mixed together in my impressions – the trees, the presence of something other. I just used to think it was the way things were, everywhere, for everyone.'

'Hm, yes, well children are supposed to be more sensitive to all these things, and of course that's another way in which it gets dismissed, because "childish" comes to mean silly or unreal again.'

His tone sounded almost perfunctory. Jessica felt disappointed that he did not seem more interested in her experience. She was at a loss as to what more to say, it seemed that everything she had ventured so far was predictable, echoing comments he had heard hundreds of times before, and now, instead of engaging with his usual generous enthusiasm, he was too tired to hide his ennui. Perhaps that was something at least, he was prepared to show his more private face to her. The sting of rebuff made her suddenly overwhelmingly aware again of his presence close to her. As she drained her glass she allowed her eyes to range over small parts of him, the way his ribbed jumper thickened into soft folds at his shoulders and arms, the slightly swarthy skin at the curve of his chin, the stubble of the day just beginning to show. The desire to touch him was almost irresistible, to feel the contours of his chest under his shirt, to kiss the skin at his neck, in front of his ears. And as quickly Richard leant towards her, taking her hand in his large hands, delicately stroking the ends of her fingers. Jessica felt a thrill of ravishment move through her and stir between her legs. His large, intense eyes looked into her face.

'And I want you to know how important your support is to me. I can *feel* your support, it's like a warm current all the time.'

Jessica nodded, not quite knowing what he meant, and not caring either. He really liked her, she felt relieved, excited.

'People like yourself, and Suzanne, and Steve, it's important, you know?'

She nodded again. Was there something odd about his expression? She sensed a whiff of need from him, the intensity of which unsettled her lust. She could not deal with neediness or insecurity. Maybe she should make quite sure. As strong now as the flickerings of desire came a backwash of repulsion. She tried in vain to find the deep well in him, to sense again the heady impact of his closeness, to see herself obeying strange rituals of the moon goddess in the dark shadows of the stones. It was all contrived: her ardour was draining out of her, uncovering the resistant ground of commonsense that lay beneath it, Paul's voice echoing annoyingly in her head. She should have drunk more Guinness.

Richard's hands were still caressing her fingers, but now she found it almost irritating. Her ambivalence must have communicated itself, for Richard stopped and closed her hand in his for a moment, smiling uncertainly at her. It was a decisive moment: what happened next was up to her.

'Darlings,' said a voice next to them. They both looked up.

'Oh – I'm sorry if I'm interrupting something –'

Cora didn't look very sorry. Jessica shook her head in guilty silence, Richard smiled. 'Only when I saw you there Richard my love I remembered there was something I wanted to talk to you about, because it's so late, and if I sleep on it I might never remember …'

'You're right Cora, it is late and it's high time I was in bed. Come and whisper in my ear as we go upstairs.' Richard turned to Jessica and for a brief moment took her head in his hands and kissed her lightly on the forehead. 'Good night,' he said.

'Good night,' she sat looking up at him now rather wistfully.

'You know it's nothing urgent, it's foolish of me really – good night my love,' Cora waved at Jessica as she put her arm through Richard's and led him away. 'It's just about the arrangements at Dayton …'

Jessica sat in the large, empty room wondering about Cora's entrance: it had obviously been done on purpose, but why? The whole episode had been strange. Still sensing the delicacy of Richard's lips against her skin, Jessica wanted to kick herself. There she went again, making a big deal about sex, convincing herself on the one hand that she wanted to break out of the relationship with Paul, and out of her too-sensible world, and then getting cold feet when the opportunity arose. Hadn't she all day been anticipating something new, longing for something different to take her over? What did it matter if she did sleep with Richard? What was at stake? If something came of it, fine, if it didn't, that was fine too. Why not? Of course, there was nothing to stop her from knocking on his door, saying that she had felt something incomplete between them …

The hall clock chimed the quarter hour. It was past midnight – perhaps it was too late now though – they had to make an early start, Richard would be tired. She was tired too, and her small tidy room with its innocent bed called to her. There was also something just a little too bold about entering his bedroom, it wouldn't be gradual enough for her to feel comfortable. Tomorrow night, she would sleep with him, tomorrow night for sure. They would be in Wales again, full of mystery and pagan currents. Tonight would be just the prelude. She would make her signs clear during the day and then, what the hell.

# CHAPTER EIGHT

THE Burton Hills rise up suddenly out of the Warwicksire plains. Covered in a tight green skin, they are strangely smooth and small, dotted with a few sheep and one or two trees. On one hillock a miniature stone turret had been built, completing Jessica's impression that the hills were really illustrations in a nursery rhyme book. Perched upon their western slope was the ancient square-towered church of Burton Dassett, and beside it, just outside the bounds of the churchyard, was an even more ancient holy well: the reason for their visit.

'All Saints Church of Burton Dassett is 12th century,' began Richard, as the group collected around him on the muddy path, 'but it is built on the site of a much older shrine, dating as far back as Saxon times, and this well would have been in use for as long if not longer, probably for healing purposes as well as pagan worship. This location was the centre of another strange outbreak of light phenomena in 1923 and '24. Brilliant lights were reported dancing around all over the region, with the activity focused on Burton Dassett. The hills around here are riddled with geological fault lines, and the church and its well are positioned right next to the Burton Dassett fault itself. We'll visit the church in a few minutes, but you might like to take some time now to look inside the well.'

A square, lintelled stone wall with a rectangular entranceway had been built into the earth which curved up in a bank around the well. In small groups of twos and threes people put their heads through the entrance to experience its dank interior. There was little to be seen. A species of dark green, broad leaved fern with silvered markings grew among the stones of the walls; the water was shallow, looking more like a pond than a well. An empty plastic fizzy drink bottle with a bright orange label floated half-submerged in one corner. Jessica stepped back into the warm air of the day and glanced round to see what Richard was doing. All morning she had looked for a graceful way to reconnect with him, but their time had been so full with visits to another stone circle close to Shrewsbury and a boulder called the Fairy Stone on Cluny Hill that she had been unable to find the right moment. She thought she sensed an awkwardness in him, but felt confident that it was the demands of the busy schedule and not a desire to avoid her that kept him from looking her way. She was sure that over lunch the right opportunity would present itself. At the moment, he was checking to see that everyone had taken their turn to look inside the well entrance before he motioned them to gather round again.

'There are over 5000 holy wells in Britain and Ireland, and probably many more that have not yet been discovered. In pre-Christian times, water was sacred, and medicinal properties were attributed to the water at many of these wells, and, like the megalithic sites, many legends have grown up concerning their use and what is likely to happen if their surroundings are disturbed. Some of the wells had small chapels or baptistries built over them and were used by Christian priests to perform baptisms. This is one way in which Christianity absorbed the pagan sites into itself. There are also several examples of ancient churches standing in close proximity to wells, as we have here.'

The church and its well appeared to exist in isolation, remote from any dwellings, yet Richard had to raise his voice to be heard above the whine and drone of the M40, just over a mile away.

Richard paused and smiled. 'So, we have the packed lunches which the hotel prepared for us, and we had tentatively planned to picnic outside, weather permitting. I'm inclined to go that route, but what do you all think?'

The day was turning out very fine indeed, one of those fresh, warm days of early June, sweetened with birdsong, and there was a general murmur of assent to Richard's suggestion.

Richard and Cora went to fetch the packed lunches from the coach while the rest idled back to the cemetery. Jessica pushed open the heavy door of the church and went inside. The church's interior seemed much larger than its outside led one to expect. Its huge Norman proportions opened up in a surprisingly bright light: an effect of the pale green wash on some of the walls, and the clear windows – the original medieval glass, Jessica read in the leaflet appealing for restoration funds. The thick walls held a shape of quiet from the motorway's onslaught, but Jessica did not find the atmosphere restful. The pale green light gave an unhealthy glow, the carvings around the thick pillars, worn so smooth by time alone, somehow frightened her. She went back outside.

Richard and Cora were already distributing cling-wrapped packages of sandwiches, apples and tins of soft drink. The grass was still too damp to sit on; a couple of people produced plastic sheets or rugs and shared them, others leaned against the gravestones. Jessica's heart beat faster as Richard approached and she found herself giving him a glassy smile.

'And how's Jessica today?' Richard was smiling too, his eyes flickering over her face.

'I'm fine, thank you,' Jessica replied over-eagerly. 'How are *you*?' But Richard had already moved on.

'Busy!' he said, shaking his head in mock overwhelm, his eyes down. Jessica felt stung: now there was no mistaking the change in Richard's attitude towards her. She had obviously annoyed him deeply: maybe he thought she was just playing games – this of course would be anathema to the kind of passionate reality of his character. Her cheeks burned, she felt exposed as a fake, or a child, running off to try out the grown-up world and not being able to pull it off. She started to chew disconsolately on a ham sandwich. Richard went and joined Terence and Suzanne on a rug, where they chatted and laughed easily together. Was there something in his expression, though, some hollowness in the cheeks, that expressed hurt as well as anger? Jessica's discomfort turned to anxiety as she started to scheme ways to make amends. She would sit with him on the coach, corner him as they were about to leave when no one would notice, or at the next site, or that evening over dinner, she would sit at his table – she could tell him how deeply she empathized with all that he said, apologize if she had seemed strange, explain how insecure she was feeling in the early stages of breaking up with Paul ...

Richard was calling for people's attention again.

'Sorry if I'm interrupting you, but Terence here has been asking about the church, and it is worth giving a bit of the sad history of this place. As you may have noticed, the church is large and sits in the middle of nowhere, but in the Middle Ages Burton Dassett was a thriving market town. This paradox is in fact testimony to the horrors of the Black Death, the plague which swept across Europe in waves from the middle of the 14th century onwards. Whole villages were wiped out, including this one. Burton Dassett never really recovered, as it has a smaller population today than when the plague hit. Over there,' Richard pointed to a far corner of the churchyard, 'you will notice that the turf curves in a slight mound, and there are no graves or shrubs or even trees. That is suspected to be one of several mass graves that were dug in and around the village.'

The group stared at the mound. Along the overgrown church wall that bordered it, old oak trees wrestled with ivy; to its side, the stone tags of the ancient graves leaned in uneven rows, a few daisies sprinkled among them. Centuries ago the villagers had died helplessly, black patches spreading across their bodies. Jessica looked at Cora; her face was pale, her bold features seemed strangely tightened. It was not difficult to sense the atmosphere here. The sad history accounted for the uneasy disquiet of the place, with no feeling of sacredness to soften it. The brutal intrusion of the motorway was the constant sound of its pain. Jessica felt gratitude suddenly flood her: she was so glad to be alive, to be warmed by the sun. It was important to live fully, while one could. She must be brave and find the right opening with Richard.

As they started to leave, however, the German woman, Uta, skipped up to Richard and took his arm, and on the coach Jessica found it impossible not to sit next to Suzanne when she smiled up at her from a window seat and asked how she was. Fortunately though, their next stop was the Rollright Stones in Oxfordshire and the journey, through pretty Cotswold villages and along fast-moving A-roads, was absorbing and short.

The Rollrights consisted of three separate features: the King's Men, a large stone circle, 104 feet in diameter, lying just south of the small country road that lead to the site; the Whispering Knights, a collapsed dolmen about a quarter of a mile south east in the same field, and across from the circle on the other side of the road, a single monolith called the King Stone. Richard sat everyone down first in the circle and recounted some of the physical and psychic monitoring and research carried out at the site. Jessica remembered some of what Richard was saying from his talk in London: ultrasound anomalies from some of the stones in early spring; abnormally high or low readings of radiation; concentric rings of magnetism, forming a spiral within the circle; an infrared glow photographed around the King Stone at dawn.

She gazed around at the ring of broken stones. They were uneven in height, some almost seven foot high, others barely grass-covered mounds. The limestone, gnarled and holed by age and weather, formed easily into grotesque features and twisted expressions as she ran her eyes over their pock-marked surfaces. Richard's evocation of pulsing energy fields and ultrasound calls at dawn were as fascinating as the folk tales and legends of petrified beings or moving stones. All suggested that the stones were alive in some way, and that possibility thrilled. It formed a gateway back to the pre-time when the elements were not so harshly divided, when magic was science and the world was more malleable to consciousness. Richard's work was important, how could she have doubted him. She looked at him again with a rush of longing.

'There's a lot more I could say about this place – its history, the legends, our work here. But I think the best thing now would be to let you experience the site for yourselves. I know some of you have felt a bit hurried at the other places we have visited so far, you would have liked more time to do your own exploring and observing, or just to be and see what you can sense. I hope that this will be possible at all the more major sites. So, it's almost 3 o'clock now, we are scheduled to have tea at about in 4.30 in Woodstock and then we head back into Wales. That gives us over an hour to spend here. I am available and happy to answer questions and discuss any aspect of the site or your impressions with you.'

Terence was sitting next to Jessica.

'I'm afraid they're all beginning to look rather similar to me.'

Jessica smiled. 'All the circles?'

'I never realized there were so many of them!'

'Nor did I, and this is only a small sampling according to Richard.'

'I'm rather glad for a bit of a rest. Do you think I'll become enchanted if I have a snooze?'

'You might do, or you'll just have some very interesting dreams!'

'I wouldn't mind seeing one of those lights though – I think that would be great fun.'

Jessica laughed as she got up. 'Yes, I'd like to as well.'

Terence propped himself up against one of the stones and closed his eyes. Jessica wandered around the outside of the circle occasionally stepping inside to see if she could feel any difference. Was there more of a sort of fuzzy feeling inside than out? She couldn't be sure. She decided to go and see the Whispering Knights dolmen. On her way across the field she overtook Stuart and Hazel who were walking slowly and deliberately side by side, dowsing rods outstretched in front of them.

'This energy is *strong* can you feel it?'

'Oh yeah, wow – it's old, this is old energy, red dragon power here.'

'It's probably a part of the Aquarian grid.'

'Yeah, we could test it out.' They both ignored Jessica, who altered her path so's not to interfere with their dragon lines.

The large stones of the dolmen were enclosed in a circle of iron railings, around which the young corn swayed in the wind. Beyond them stretched a view of patchwork fields. As Jessica approached, Richard appeared from behind the dolmen. In the moment of surprise, she smiled at him with delight.

'Richard! I didn't see you there! Were you hiding?' Her spontaneity seemed to reconnect them. Richard smiled a little sheepishly.

'Kind of. I thought I'd take a few moments to meditate on the view.'

'I don't know, I always seem to be bursting in on your moments of sanctuary.'

'Well I never feel that way.'

Jessica hesitated. None of the things she had planned to say seemed relevant now. 'This is an amazing place –'

'Yes, isn't it, I love it, especially when the weather is like this.'

'I suppose you've seen it in all conditions.'

'Yep, it can be pretty cold at four on a February morning!' Richard glanced behind her, and his face took on its welcoming smile. Stuart and Hazel had finally reached the dolmen. 'Hi, how are you doing?'

'Great, great.' Hazel's eyes glowed with fierce enthusiasm. She did not seem to register Jessica's presence. 'We're getting very significant signals, Richard.'

'Are you?'

'It's phenomenal, isn't it Stu?'

'Pretty cosmic, I'd say.' Stuart smiled apologetically.

'Great, good, well – enjoy!' Richard put his arm around Jessica's shoulders and moved her off back towards the King's Men.

'What are they doing, Richard?'

'Dowsing energy lines.'

'What does that mean?'

'No-one really knows. There is some kind of theory that ley-lines, the alignment of stones or ancient sites upon the landscape, form part of a worldwide grid of planetary or cosmic energy.'

'And do they?'

'There may be some truth to it, but I'm afraid it's one of the vague ideas that Simon is so dismissive of, that attracts virulent embroidery by the loony aspect of the new age. But don't quote me!' Richard turned intense eyes to Jessica.

'Oh no, no, I won't, don't worry.'

As they approached the stones again, other members of the group turned to speak to Richard. 'I'm back on duty,' he said, and squeezed her shoulder gently. Smiling, she gracefully ceded him to the group and then walked across the lane to visit the King Stone. Now she felt as sunny as the day: it was as if she and Richard were already lovers. Last night had been no more than a hiccup, she had blown it out of proportion. Either that or Richard was as gracious and sensitive as she had always thought.

A gap in the hedge and a worn path signalled the way to the monument, situated over a slight curve in the land, and to the side of the field. The monolith was strangely curved, as if the king were leaning over on his side. It too was enclosed in its own little ringed fence of black iron spears. She walked round to the other side. From this angle, the megalith looked like two forms ecstatically entwined.

She felt an irresistible desire to get back to the circle again, and hurriedly retraced her steps out of the field and along the road. As she emerged through the little wooded path that obscured the circle from the road, she saw Richard's tall form bent slightly to hear Bahira. Jessica felt a flicker of desire go through her. She had longed for someone who would transport her to deeper levels of herself, even while she was frightened of it. Sometimes the threshold to greater depths appeared. If you did not step over, the opportunity was lost, perhaps never to recur. When the fairy beckons with his golden cup, or the drawbridge is lowered to the Grail castle, you had to approach. The process was not about avoiding hurt, it was simply to do with going deeper. She realized now that what she had mistaken as neediness in Richard, that strange, almost shaky intensity, was actually his vulnerability to these other realms. The waters of the dark ran close to the surface in him, like the sudden and disconcerting appearance of a god, a Dionysius, who knows not logic nor morality, whose black eyes see only a another kind of dimension, where elements fuse and blow apart according to subterranean, unknown, forces.

'I can see that coach tours are definitely a way to get very fat,' said Suzanne, as she bit into a scone loaded with cream and jam.

'That's right, they *are*,' agreed Jessica. They both giggled and looked accusingly at Richard.

'All you do is sit on a coach while you drive from one lot of old stones to another, and in between, you eat,' elucidated Jessica.

'A lot of old stones!' Richard feigned outrage.

'That's what this is about, isn't it?' went on Suzanne, 'you're fattening us all up and then you'll offer us as sacrifices at some really spooky and remote site.'

'Yes, or that weird community we're all going to. Come on, admit it.'

Richard laughed and choked a little on his tea. 'Now why would I want to do that?'

'Well, you're not in this for the money, are you?' Suzanne said, wickedly. 'So there must be some other blood curdling reason.'

'But Suzanne,' said Jessica, 'no-one is actually making you spread your cream one inch thick on your scone, you know.'

'Oh yes they are,' Suzanne retorted, motioning to the frazzled waitress to bring another dish of cream. 'We're all so starving. Those sites are all mystical, for some reason they make you very very *hungry*. Do you like your women fat, Richard?' She shot him a sudden startling glance, and then smiling said, 'come on Jessica, you're not eating enough of this cream.'

'Mm, I'll have some more.' Richard helped himself to the newly arrived dish. 'As you seem to be eating the most, Suzanne my love, I'll make sure you go to the top of the fattened sacrificial victims list.'

Suzanne giggled into her cream scone. Jessica laughed, sneaking a delighted look at Richard, and at this point Helen, late from a shopping errand, sat heavily down at their table.

'Jesus, I'm bleeding like a pig,' she said with all her visceral intensity.

Suzanne giggled some more. 'Here, have a scone.'

'Thanks, is there any tea left?'

'Have some of mine, my dear, and I'll ask for some more. Do you want cream, and – jam?'

'Oh boy yes, I feel shaky with hunger.'

'You see, it's affecting her too.' Suzanne looked sternly at Richard.

'What's that?' asked Helen.

'We've just been saying how hungry we've been on this tour, and how much we're eating.'

'God, don't I know it, I feel like I've put on pounds.' Helen drank some tea, then fixed her eyes on Richard. 'Now Richard,' she began, 'I think you've been avoiding me.'

Jessica and Suzanne looked at Richard, who raised his eyebrows.

'Helen, what do you mean?'

'Because you don't want to discuss my idea of writing a book together. Either that or you don't want to do it at all.'

'Of course that's not the case, I mean, obviously I am a little busy with other things right now but I'd love to talk it through with you when this is all over.'

'I know that, but don't avoid me because you *think* I want to talk about it.'

Jessica and Suzanne looked at each other. Jessica raised her eyes heavenwards, Suzanne turned down the corners of her mouth. They laughed again.

'Sometimes I think you're trying to pander to the scientific community too much you know, Richard. I know you're trying to tread a middle path and all that – but the psychic component of these sites *is* very important.'

Insensitive to Richard's tacit request, Helen launched into a detailed account of her book idea, oblivious now, it seemed, of their presence. She had a maddening way, thought Jessica, of inviting intimacy only to rebuff it.

'I talked to Steve last night,' said Suzanne.

'Oh yes, how are things with him?'

'Busy, very very busy. He's planning to meet up with us all in Cornwall.'

'Oh right, the film. I'd almost forgotten.'

'He says Paul's coming with him.'

'What?'

'Have you forgotten him too?'

'No, I mean – what's he coming for? He loathes all this!'

Suzanne shrugged. 'Steve didn't say, just said he was helping him out.'

The mention of Paul's name was like a shadow falling across Jessica's newly reclaimed evanescent world. She felt on edge at the thought of him coming, and appalled at her own reaction. How could she have grown so distant, so quickly. Yet was it quickly? Yes, she had only been away three days, it was just that it seemed so much longer.

'He probably wants to make things up with you.'

'Hm,' Jessica masked her feelings with a sulky anger. Magnetized as she had become to Richard's presence, she felt Paul as an intrusion. At the moment, she had no interest in reconciliation.

'I thought you'd be pleased,' said Suzanne.

'Well,' Jessica wrinkled her forehead, 'I just feel like I'm in another world. I feel confused at the thought of him coming.' Unconsciously she lowered her voice. She did not want Richard, still wrapped in Helen's monologue, to overhear them. 'This time is important for me, to find out what's really right –'

Suzanne nodded. 'And whether you want to be together still.'

'Yeah, that too, I suppose.'

'It's funny, 'cos *I've* felt very different since I've been on this trip. I feel sort of excited, or something.'

'Yeah? You know you look different too.'

'Do I?'

'Yes, you look really well, and happy.'

In fact Jessica could not remember ever seeing Suzanne look so blooming. There was new colour in her face, her eyes had softened, her hair was glossier than ever.

'Is it all the food do you think?' asked Jessica, and they both went back to their giggling.

For the next leg of their journey Jessica was content to let the pattern of people fall together as it would on board the coach. Secure as she now felt in her complicit intimacy with Richard, she no longer anxiously contrived to be close to him. She desired only that she have space to go deeper into herself and savour her now blood-tingling anticipation of the dark mysteries that might await in the mist-filled valleys of Wales and the night that lay ahead.

'Is this seat taken?' Jessica's new found equanimity seemed all too easily upset as she turned to see the monk-like Bill.

'No, it's not,' she said, hardly disguising the resentment in her voice, knowing that Bill would not notice it anyway. His presence was doubly unwelcome: not only would he talk incessantly on the three hour trip, spoiling her hoped-for meditative silence, but he was also another reminder of her former life.

'Jessica, this is great, you know I've been feeling a bit guilty because I know I owe you a report about that proposed West Penwith development – I hope you don't think I've been avoiding you?' he looked anxiously at her.

'No, no, of course not.' Jessica felt another shock of anxiety pierce through her – she had almost forgotten about the oak trees. 'I mean it's been a very full time so far.' She was excusing herself as much as him.

'I did contact the planning authority, and I was diplomatic, like you said. I mean, I basically did our standard approach, plus a couple of extra phone calls really.'

'Yeah, and what happened?'

'They were fine about it all. You know, they said they would process the application as they were bound to do in the usual way, but would take very seriously our written and spoken objections and alternative propositions.'

As she listened to Bill, Jessica felt as if she was having to rein in her mind from a great distance. Instead of her previous urgent intent around the proposed development, she felt only a heavy dutifulness. It all seemed so old and irrelevant now. What was happening to her?

'Oh, pretty standard reactions then – any outcome?'

'No, I'm afraid not – not that I've been able to find out anyway.'

Jessica nodded her head. 'So it's still in the balance then.' She frowned, feeling doubly guilty – she was away from her office, and unable to do anything herself, but even worse, she did not want to deal with it any more, had been happy to forget about the situation, along with the rest of her former life. 'Oh well, thanks for letting me know anyway.'

Bill smiled distractedly. 'That's OK, Jessica. How are you enjoying the trip?'

'Very much.'

'So am I, I have definitely decided to leave FOE now, in fact this trip has helped me make the decision.'

'Uh-huh,' Jessica nodded, uncomfortably aware again of the parallels between her and Bill's experience.

'Yes, I've felt really inspired – by the places we've seen, by Richard, by the people on this trip, and by some of what I've sensed at these sites.'

'Really?'

'Mm. It's the power of positive thought that's needed, not negative protest and anger. Deep meditation – allowing the earth to be sacred again.'

'Yes,' Jessica murmured neutrally.

'You agree then?'

'Well, I'm sure there's truth in what you're saying.'

'Yes, yes. Have I ever told you about the retreats I run?'

'Yes Bill, you have.'

'You ought to come on one you know, Jessica. I mean, if you're enjoying this tour, I think you would find it really helpful.'

'Maybe. This will probably do me for now.'

Bill talked on, telling her again about the retreats, expounding his philosophies of the spiritual life. Eventually Jessica felt she had fulfilled her duty.

'Look Bill, I'd really like to be quiet now for a bit, do you mind?'

'Oh no, I understand. The power of silence,' he said, and abruptly closed his eyes and fell asleep.

By now most of the coach party were reading or dozing. A few muttered conversations still blended in with the changing revs of the diesel engine as the old coach shuddered and shook its way up the increasingly steep and winding roads. The Welsh hills and the soft blue of evening were closing in around them. Jessica shifted in her seat, rubbed her hands across her forehead and eyes. With Bill quiet at last, she felt at least temporarily discharged from her past. Paul would meet them in the remote future when they arrived in Cornwall. Beyond that, all was unknown, and was waiting anyway to be borne out of the trembling intensity of the present to which she now wished to commit herself completely.

The Abbey Hotel, in Llanthony, Abergavenny, was built out of a ruined 12th century Augustinian priory, set on one of the softer folds of the Black Mountains, with higher darker hills rising up all around it. At nightfall, with the ruins of the priory picturesquely piled up to one side, square towers and arched doorways still clearly defined, and the lights golden from the hotel's windows, the whole rambling stone edifice looked as inviting as a medieval romance. The hotel had agreed to serve a late supper to the tour and there was time to change and freshen up before dining. An original spiral staircase led up to the sparse, white bedrooms, which had been converted from what remained of the Norman church's west front. Having found her room, Jessica ordered a glass of wine from the bar and tripped back up the worn stone steps to get to the bathroom before anyone else. She filled the old-fashioned cast-iron tub almost full and lowered herself slowly into the clear absolving heat.

She sat in a state of semi-ecstasy, motionless except for sipping her wine, feeling herself baptized into her new state. The hotel setting excited her imagination, symbolizing as it seemed to a literal marriage between past and present, between the sacred and the profane. Who knows where she would end up if she followed the spiral stairs all the way to their top; and those shadowy doorways, in the jumbled cliffs of masonry, looked like they might lead to another dimension altogether. She wondered where Richard's room was, and then realized the corridor outside had gone quiet: no sounds of people brushing past, no toilets flushing, no snatches of conversation. Everyone was at supper, and she was still in her bath! She had to hurry through her carefully planned beauty routine – hairwash, body oil, a minor facial, and finally, anointed and wrapped in leggings and a soft clingy jumper, she arrived in the dining room. Feeling a little panicky, she looked round to see where Richard was. His table was full, he was engrossed in conversation with Suzanne. She found a space at another table, the waitress brought her cottage pie and she ordered more wine.

As dinner drew to a close, Richard lingered at his table, chatting with Uta and Suzanne. Jessica, later than most, kept an eye on them while she finished her dessert. As Richard pushed back his chair, and started to get up, she got up too and went over to join them. Just as she arrived, Richard had stopped to talk further with the two women, leaning with his hands against the back of his chair. For a few moments Jessica had to hover awkwardly, not wanting to interrupt, and they, somewhat unnecessarily it seemed, delayed in acknowledging her. Then Richard turned around.

'Hallo there, I hope you've been eating as well as Suzanne has.' Jessica and Suzanne both laughed.

'They have been complaining that the ancient sites are making them eat too much,' Richard started to explain to Uta.

'Ah yes, is that what it is,' nodded Uta. 'You are not by yourselves, I have also been very hungry –'

'Richard, can I buy you a drink?'

Uta closed her mouth, and looked from Richard to Jessica to Suzanne. Momentarily Richard seemed to hesitate, making more awkward the gash in their chat that she had made. Jessica was seized with the dreadful fear that he was going to turn her down.

'Sure,' he said in a kindly way, which, as she paid for his beer and her wine, Jessica realized was not a comforting note to sound. They sat down at a corner table of the bar, and Jessica thought she saw Richard give a sideways glance, as though checking on something. However, having previously disavowed what she regarded as a tendency in herself to over-interpret the minutiae of social interchange to the point where she was rendered virtually inert, Jessica decided to advance in defiance of the feedback from her cautious perceptions.

'Quite a place isn't it?'

'Richard, it's just so perfect – I feel as if I could walk through to fairyland from here, like *The Lion, the Witch and the Wardrobe*, you know – where does the spiral stairway lead?'

'To my room,' he replied, staring intently at her face. She faltered a little.

'Oh, just the one room up there?'

He nodded. 'Yep, 62 steps to the top.'

'Wow, that's quite a lot.'

He smiled, his eyes still on her face. Then suddenly, leaning forward, he asked, 'What do you want to *do*?'

Jessica was taken aback. She felt challenged, scared, but she was also drawn in by his eyes, and by the wine and the lateness of the evening.

'I want to go for a walk –'

'A *walk*?'

'Through the ruins at night, I want to walk through that big doorway and see where it leads.'

'Now?'

'Now.'

Richard drained his beer. 'Come on then.'

'I'll have to get my coat first.'

'OK, hurry up.'

The moon was up now, its semi-circle turned concave, chased by high, dark purple clouds. Richard walked out ahead of Jessica, his feet crunching on the gravel path. Jessica felt in slow-motion – buffeted by a tumble of sensations, damp fragrance of earth and grass, the chill wind-filled meditation of the Welsh night. The cool wind tugged at her wine-muffled perceptions. She shivered from cold or uneasiness and hesitated. She could no longer hear Richard's footsteps, he had stepped into the grass-floored ruins and disappeared.

The moon surfaced again from behind clouds: in front of her a small raised doorway in the massive stone wall led into the remains of the priory. The moonlight dimmed and brightened with the play of clouds, the stone landscape now pattinaed silver, now grey. Looking at the small black shape of the doorway, Jessica felt the up-gushing again of the dark, the swooning desire to descend: now she wanted to go through. She had to bend her head down as she climbed over its threshold. On its other side, the massive serried walls blocked what silver light the moon gave. At first it seemed as if she was entirely enclosed, but gradually she made out a softening of the black ahead of her. There was no sign of Richard.

The softened patch of dark turned out to be another more open space beyond, where two of the old walls were mostly tumbled down, just the corner stacks in place. Attached to one of these, the arched and battlemented doorway stood open to the night. Jessica could see stars through it.

As she walked through she called out quietly, 'Richard.' His name echoed in the thick stone arch. She stepped out into the clearing beyond.

'There you are.'

The words startled her, seeming to be spoken out of the night itself. Then she saw him, a black figure, leaning against the black wall to the side of the entrance. With a slight jolt of fear, Jessica turned towards him; he took her arm and pulled her into him. Now she was against his body, her face pressed up into his. He twisted her round, pushing her back into the wall, leaning hard against her. At first Jessica felt only the shock of illicit intimacy, the touch of skin, the twisting of tongue and lip; but then she was aware of a descent into blackness, long, timeless. They parted again for a fraction, letting in the brightness of night, of stars, and then again, faces and bodies merged together, going down, it was definitely there again, the compelling depth, the dark. They were there forever, in the grey and silver landscape, lit by a fitful moon, diving into the black, deeper than oceans, deeper than rock and bone, surfacing again almost breathless. For Jessica, it was like stepping through a tangled beach to enter the ocean: somehow the sheer physicality of their closeness was almost distasteful, but the depths were hers, demanding every tiny part of herself be present. But she could not sustain it; she did not have the stamina to keep descending, she must have air. Jessica pulled back from their embrace. Richard ran his hands across her shoulders, down her back, up under her jumper. The exultant awe had gone from his eyes, they were deadened now by indiscriminate desire.

'Shall we go to my room?'

Jessica stared at him. He pulled her jumper up and started kissing her breasts. She shivered.

In the subdued warmth of the hotel foyer, the air around them seemed to crackle with energy. 'Do you want another drink?'

'Yes.'

'I'll get it, you just keep climbing till you reach the top.'

As she spiralled up, Jessica tried not to think about what she was doing. Perhaps she should just bolt into her room and hide; perhaps she should confess to Cora, ask Suzanne's advice, tell Richard she felt exhausted.

She hoped no one had seen her as she climbed beyond the last corridor of bedrooms. Richard caught up with her as she arrived at his door. He was carrying a bottle and two glasses. He switched on the bedside light and poured her some wine. She drank it gratefully.

'How're you feeling?'

'Fine,' she held out her glass.

'Is it warm enough in here?'

She nodded and sat down on the edge of the bed.

'I wanted to make love outside.'

'In the ruins, under the moon?'

'Yeah, but it's too cold I'm afraid.'

'Yes, yes.'

She drained her glass. Richard bent down and switched out the light again. Crouching in front of her, her pulled up her jumper and ran his fine fingers over her breasts while studying her face. He leaned into her, kissed her neck, began to suck her nipples. Jessica felt a kind of helpless fascination. He lay her down on the bed, pulled down her leggings and pushed her legs apart. He snaked his tongue down around her belly, in the softness of her inner thighs and then inside her. Jessica cried out.

Hurriedly they wrestled off their clothes, he rolled her over then pushed inside. He came just before she did, gasping, gripping the sheets. It was all over so fast, all the sensations used up in a spree of indulgence, flown out the window. And then they were just two sweaty bodies on a bed.

Jessica lay for a moment, feeling the little curl of disappointment inside her, not wanting to acknowledge the blank disconnection she now felt with the alien body next to her. She sat up, folding her legs delicately under her, trying to remain undetected. Richard's body lay sprawled in front of her. He turned his face. 'Are you all right?'

'Yeah,' she said softly.

'That was good, Jessica, I guess we rushed a bit, didn't we?'

She smiled. Did he realize they had left the depths behind?

'I think I'll go back to my room now.' Richard nodded, his eyes glittering in the dark. Jessica pulled on her clothes and left.

She had to wash herself again, filling the bath at low speed so as not to wake people. Her head was starting to ache, she felt dehydrated and generally sickened. Images of her love-making with Richard kept flashing across her mind, and she wanted to wash them away. She scrubbed her teeth at the sink then stepped into the bath and submerged herself and her hair. She lay for a while as though floating in the water, hoping to find an inner stillness, but there was only a leaden tiredness. That would do though, she thought. She pulled the plug, towelled herself and downed a large glass of water. Finally she went to bed, grateful for the promise of sleep's amnesia.

The deep, unconscious fathoms of sleep became the dark bar of the horizon which detached itself and started to ripple inland. The bar grew larger, building into a shimmering wall, a huge curve of demand and desire. She was swimming out in the bay of her favourite beach, the tide was high, she was swimming naked in the smaller waves, rocked in the rhythm. The sea was male, strongly male, it had her in his grip, rocking her in a massive swell; taken over, her body responded orgasmically with the motion of the waves. She had to get ready now for the next even more immense roll of water, the pull so strong it had to be resisted just to find a way to be taken by it, without being broken apart by its force. The sea was making love to her.

Jessica opened her eyes. The surge and pull of the ocean was still in her body; she felt shaken, and madly desirous. She heard Richard's words again, 'We rushed it a bit, didn't we.' Maybe she should have stayed, and they could have gone to depths together. There was something unfinished between them, that must be what the dream meant. Unsteadily she got out of bed, still dazed by the violent awakening out of deep levels of sleep.

She needed to go to the bathroom first anyway. She relieved her bladder and drank some more water.

Turning away from her face in the mirror, Jessica still felt the impulse to climb back up the stairs. Her rational self was held at bay by the power of the dream and the dislocation that waking so recently out of sleep brings. The first time was always awkward, she told herself, you needed longer to get it right. His comment had implied as much.

Suddenly she froze – there was the sound of footsteps outside. Perhaps someone needed to use the bathroom. She opened the door, just in time to see Suzanne's back as she disappeared out of the corridor and up the winding stairs. She must have decided to try the bathroom on the next floor. If Jessica hurried, she could get past before Suzanne returned.

Barefoot on the stone steps, Jessica made no sound; she was more awake now. But Suzanne did not stop at the next floor, she kept going. Jessica followed. At each step her dream's compulsion and her hazy detachment diminished and were replaced by an extremely alert and enlarging sense of alarm. Suzanne went all the way up: as if hypnotized by dread, Jessica followed. At the last turn of the stairs Jessica stopped. She heard the gentle knocking at Richard's door and the quiet click of the catch as Suzanne closed it behind her. Jessica waited, terrified lest Suzanne come back and find her there, and horrified that she might not, that she might stay in Richard's room, removing any last faint traces of rationalization that Jessica could think up to explain away the otherwise unthinkable and ugly fact that stared her in the face.

After a while, Jessica crept up to the door and put her ear to its keyhole. She could hear Suzanne's muted giggle, the muffled tones of Richard, just a few words, and then the rustle of bedclothes, the creak of the floorboards. Jessica was trembling, with shock, with lust, with rage. Should she burst in and make a scene? What about – Suzanne's ignorant and airy promiscuity? Richard's amoral duplicity? For a moment the prospect of completely losing her self respect welled up like a strange temptation. She had never known herself like this before, but gradually her trembling turned to forlorn shivering. She was cold, she had been duped, she had allowed herself to be duped: she would go quietly back down the stairs, and pretend nothing had happened.

The rest of the night passed in a hallucinatory procession of images between sleep and waking. Her body turned hot and cold as her emotion ricochetted from one scene to another: the arched silhouette of the ruined doorway, the dark bar of the wave, Richard laughing with Suzanne at dinner, Cora on the coach speaking about lust and sensation at the stones, Paul's face smiling a welcome. She felt contempt for her emotions, fearful that their violence proved her unable to interact on her own terms with life. She was weak and would always be dependent on the patronage of Paul or someone else. Yet a more rational part of her mind argued that despite the painful humiliation of her night's adventures, the reaction she was experiencing now was disproportionate to that cause. Gradually she realized that a larger process was at work, that the force of the symptom had exposed an underlying ill and she was being purged. In her mind's eye she saw projected out from her, like a shadow from a building, a pyramid-shaped map, etched in black. It was the map of the fault-line that ran through her character and erupted at times of crisis. More scenes from the past played out before her in full colour: times in childhood, at college, the row with Paul before he left for the oil slick. But the shadow map was the software behind the action. She saw clearly that she had a taste for melodrama, even petty deception. She got lost in her own internal process, wallowed in emotions. It felt sharp and clean to look at the map and understand. Being able to see it so clearly meant, she knew, that the coding was no longer so entwined with her psyche. Jessica visualized it as a pattern of immaturity separating out from her, peeling off and fading away. Then the picture shifted, and she saw that the pattern formed not a presence but an absence: as if a patch of her personality had been stunted. Now it was uncovered, and blood and life started to throb through, awakening growth, it hurt. The black etchings of the map blurred into movement: back in the wood of childhood, she saw light playing through the trees, and felt suddenly an old fear, there by the roots of a 100-year-old oak a dark opening; and finally she allowed herself to recall the descent into black depths with Richard, before mere sensuality took over. Outside, the first wide-spaced chirrups of birds began to punctuate the dark. The turmoil of thoughts and images swirled away out of the room. Jessica was left holding a piece of her own power, which at once frightened and reassured her. Everything fitted back into the right perspective. She yawned, feeling at last wholesomely tired, and fell into a deep, dreamless sleep.

# CHAPTER NINE

To the east the South Wales countryside stretched away in chequered green abundance, rows of cumulus charging across it. To the west, the sea was a gun-metal grey sheen in the distance, out of which black bars of cloud were now speeding towards the hillside, rain-mist billowing in their van. Soon the summit was enclosed, the views extinguished. The clouds emptied out large hailstones, then, with another cold gust, came the rain: spaced dollops turning to a fine, steady downpour. Jessica trudged in resignation up to where a mass of craggy rock broke out of the gorse and heather skin of the mountainside like a section of dislocated spine. The wet huddle of the group was attempting to shelter in the lee of this volcanic outcrop known as Carn Ingli.

'Welcome to the Welsh summer,' she heard Richard saying. She leant against one of the volcanic extrusions. Uta and Suzanne were the last two stragglers, sitting down next to her. Richard smiled in their general direction.

'As some of you know, this area is close to home for me, so I am able to assure you that Mother Nature does not have it in for us, this kind of weather is not unusual around here.'

Some of the group smiled sadly. The whole day had felt sodden, even before the rain; cloudy and damp. Some had complained about how steep the climb was or had wanted longer for lunch; a disgruntled air had begun to hang about them. Jessica thought back to the visit to Richard's home: the coal fire glimmering, the books, the pictures, and her wondering excitement about him and his work. She had felt as if some marvellous revelation was imminent, towards which she yearned and pushed as through a gauze veil, past separation to the burning core of life. That naïve longing was now mired and compromised.

'I had planned to let this be a longer stay again,' Richard went on, 'so that we could explore and experience at our leisure, but obviously conditions don't allow for that, so I'll keep it brief and, as before, we can discuss this and the other sites we've seen today back in the comfort of the Priory tonight. As you can see, Carn Ingli is one of the most dramatic outcrops of igneous rock on the Preseli Hills. Around it neolithic man built stone walls, enclosing a series of terraces. Today their remains blend in almost imperceptibly with the rock itself.'

As she had done all day, Jessica found it difficult to look at Richard: his face had become her jadestone. She had been deliberately late for breakfast, hoping to avoid him; but in the pre-departure shuffle, he had cornered her briefly in the hall and asked how she was. 'I had strange dreams,' she'd replied, without stopping. 'How about you?' She glared from the stairs. 'Feeling a little tired this morning?' Richard had said nothing, only his eyes veiled over.

Jessica had hoped her pre-dawn vigil might have absolved her of any human emotion, leaving her nobly objective; but the sting of last night was still there. Pangs of vulnerability and jealousy vied with a restless discontent as she watched him speak. Everything was adrift in her new uncertainty. The two standing stones and the Gors Fawr stone circle already visited that day had left her unimpressed. Ancient they evidently were, but she could no longer vouch for their potency. She debated whether the intimations of power at the previous sites had their source not in the stones but in her infatuation with Richard. Now that spell had been weakened, she found herself returned to inert mundanity. In some ways the sites struck her as veritably threadbare, debased as marketing ploys for small time new age commercialism. Was Paul right after all? Was the tour really just a fake, an overblown and gimmicky sideshow, with no solid punch to it?

'Carn Ingli translates as the "peak of angels", and this name arises from the experiences of a sixth century holy man, St Brynach, who lived on the peak as a hermit and was said to converse with angels. Today we might say that St Brynach experienced an altered state of consciousness, due to anomalies in the magnetic field.'

Should she talk with Cora, or with Suzanne about what had happened? But it was probably no big deal for Suzanne. She would just find it amusing. How long had she been sleeping with Richard? It was obviously not the first time. Jessica looked at Suzanne's face: she noticed that a wash of anxiety had chastened its bloom.

'At many points among these extrusions a compass needle will move off the magnetic north. In some places by tens of degrees, in a few spots by a full 180 degrees. This is due to the minerals in the rock being 'frozen' in the direction of the earth's field at the time the rocks were formed. In other words, when the poles were reversed.'

Jessica could hear Uta whispering something to Suzanne who was now looking very pale with her head in her hands. Uta motioned to her to sit up and put her head between her legs. Suzanne attempted to move but slumped over instead.

'What this reversed field effect causes of course is a disturbance in the magnetic field, and there are numerous reports from people who've experienced odd phenomena around this site: feeling strange wave effects, hearing inexplicable sounds, seeing rainbow lights at night ...'

Richard had not noticed Suzanne's collapse, but the little commotion spread through the group until it reached him.

'What's the matter?'

'She's fainted,' said someone. Uta was struggling to her feet. 'We must get her away from here.' Peter and Jessica helped her lift Suzanne and half-carry, half-drag her down the slope away from the peak. Richard watched the proceedings warily.

'OK, I guess that's it folks, point proven rather dramatically, I think we can call it a day.'

People were already starting to trickle back out into the full gusting of the rain and head into the mist. The rain and cold soon revived Suzanne who was deeply embarrassed and insisted she was fine and able to walk on her own. Uta stayed by her side, however, with a warm kindness that was easy to accept, while Jessica and Peter walked behind, at just the right distance to demonstrate respectful sympathy.

'Well, I'm looking forward to a hot bath and a strong cup of tea,' remarked Peter as he pulled his anorak hood tighter around his face.

'Mm, yes,' agreed Jessica, 'tea with lots of cake would definitely be welcome.' Her anticipation of such physical comforts was however mingled with dread at the return to the scene of last night. Staring out at the rain-blurred countryside, an overwhelming homesickness rose up in her; but that feeling became itself a source of more perplexity, for where did home lie? She no longer knew if Paul's flat was her home, or what her connection with him was any more. And with no clear place to which to attach her longings, they funnelled into a strong, instinctual negative, an almost physical desire *not* to be there where she was.

'Did you say something about cake, Jessica?' Suzanne turned to her.

'Yes,' said Jessica, blowing her nose, realizing she was back in the swamps of self-pity again, images of Paul and Caroline going through her head.

'I think that's probably what was wrong with me – I just didn't eat enough today.' She smiled wanly.

'Ooh no Suzannah, I know it was the magic mountain, we want some prophecies now,' said Uta, and winked at Jessica.

'Yes, come on Suzanne, didn't you hear any angels, or see any strange lights?' joked Peter.

'No, I just felt nauseous, started to black out and then fainted.'

'But you must have felt the energy waves, like Richard was saying,' Uta assured her earnestly.

Suzanne shook her head. 'No, sorry to disappoint you folks, absolutely nothing mystical about it.'

Peter turned to Richard who had caught up with their little group,

'She says it was nothing mystical I'm afraid Richard.'

'That all depends on what you mean by mystical. Most of science is pretty mystical these days if you ask me. How are you feeling, my love?' He put his arm around Suzanne's shoulder and trudged in step with her. Jessica tried not to notice every detail.

'I'm fine, really Richard. I think I just didn't eat enough,' she tried a giggle, 'or maybe it was you know, the wobbly magnetic field.'

'Well, the important thing is that you're OK now,' he said, pressing her into him. Jessica looked at the ground.

'So it wasn't a set up then, by you two, to impress us all?' said Peter.

'Tsch, what a terrible thing to say,' scolded Uta.

It *had* been impressive though, Jessica acknowledged to herself. Suzanne's fainting fit had had the effect of re-validating both Richard and the sites. It had checked her own creeping disillusion, and dispelled the subtle resentment at what might prove to be pointless suffering that had begun to take hold of the group.

'It's amazing to think that this cold, quiet green countryside was once covered with eruptions of boiling lava, with all kinds of cataclysms going on, I mean what happens when the poles reverse?' Jessica still had her eyes on the ground as she spoke, picturing the pre-historic landscape in her mind's eye while walking through the present. 'And we worry today about environmental disaster.' As she lifted her head she found herself gazing into Richard's face. His eyes caught her look and he smiled secretly at her even as he was holding Suzanne. Jessica looked quickly down, but something relaxed in her. Perhaps it wasn't such a big deal after all; why should she expect to be singled out to live an immaculate existence, where nothing sordid or messy intruded. She could not expect special treatment from life, as if she were somehow different from everyone else. In an unexpected minor miracle, the calm of acceptance settled over her: the vein of assurance she had tapped into early that morning – she would get through the evening somehow; the journey was more obscure than pristine. There was a kind of relief to be had in joining the muddled ranks of the human species among whom all manner of odd situations occurred, for most of which there were no neat explanations or resolutions.

Never had their coach looked more welcoming as the cold, wet pilgrims clambered aboard and sank back in their seats knowing that no further effort would be required of them that day, save to prepare themselves at their leisure for a supper cooked by somebody else. The rain had set in all across South Wales and for the whole journey the land was wrapped up in obscuring grey mist. Uta sat next to Suzanne and continued, intermittently, to marvel at the mountain and Suzanne's sensitivity. Peter fell into a steady murmured conversation with Simon; and Jessica, exhausted from lack of sleep, physical exertion and above all from the polar reversals of her own emotions, curled up and went to sleep.

Hot baths, tea and pre-dinner drinks were duly taken or drunk by all who wanted them, and the dining room was fizzy with conversation. No hint of mutiny remained. Now the group exuded the committed and celebratory air of those who had undergone an initiatory rite of passage, and achieved a deeper level of engagement in their quest. At Richard's table the talk was of the new research linking anomalies in the magnetic field with altered states of consciousness. Over in the corner, Peter March was telling Suzanne and Uta about the history of the Black Mountains: 'It has always been a strange place, a lot of bad feeling from the conflict with the English, rumours of incest, inexplicable suicide, witchcraft;' while Cora was explaining to Jessica, Adam and Terence that the planets were currently in an unbalanced configuration. 'Oh dear,' said Terence frowning as he listened earnestly.

'What does that mean Cora?' asked Jessica. Cora shrugged her shoulders. 'It means that unbalanced things can happen, Jessica dear.'

'Is that bad?' asked Terence.

'It depends. It can be a time when breakthroughs occur, simply because the balance of the status quo is precarious.'

A little later, as dinner was cleared away and the conversations started to ebb away, Cora asked Jessica how Paul was. 'What's happened to him?'

'I don't know,' replied Jessica a bit sulkily. 'Apparently he's going to come with Steve, they'll meet us in Cornwall.'

'Ah!' Cora seemed pleased.

'He's very dismissive of all this.'

'Hm,' Cora nodded her head. Adam and Terence got up from the table. Jessica hesitated. Since Cora's unexplained, late-night apparition one hotel ago, Jessica had avoided her, assuming that for some reason Cora did not sanction a liaison with Richard. It was not disapproval that she shrank from, for instinctively she knew Cora did not speak in that tongue. Rather she sensed Cora would not believe in her affair with Richard, and feared being called on her motivation. Jessica had unconsciously acknowledged that her relationship with Cora, though minimal in outer terms, set off major resonances in her inner world. She had come to think of it as existing in an archetypal universe, parallel to but not particularly well delineated by the modern present day reality. Automatically she pictured its inner scenarios in mythical terms: she was now the reluctant nymph, in service to the goddess, summoned to give account of her actions in the temple. On first meeting Cora, this inner dimension had liberated and nourished her. Now her more wary, outer self resisted coming into line with the archetypes. She was no longer sure she believed in them, or wanted to obey their demands.

'Cora, was it only Richard's work that caused his marriage to break up?'

'I think it was the main reason, darling.' Cora seemed completely uninterested in the subject. 'But, he hasn't been lonely since. People experiment, you know.'

'Cora do you – why did you come back down to the hotel lounge the other night?'

Cora looked at her, puzzled, then her eyes lit up with remembrance.

'I couldn't find Adam, darling. I wondered if he'd strayed off somewhere, he's a bit whimsical, you know.'

'Oh –' Jessica stopped as Richard came over and laid his hands on Cora's shoulders. As Jessica watched Richard's long fingers massage Cora's neck, she was turning over the surprise she felt at Cora's reply. So the incident had been mere coincidence, not archetypal intercession. Cora had simply been following out her infatuation with Adam, not over-seeing the antics of her nymphs with foresight and prescience. Jessica felt more confused than ever: certainly this seemed to remove any remaining reason for her not to yield to her own impulses.

'Ah, that feels marvellous,' said Cora, as he gave her an impromptu massage. 'How's Suzanne?'

'She's fine, but she wants to have an early night. She's gone to bed with a book,' Richard replied, his eyes on Jessica.

'That sounds like a wonderful idea. Maybe I'll do the same.' Cora stretched and smiled and to Jessica's dismay got up from the table. 'Good night my loves, I'll see you in the morning.'

Richard sat down opposite Jessica. 'You've barely looked at me all day Jessica, what's wrong?'

'I suppose I'm not very good at experimenting yet.'

'Experimenting?'

'Richard,' Jessica raised her eyes, 'I saw Suzanne go into your room last night.'

'How did you see that?'

'I'd gone to the bathroom.'

'But that bathroom's three flights down. Did you follow her?' To Jessica's irritation, Richard seemed riveted by the logistics of her discovery and oblivious of its implications.

'No I *didn't follow* her.'

'Then how did you know?'

'What does it matter *how* I know?'

'You were going to come back.'

Jessica felt her cheeks flush. 'Never mind what I was doing, what about you?'

'Yes I slept with Suzanne, she came to my room. What was I going to do, throw her out?'

'I felt tricked.'

'Why – we hadn't sworn some oath of fealty to one another had we? Suzanne predated you.'

'Then why -'

'Why not? There aren't any rules about this.'

'But, what about Steve?'

'What about him, that's Suzanne's problem, not mine.'

'But he's coming to make a film about you, supposing ... if it all comes out, I mean, isn't it a bit irresponsible?'

'I don't know – it's not my responsibility. I assume Suzanne and Steve have whatever arrangement they have.'

Jessica pressed her lips together and said nothing.

'You're a little bit precious, aren't you. You don't really care about Suzanne and Steve, you're just miffed that you seem to be caught up in something a bit messy.'

'Yes! No – I, ... It's not the mess. It was – I thought ...'

'Look Jessica,' Richard stretched out his hand and took hers, 'I've never experienced that before. We lost it I think, later on. I feel a bit lost now, I don't know what to do with it all.'

Jessica felt helpless again. She did not want this. She wanted an open and shut case. She wanted to write Richard off. She wanted to go to her room with those old copies she had found of *Country Life* and *National Geographic* magazines and read about things that were nothing to do with the here and now of her life. His appeal surprised and terrified her, requiring as it did that she now face her own responsibility. She had opened up the depths, and that had certain consequences. In the inner universe one did not summon up the dark waters merely to flirt with their possibilities. They demanded a response.

'There's a place I want to show you.'

'Where?'

'It's not far, a short walk. Get your coat.'

Richard headed past the ruins, down the steep narrow road that led from the priory. Jessica followed reluctantly. The chill air returned her to uncomfortable mundanity, making the prospect of a cosy evening in her room seem even more desirable, and weakening the ghostly claims of the archetypes. About half way down the hill, hidden by the dense black foliage of oaks, an old gate was set into the crumbling wall that lined the road. The gate creaked as it opened, and a path curved through an overgrown tangle of briars to a small, huddled stone building, with two Celtic crosses stood up at the two peaks of its eaves. Richard took a large, ornate key from under a stone and unlocked the arched wooden doors.

The moonlight barely penetrated the darkness inside through the thick-paned, slit windows set into bulky walls. Jessica caught the scent of something sweet mingled with the musty smell of damp stone. She stood still while Richard felt in his pockets for a match. The flaring light showed a plain altar at one end, covered with a white cloth and faced by rows of wooden benches. There were two candles on the altar which Richard lit. Jessica noticed there was no crucifix or Bible or other church accoutrements. Instead the altar was piled with bunches of faded flowers and herbs.

Richard sat down on one of the benches and smiled up at her: 'This is one of my favourite places.'

Jessica walked to the front of the benches and sat down opposite the altar.

'What is it?' she turned to ask.

'It was just a little abandoned Welsh chapel, and some of my pagan friends somehow got permission to use it for their ceremonies.'

'Pagan?'

'Yes, hence the flowers. They offer tributes to the spirits of place, the devas of the plant kingdoms, and they hold ceremonies to mark the ancient solar calendar – Lammas, Beltane and so on.'

'Why do you like it so much?'

'I just love the simplicity of it, the atmosphere – the mix of Christian and ancient worship – to me it's the chapel of the Grail quest. I come here for insight and revelation.'

'How do you mean?'

'I do – I come here sometimes, in the very early morning, or at night and just sit and think. I get ideas here.'

Jessica recalled vaguely that in the Grail quest it was known as the Perilous chapel, where knights faced death-like initiation rites.

'Do they offer any sacrifices, your friends?'

Richard laughed, 'I've never seen any blood.'

Jessica was silent, watching the flickering lights of the candles, trying to gauge the atmosphere for herself. The chapel seemed oppressive at first, small, slightly damp with the almost sickly smell of the withering flowers. Richard had closed his eyes. She shifted in her seat, and then she watched how the silence started to weave between them, a heartbeat filling the small space. The quiet darkness intensified, the chapel was filling up with the overlapping of their presence. Jessica breathed more deeply, the rising and falling of her chest was an acute longing, a massive disturbance of the stillness.

The night outside was pouring in now through the windows and their energy was spilling out under the doors. Richard opened his eyes. Jessica swallowed. One of the candles was guttering, he got up to steady it. He turned to her. She did not meet his eyes, but watched in an unfocused glaze as he moved towards her. She stood up, straining to know what should happen: the energy was pulsing around them, but there was no haze of alcohol to ease perceptions. Richard ran his fingers down her throat, loosened her coat from her shoulders; she pressed forward into his body, they went into blackness, mouth against mouth, body against body. When they emerged, the chapel was cavernous, its spaces dancing around them in the flickering light. Jessica hesitated, turned to look at the candles, but Richard pulled her to him again. The depths were still there, each time was a dive into caverns and narrow passageways to where dimensions shifted, the bottom fell out the world. But she didn't feel safe. Now the chapel seemed small again, its stone walls folding in around them. Richard was unbuttoning her blouse, opening his fly. He turned her back to the altar. Then she saw it, clearly in her mind: his fantasy. He wanted to have her there over the altar, this was his erotic dream: white skin, red blood, the illicit union on hallowed ground – but this was contrived. She observed him soberly as he touched her skin, kissed her neck and breasts. She sensed his neediness again: he was an energy vampire, he fed on people's life-force. It all seemed a little pitiable now. She felt disinterested and wondered only how to extricate herself. She had fulfilled her part, she had opened up the depths. Now she had to be guardian over them.

'Richard.'

He lifted up his head. 'What is it?' He was caressing her thighs. Her body responded. She could still go with him, it would make things easier – but this was not the point, not any more. She struggled back to consciousness. She had already tasted the bitterness of simple gratified lust. The depths demanded surrender, not fantasy. Richard could not go there with her. She realised that he had been the screen for her own projections, not really the man she'd hoped for.

'Richard!' She pulled away, pushing her hair back from her face, clutching at the open panels of her shirt. 'Richard, this isn't working for me.'

Richard blinked, he looked dazed.

'I'm sorry – it's like, it only works so far – you know? And then it goes.'

He frowned, moved towards her again. 'It's OK,' he said, taking hold of her arms again. 'It's OK.'

'No – no, it's not. It doesn't feel right. It … it's dangerous.'

'Dangerous?' he let go of her and pushed his hands over his forehead. 'Maybe you just need a drink or two,' he said darkly.

'Yes, maybe – to carry on. To blur things over.' She disengaged from him and sat down on a bench. She started doing up her buttons. 'Look I'm sorry, I'm not trying to be a tease or something chronic like that, I really wanted to feel what was right. I don't know, if we'd been together longer, or something, I'm not sure – maybe we could sustain that space – but it only goes so far.'

Richard leant back against the altar. 'This is too mystical for me.'

'I'm glad we've done what we've done – you know? I'm really glad we experimented. I've learnt something about myself – I don't want things to be sour between us. This place, you know, it's not for me.' She indicated the chapel.

Richard nodded as he zipped up his fly. 'That's cool – why didn't you say so. Place is very important. We'll find the right spot.'

Jessica said nothing. There were plenty of other women to distract Richard – Suzanne, Helen, Bahira. She could safely bow out of the picture, now that she saw things clearly.

She experienced a new lightness of heart as she and Richard walked back up the windy night road. She could not tell what Richard was thinking, but there was no awkwardness between them. At the turning to her room, she gave him a peck on the cheek, bad him goodnight and went to her bed smiling and alone.

The sun was back, with small clouds scudding across it, and Jessica alternated between relaxing in its warmth and tingling with goosebumps in the breeze. She was staring into a black fissure in the 20 foot megalith that stood on the grass in front of her, wrapped in its own thick enigma. The deep, curved fissure and nearby notch looked like the down-turned mouth and unseeing eye of a whale; then like the crumpled blank features of the hag. It was one of a line of megaliths, alternating curiously between narrow pillar shaped and wide angular stones like this one, that formed the West Kennet Avenue of the Avebury complex.

By its magnitude and mystery, Avebury dispelled any lingering doubts about the specialness of the ancients' legacy. Whatever the megalith might look like to Jessica's inner eye, its solid, 40 ton reality was strictly objective. From her vantage point she could look back the way she had come, to the main henge circle and ditch, with its peculiar backdrop of village shops and cottages. The very fragmentary nature of the huge neolithic complex was appealing. Poignant though it was to hear of the 16th and 17th century acts of vandalism, when stones were toppled and buried, or broken up to build farm houses and the village itself, yet its ruined grandeur, mingled with the dainty English village, formed a marvellous interweaving of the ancient and present day. The High Street and A-road quartered the centre of the henge, and drove between its two inner circles. The name Avebury denoted both the village and the megalithic landscape, depending on who was using it, making it a perfect symbol of English consciousness, Jessica mused. A pretty village, full of 18th century and Victorian houses; the busy A-roads with modern, over-powered cars whipping too fast through the quiet; both surrounded by and yet helping to obscure the millennia old monument, its stones penetrating the mists of prehistory, not completely censored by religious fanaticism and greed, and giving no answers to the curious 20th century mind. Jessica moved closer to the monolith, and stroked the creature's mournful cheek. The stone felt velvety smooth under her fingers. She was glad they were both there. Jessica realized that she felt thoroughly happy: no longer distracted by what Richard was doing, no longer trying to prove something to Paul. She was liberated to enjoy in an uncomplicated way the windy, sunny morning, the wonderful physical and spiritual mix of the site.

'Do you feel any strange emanations?'

Jessica turned to see Terence ambling, stiff backed, towards her. She smiled and shook her head. 'It feels almost soft.'

Terence came up alongside her and paused for breath. 'You know I hadn't realized how extraordinary this place is: I've been here before, quite a while ago now, but I suppose I wasn't as aware as I am now.'

'I don't think I've ever been here before.'

'Makes all the other places seem small fry, doesn't it?'

'Well, you could also say it lends them dignity.'

'Mm, true.'

They started to walk towards the henge and the village.

'I'm feeling rather pleased with myself this morning, I've walked to Silbury Hill and back. Very intriguing.'

Jessica looked back at the innocuous looking, flat-topped mound that seemed to peep up from every angle on the sky line.

'Did you climb to its top?'

'Yes, wonderful views, wonderful views. They found grass, you know, when they excavated, perfectly preserved, still green, and insects. Did you read that bit?'

Richard had handed out information sheets and let the group wander as they liked around the 12 square mile area of the henge with its two inner circles, and the more far flung barrows and clusters of stones.

'No I haven't, how amazing.'

'I'm headed for a cup of coffee myself.'

Jessica walked with him to the café and gift shop, where she got distracted by the plethora of books, postcards, posters, tarot cards, new age tapes, crystal balls, silver miniatures of dragons and wizards, crop circle earrings, Celtic brooches, statuettes of the goddess. The range of goods was amazing: who produced all these things, how had they proliferated so wildly? She was tempted by the crystal balls and a little clay figurine of the earth mother, but then she picked up a green tourmaline pendant, set in silver. The gem's viridescent translucency was resonant with associations: the colour of toppling Atlantic waves, transparent in sunlight; or early morning lush fields, still wet with dew; reminiscent of *acqua minerale* in green bottles and smoothed glass pebbles on the beach; but it also exuded its own essence of preciousness, of exotic potency: Jessica felt it to be the colour of her well spring.

'That's pretty,' Helen brushed past Jessica as she turned the pendant in her hand. Helen was carrying one of the goddess statuettes. 'I shouldn't be doing this, I'm broke, but I had to have her.'

Jessica smiled. 'I wanted one of those too.'

'You coming for lunch?' asked Helen at the cash desk.

'Gosh, is it that time already?'

'Yep, almost, it's in the pub.'

'Listen Helen, what's happening after this?'

'We drive to Bath, after lunch.'

'Oh! You know what, I think I'll skip lunch then, I can always pick something up later in Bath.' Jessica was thinking out loud.

Helen turned down a bag from the cashier. 'See you later.'

Jessica fastened the pendant round her neck and went off to see for herself the green slopes of Silbury Hill.

Concerned that she be back in time for the coach's departure, Jessica tried to hurry, but could find no easy route to the mound. Unsure whether there were paths through the countryside by Waden Hill, she ended up walking the long way round on the edge of the busy A-roads. Silbury Hill rose up right next to the road, a tarmac carpark at its base. The mound surprised her with its immensity, and its bare 130 foot high slopes were unexpectedly arduous to climb.

On reaching the summit, she sat down and took out Richard's notes, but the paper flapped wildly in the breeze that blew much more strongly across its 100 foot diameter flat top than down below. Jessica gave up and allowed herself to gaze out at the views: the blue ridge of the Marlborough Downs floating far to the east, the dark green rim of Waden Hill in front. Curls of green trees outlining Windmill Hill and the long low barrows subtly moulded into the landscape. It was very silent on the summit: the traffic below could barely be heard, even the wind, slithering invisibly through the grass, made little sound. Jessica lay back and shut her eyes. She was tired again from the night's adventure, and it suddenly seemed a long time since she had been alone.

She sighed. The sun beat down onto her closed lids, the wind gently buffeted her body. She recalled vaguely one of Cora's relaxation exercises when she had to merge into the floor. Her body released its tension into the ground, and became seamlessly contoured into the earth. The silence whistled past; the hills and fields displayed their grave vistas to the sun. In her mind she pictured the landscape slowly floating through its own seas of light, as the sun processed through the day, the seasons, marking changes of shadow and brilliance. Clouds rolled by, hills moved closer or further away; misty mornings, harvest gold, winter brown.

Jessica started: she heard voices, carried intermittent and staccato on the wind. Other tourists must be coming to join her. She sat up, blinking in the bright light. She thought she heard them climbing up the same way she had. She got to her feet, brushed herself down and walked to the edge of the summit to look over. Momentarily she was confused: it was the opposite side to the slope she had climbed. She had got mixed up.

She walked back across and looked down again: to her surprise she saw Cora, just disappearing round the stepped ledge that circled the hill 17 foot below its summit. Was Adam with her? It must have been their voices she had heard.

'Cora!' she cried. She ran across to look down on the ledge in the direction they were heading, but could see no one. She scrambled down to the ledge, and jogged back around its curve. 'Cora, Cora!' she called. There was no one there. A chill touched her. It was impossible to lose anyone on the mound: the only feature on its exposed slopes was the ledge. Nothing grew on the hill except grass. The chill became edged with panic. Jessica looked at her watch – nearly 2 o'clock! She had been much longer than she'd intended. When was the coach due to leave? Would they wait for her? She needed to get off the hill. She started to clamber down, not giving too much weight to the feeling that she was being followed, but too scared to look back and check. At the bottom she set off at a run back along the road to the village.

The coach was already throbbing, Richard and Cora were conferring anxiously at the door and looking round to see if she was coming. She called out to them, they waved, relief on their faces.

'I'm so sorry,' she said, breathless.

'It's OK, it's OK,' smiled Richard, patting her on the shoulder.

'Come and sit behind Helen and me,' said Cora. There was an empty seat beside Jonathan. Jessica smiled at him.

'Did you get lost?' he asked.

'Sort of.'

Jessica hesitated to speak to Cora about her experience in front of Helen and Jonathan. Instead, she sat back and started to read Richard's notes on Silbury Hill. He listed statistics and dates first: 'The mound was started around 2700 BC; ... the first layer was built out of thick layers of soil clay, chalk and gravel; the rest out of honey-comb walls of chalk blocks, filled with chalk rubble. Legend spoke of a king Sil who was buried in a golden coffin, clad in golden armour. However excavations between 1968-70 showed Silbury to be a Neolithic not Bronze Age structure, found no burial remains but revealed the complex construction and that the original turfs – cut off from sunlight for nearly 5000 years – still contained green grass, as well as the flying ants that had been busying themselves in them that day in late July or early August when the turfs were first covered up.'

'Isn't this amazing? About the grass – have you read this?' she turned to Jonathan.

'Aha,' he nodded.

'How could the grass still be green?'

'Isn't it that orgone energy effect that Reich wrote about – the layers of organic and inorganic material, preserve or store energy or something.'

'Oh, I've heard of that vaguely.'

Jessica read on. Richard gave some of the theories of Silbury's significance. There were associations with the sun, the harvest and with the goddess.

'*Sil* was an ancient word for harvest festival; ... construction of the original mound was begun at harvest, or Lammas time, as the flying ants demonstrated ... at the same time of year a double sunrise can be seen: first from the mound's summit, and a few seconds later, from its ledge, due to the way the hill is placed in relation to the far eastern two-fold horizon of the Marlborough Downs and Waden Hill ... 'Sul', a word associated with 'Sil', meant the British goddess worshipped on hilltops above springs ... the shape of the land being associated in ancient times with the body of the goddess ... In ancient Britain, as elsewhere, the sun was seen as feminine ...'

The coach gave a lurch and stopped, engines shuddering. They were already on the outskirts of Bath, enmeshed in its summer traffic jams. Jessica looked up, her head spinning. Silbury Hill was the goddess! She put her head through the gap at the top of the seats in front.

'Cora – Silbury Hill is the goddess – did you realize that?'

'That's what we've been talking about,' Helen looked up at her. 'We want to do a dance about it tonight at the community.'

'Oh,' Jessica said, uncomprehendingly. 'Great.' She frowned, 'but it doesn't explain –' The coach started up again, and she lost her balance.

'Doesn't explain what darling?' asked Cora, but the coach was pulling into their drop off point. Jessica sat back in her seat, letting the others get off first. If the mound was a celebration of the golden presence of the goddess, why had she felt so frightened there?

Jessica followed Cora and Helen off the coach and attached herself to them as they strolled, still absorbed in their plans, into the town centre. They came to a gradual stop in a pretty, thronging pedestrian crescent. Flower baskets hung from elegant lampposts, a small fountain bubbled by wooden benches, and a pageant of gift shops, tea rooms, bath and body shops, jewellers and bookshops coloured the street. Jessica, distracted by her questions, felt bewildered by the sudden return to city dazzle. Helen and Cora finally paused and took stock of where they were.

'Do you two want to have some tea?' Jessica asked anxiously.

'Tea, that would be good, very good,' said Cora.

'Yes, OK, but no more cake, and I don't want to be too long, I want to visit the Baths, and there are some good book shops here.'

Jessica felt irritated by Helen's attitude that she was doing her a favour. She would rather have talked with Cora alone, but saw no graceful way to exclude Helen. As they walked up the curving street to choose a teashop, they came across Suzanne walking swiftly in the opposite direction. She almost didn't see them.

'Suzanne,' Cora called out. Suzanne looked startled, almost guilty, then smiled.

'We're going to take teee – would you like to join us?'

'Thanks no – I've got errands to do: it's so long since we've been in civilization! They've got a good Boots here – I can't wait.' She laughed and hurried on. Jessica wondered why her face had flushed on seeing them. Did she know about Richard and herself?

Jessica poured tea into the floral cups, and watered hers down from the small stainless steel jug of hot water. The teashop was crowded, they were wedged into a small table against the wall.

'You know, it's very odd, but I thought I saw you, Cora, on Silbury today.'

Helen looked sharply at Jessica.

'Oh, I was there this morning –'

'No, but she went there over lunch time, didn't you?' Helen narrowed her eyes. 'That's why you were late.'

'Yes, that's right.'

Cora looked at her.

'I was lying down –'

'Where?' asked Helen.

'On the top. I was resting a bit, having a sort of reverie. Then I thought I heard voices – do you take milk?'

Both women shook their heads. Jessica poured milk into her cup, frowning in concentration. 'I went to look – at first I was a bit disoriented. Then I looked over and I saw someone – it looked like you – just as they disappeared round the corner of the ledge. I went down to the ledge and kept looking, but no one was there. And, and anyway –'

'She was having lunch in the pub.'

Jessica looked at Helen.

'Yes,' she said. There was a pause. 'So then I, I started to feel really afraid. I wanted to get away as fast as I could, but I also had this strong sense that I had to be careful, not to panic –' Jessica drank some of her tea. No one said anything. She went on. 'So you see, I don't understand – I mean, I know it's possible to imagine things, or maybe you came into my mind then for some good psychic reason – but, if Silbury is the goddess – why did I feel so scared?'

'Wow,' said Helen, shaking her head.

'I think you did see me for a good reason, my love,' said Cora.

'You know, this is so amazing, this is in my book –'

Jessica's heart sank, the last thing she wanted was a diatribe about Helen's theories.

'It's all about the psychic experiences people have at the ancient sites. Something Richard did not include in his notes – because he's too chicken or is frightened of what people like Simon will say, or something –'

'Or maybe because he doesn't want to prejudice or scare people,' Cora admonished.

'Well, I don't know about that, I keep telling him that he should include more –'

'What, what didn't he say?'

'The impressions of a *very* well-known psychometrist – one of the best a woman naturally, called Olive Pixley. When she visited Silbury, she felt that the mound had been erected over a stone circle where black magic had been practiced. The place had such an evil atmosphere and so potent an influence that the only solution was to destroy the circle and bury the stones.'

'But why slot it into the landscape so precisely?'

Helen shrugged. 'The circle would already have been carefully placed in relation to the whole site. They covered the degenerate stones with the mound, with the body of the goddess, and turned it into an opportunity to honour the goddess, bringer of life and healing.'

'So symbolically the goddess took into herself the evil –'

'And annulled it,' said Cora.

'So why was I frightened? Did some of the evil remain?'

Cora shook her head.

'Who knows?' She looked at Jessica. 'Sometimes it's disowned parts of ourselves that we are frightened of.'

'What do you mean Cora?'

'Sometimes what we call evil is just a shadow in ourselves that we have not included. Sometimes we just label things evil because they frighten us.'

'Like women themselves,' interrupted Helen, 'labelled wicked witches when they were just intuitive or clever with herbs, or uninhibited sexually – all of which used to frighten men so much they burnt them. Still frightens them actually, I think that's partly the problem with Richard not wanting to acknowledge properly what I am doing …'

'But how do you learn the difference?' Jessica turned to Cora again. 'Between the shadow and real evil, I mean.'

'We have to re-learn the art of the shawoman, we have to descend and own the depths of ourselves.'

'Like Inanna meeting Ereshkigal,' said Jessica, a smile lifting the corners of her mouth.

'Wow, this is cosmic, we must do something about this,' Helen said, happily biting into the thick slice of Dundee cake that lay untouched on Jessica's plate.

# CHAPTER TEN

'So welcome to our living circle tonight. Some of us have been seeing a lot of circles recently, mainly stone ones.' There was a slight ripple of laughter from the living circle: the tour group, joined by 20 or so from the Dayton Community, who were seated, some in chairs, some on the floor, in a wide circle around a spacious room of unplastered stone. The eastern wall was formed almost entirely of sliding glass doors, allowing for a wide view of the green, stirring garden outside. An ancient, rather battered grand piano stood in one corner, and in the very middle of their circle a squat, white candle sat on a chipped saucer next to a box of kitchen matches. The speaker was Gabriel, his tone as always smooth and silvery, a little too at ease in the situation. He had obviously done this kind of introduction many times before. There was no denying though the sweet atmosphere that hung around the large, shambly Victorian house, once the village rectory, in which the Dayton Community were principally housed. Not just the sweetness of an old-fashioned English country house, furnished with worn floral sofas and slightly battered antique furniture, accented with vases of flowers from the garden and with mullioned windows that made the light look like water. There was a lift to the sweetness, so that it carried more than tones of nostalgia, but uncovered a place in which it was possible to feel content, unconcerned about the details of things. There was nothing ethereal about the place, it seemed robust, an everyday space in which new forms could flower and uncomplicated pleasure be had in the cadences of present experience.

'We who live here at Dayton would like to warmly welcome those on the tour of ancient sites, we're very happy to host you and share in your experiences, and we look forward to creating this time together.' Gabriel paused, and smiled at Bahira, who then got up in his place. She was dressed in a white Egyptian robe, with gold jewellery at her throat. Her perfectly made-up face as mask-like as any dead pharaoh's.

'We thought it would be appropriate to begin our time this evening by creating an altar together. Don't worry,' she raised one hand magisterially, 'it's very simple and easy. At supper time, we asked if you could bring something with you this evening that symbolizes your current most sacred experience. We'll start the music, and then, whenever and in whatever order you feel moved to do so, come up one by one to place your object here in the centre, again in whatever relationship to the other objects seems right to you. So, could we start the music?'

She nodded to the back of the room, and some synthesized flute started to meander softly around the walls. Bahira bent down and lit the candle, then placed a sprig of basil close to it on the floor. After she sat down, the silence gathered in uncomfortable folds until Edwina suddenly gathered herself up from the floor and, long skirts rustling, placed a smooth white quartz stone south from the candle. Her compliance started a flow going, and soon there was a small pile of disparate objects in the middle of the room: a posy of wild roses, a piece of lichen-covered bark, someone's turquoise ring, a notebook. Cora placed a branch of coral by the bark, and Jessica hung her green pendant from it. Towards the end, people came forward more quickly, no-one wanting to be last, and very soon all the symbols had been offered and the altar built. Bahira stepped into the circle and graciously thanked everyone as the wave-like hum of the music ebbed away.

Richard got to his feet. 'I've been asked to say just a few words about our tour, which I'm happy to do. The idea is for me to give an outline of what we've been up to, and then leave space for anyone else who wants to share their own thoughts and experiences so far. But before I begin, or we begin, there's something I just want to acknowledge. We're here tonight to create a ritual space together, in which something of the sacred dimension of life can be touched and shared as a group. Now this kind of ceremony is not for everyone, and I want to emphasize strongly that we definitely have options this evening: some may prefer to watch the television or go to the pub and hey, that's cool, that's really OK, that's another kind of circle if you will. We are the intermingling of different tribes here, on this tour, and in this community, and *that* is sacred and to be respected. And so I hope no one is here because they feel that they ought to be for some reason, and if you're here because you're just curious, that's OK too.'

Jessica shifted in her seat. She wasn't sure she understood what Richard was saying. She had the impression that the Dayton community focused an informal network of people with which Richard, Bahira, Cora and one or two others on the tour were familiar, and that the evening offered an implicit invitation to others to connect with this web. She sighed: she didn't really like organized togetherness, it reminded her of the Girl Guides, or discussion lessons at school that never took off. She half-wished she had joined Peter March and Simon Graves at the pub, sipping local ale in the mellow light of old stone and evening sunlight. On the other hand, she was quite enjoying the odd ambience of the occasion, even though she was not much interested in hearing people's accounts of the trip. Nothing was being required of her, yet at the same time the possibilities of the agenda-less evening lapped with gentle potency at her feet. If she chose, she could throw in a stone, dip her feet or wade right in and see what happened. Equally, she could allow her mind to wander, sometimes glancing out at the slow-moving foliage of the trees in the garden and beyond; sometimes focusing in on the circle and its speakers, speculating about their lives and inner worlds.

After Richard completed his overview, Gabriel was the first to get up – the professional dancer seeding the floor for the rest. He expressed his awe at the megalithic heritage, his gratitude to Richard for opening up the sacred world of the ancients, the importance of his work. Then Edwina rose to her feet again. She spoke in a shy, little girl's voice.

'Em, yes, I too just want to *thank you* Richard. This tour has meant a lot to me, I feel inspired – I mean it's just so wonderful to know that … that in the beginning this country was shaped by *true mystics*.' Her last two words were squeezed out as if under pressure, and quavered with emotion. She blushed and sat down abruptly.

What a peculiar exercise, thought Jessica, unsure whether Edwina's intensity expressed deep feeling for a spiritual heritage or simply the ordeal of speaking in front of a group of people. If the latter, the evening's apparently easy and open-ended framework could be viewed as a manipulative way to force a 'happening' by exerting pressure on whichever the weakest and most unquestioning links might be. Either way, the steam blast of emotion threatened to penetrate Jessica's airy detachment, engendering as it did some kind of response and therefore participation.

Uta stood up, and began to speak, her deep even voice mellowing out the atmosphere. 'So what we have learned, on our tour, sorry, *some* of what we have learned, is that the builders of these places we have visited were very skilled and wise. They knew about forces of the earth, perhaps even of the interaction *between* the earth and the mind, that we do not understand. And I think it is important to know these things so that we realize our civilization is not as clever as we think, and that the past and our planet have many secrets to teach us, and this can help us stay humble.' Everyone relaxed again. Yes the circle could also be this quiet reasoning together, the tribal ritual of collective thought, where thought and feeling mingled together like the melody and discord of improvised but purposeful music. One or two others spoke, then Cora and Helen stood up with the assured air of pre-arranged intent. Helen spoke first:

'Legend has it that the ancient sites – the stones, the holy wells – form doorways to the 'otherworld'; that they are places where at certain times and under certain conditions, it is possible to cross the threshold of our ordinary, everyday world and step into a different dimension. Some of you know that I am working on a book about the high numbers of people who have psychic experiences at these sacred sites: they hear voices, see lights, experience time loss, or feel a kind of *presence*. I believe that the forces at the ancient sites help us get in touch with the power of our own subconscious minds, or, more radically, that at some deep level, not fully understood, our subconscious minds *become* the otherworld.' Helen stopped, as if she were overcome by her own thought process. She looked at Cora who smiled and started to speak, or rather intone in the chant-like voice she used in her workshops:

'Our minds and our bodies are the earth, the earth is our body, our mother. Many of the sites were places of worship where the ancients would commune with her: they honoured her dual aspect of night and day, hag of terrible truth, and goddess of love and fertility. In ancient times, women were the first shamen, shawomen, it was their sacred responsibility to travel into the different worlds. One of the earliest myths tells us this: it is the story of Inanna, goddess of heaven and earth, and her descent into the underworld where she meets her dark sister, Ereshkigal who stares at Inanna with the eyes of death, killing her, and hanging her on a meathook to rot! But slowly Inanna resurrects, helped by Inki, god of water. She returns to the overworld, forever changed by her encounter, and the dance of creation begins anew!" Cora shook her head. 'Oh, dear, so many words! Words are wonderful but the otherworld demands that we use all of our body – not just this top bit!' Cora cut off her head with her hand, a few people chuckled. 'Dance, music, poetry – these are the languages of myth.'

Cora walked into the centre and stood by the altar pile. She was dressed in her black leotard and skirt. Helen was wearing orange leggings and a long yellow shirt. 'We want to dance our experience for you,' said Cora, and she lay down on the floor, curled in a foetal position. Helen started to pace round the edge of the circle, picking up speed as she spiralled in towards its centre. As she moved she looked back over her shoulder and gestured in fear as if something was following her. A man whom Jessica took to be a member of the community jangled fast discordant chords on the piano, his playing keeping pace with Helen's circles. At the centre, to a climax of base chords, Cora uncurled herself and sat up, eyes closed, as Helen froze in fear before her. Now instead of the music, Cora began her death rattle breathing. Slowly she snaked and twisted her body round until, rearing up in front of Helen, she opened her eyes and immediately Helen collapsed. Cora stopped her breathing and sat inert while quiet rivulets of piano started to ripple over the floor. Eventually one stirred Helen, who now could return the gaze of the black goddess. The two mirrored each other's movements as they rose to their feet; then, still in slow motion, they intertwined their arms and stood for a moment hinged like the fragment of a frieze. The piano music began again, only now the chords were strong and melodious, bass and high notes interweaving, and Helen started unwinding back through the spirals of the circle, while Cora remained at the centre. The two figures, gold and black, moved in strange rocking motions, Helen flinging her arms up as Cora crouched low, Cora standing up while Helen crawled on the ground. Up and down they alternated until Helen stood at the edge of the circle once more and their dance was finished.

There was a hush, then came the applause, not just a polite, obligatory rattle, but vigorous and sustained. Many were clapping their hands out of relief as much as appreciation: that the dance had been good, not embarrassingly inept; relief too, that the dance had ended, for it had been powerful enough to provoke discomfort; and again, relief that nobody would be expected to follow this act, and that therefore the evening, with all its attendant dangers – of involvement, of exposure – was over and people could relax.

Jessica applauded out of genuine pleasure, and sat in a contented haze watching the circle and its altar gradually break up as people retrieved their symbols and processed slowly out of the room. Continual movement, like waves, in and out of the underworld – this was not only essential, it was *natural*, she realized. Down into the chaos of the dark feminine, and up into the order of the above ground world: the dance, the *dance* of life! Is this how everything is, like a garden that dies away, goes to seed, looks a ruin in winter, but blossoms again in the spring? Like barrenness in oneself, places that can come back to life. For a moment she thought of Paul. He still seemed a long way off, struggling somewhere through hardened ground. Jessica realized that the room was almost empty. The gold and black figures of Helen and Cora were at the doorway.

Helen called to Jessica. 'What's happened Jessica? Are you entranced?'

Jessica started out of her chair. 'Yes, yes, I am.' She walked over and gave them each a hug. 'Thank you so much for that dance, it was beautiful.'

Herb tea and digestive biscuits were being served in the lounge next door. Turning from the tea table, cup in hand, Jessica found herself looking into the chest of Richard. On impulse she reached up and kissed his neck. 'Oh Richard, I love this place, I'm so glad you brought us here.'

'Jessica! Good! Look, how are you?'

'Couldn't be better,' she said, and moved off through the throng, as Bahira closed in on him, bearing cups of tea. Jessica made her way over to an old comfortable-looking armchair, part of a configuration of empty chairs gathered round a large coffee table. Most of the group were standing in small chatting clusters.

'I was so interested,' Jessica could hear one large and elderly woman in olive green tweeds saying to Cora, 'in what you mentioned about women being the first shamen ...' Suzanne, still with her air of suppressed agitation, was talking with Jonathan and Uta, the three of them pressed up against the wall in the crowded room. Jessica sat silent amid the buzz, nourished by the collective presence, but grateful to be left alone. She wanted to think about her new insight. Yet she found herself noticing as Gabriel, perched on the arm of one of the sofas, conversed earnestly and deliberately with Edwina, curled up in its corner. As she watched him, Jessica saw suddenly that his silvery exterior had been almost dutifully manufactured to mask a genuine sincerity, as if he did not believe his natural self would be considered sufficient on its own. Intrigued, Jessica looked away and sipped her tea, intending to return to her own thoughts, but this time her attention was caught by Richard. He had put his arm round Suzanne in a kind of lassoo as she was pushing her way through the thickets of people. Suzanne was all smiles and compliance, but Jessica could tell that she ignored his secret entreaty, moving on, face down and determined. Bahira appeared at his side again, and he allowed himself to be led away, deep in conversation. He needed groupies, Jessica confirmed to herself. He drew his strength from people's, especially women's, response. Were the stones the same? Do we feed the ancient sites with our own energy, and then wonder at it being reflected back to us? Jessica frowned; she had lost her moment of equilibrium. Now insight had given way to legions more questions and uncertainties. Either that or her thought was fraying out of coherence now that the adrenalin of the evening had subsided and the depth of her tiredness suddenly uncovered itself.

Her cupboard-sized room was at the end of a long red brick wing tacked on to the original stone Victorian building. Jessica was now so sleepy she felt almost drugged. From her bed, she watched the moon sailing above the grey shaded lawn and flower beds with a pleasant blankness. It was as if she saw the scene directly, without thought shifting the clarity into simile that confused or led away from the experience of the moment.

In the morning she knew she had dreamed, although it had not seemed like a dream and she did not remember waking. It had been a singular, simple dream: she had seen a face, that was all. A face that was archetypal: dark curled hair and beard, but with its own human peculiarities: the nose and forehead a little shiny, shadows under the eyes, a curve of humour at the mouth. It was a face to touch, the skin was right in front of her: a fragile delineation of features. Jessica had felt her head tingle with recognition: that blessing confounded its sterile symbols of gesture and dogma, chalice and cross; a benign undergirding, a kind of molecular pulse or heartbeat. No words were actually spoken, but the expression, the eyes in the dream reached into her so fully, communicated his presence, resonating still within her, she had known it already, it was familiar, it was hers.

Jessica blinked, and turned to the window: the sky was a very pale, hazy blue, the garden glittered with dew. Everything was refreshed, everything bore this subliminal smile of creation, of the vibration of being alive. Millions of pounds could not buy this morning, paradise came out of the heart. How could she sustain this feeling, she wanted always to live this way. And as soon as she thought this, the moment changed. A cat strolled out onto the lawn and twitched its tail at the bird-bearing trees. A veil of ordinariness inserted itself back into Jessica's vision, and she was in the process of coming to terms with the return of mundanity, realizing that coffee and toast was part of it, when there was a tapping at her door. Startled, she at first made no reply, apprehensive lest it be Richard. Then she told herself that in her new state of mind she could handle anything, her doubts diminishing further with the thought that Richard was unlikely to merely tap on a door.

'Come in,' she said, realizing as she spoke that the tapping reminded her of a similar sound, heard from the other side of a door, at the top of the Priory's winding staircase. The scene re-etched itself across her mind as Suzanne slipped into her room.

'Hallo!' Jessica was awash with surprise and memory.

'I haven't woken you up have I?' asked Suzanne distractedly. She still looked agitated, but the gleam in her eye was of excitement, not anxiety. 'Look!' Suzanne waved a tiny white plastic spatula at Jessica.

'What?'

'It's pink, it's *pink*!'

'You're pregnant!'

'Yes – my period's two weeks late, so I'm one month if you count from ovulation, six if you count from the last period – and mine are like clockwork.'

'You're pleased –'

'I'm *thrilled*, I'm so excited. I just,' she frowned,' I just feel a bit strange though, because I've been sleeping with Richard ...'

'Ah.'

'I'd been feeling really magical, and my period was late, so part of me knew, but the other part sort of glossed over it, and now I don't feel right about it –'

'About what?'

'About sleeping with Richard when I was pregnant –'

'Is it Steve's?'

'Oh, I think so. I mean there hasn't really been anyone else, for a while …'

'How do you think Steve will take it?'

'Oh – I don't know, I think he'll be pleased. If he isn't, it doesn't say much for our relationship, does it?'

'But Suzanne! You're the one who's always talking about not being tied down. You're the one having an affair now!'

'Not now, not any more. Well maybe it's time to be more committed – anyway, it's mainly *my* baby.'

'So you'd have it anyway, even if Steve doesn't want to know.'

'Of course. I mean what's all this talk about the mother goddess if it doesn't dignify single mothers!'

Jessica smiled and took Suzanne's hand. 'I'm really glad you're so happy about it – it *is* exciting.'

'Thank you,' Suzanne smiled her sweetest smile. 'Well, I suppose I'd better get dressed properly.'

'Are you going to phone Steve, or wait till you see him?' Jessica swung her legs out of bed.

'I'm not sure – it might be best to wait.'

Jessica nodded and Suzanne was gone.

Richard had warned them over breakfast that the Stonehenge they were going to visit would not look like the many photos they had seen of it: carefully framed to isolate the great stones from their modern encumbrances and evoke their remote and pristine past. Nor would they be able to get close to the stones, long fenced off from Druids, hippy travellers, midsummer festival goers, souvenir hunters and general public alike. The coach pulled into the carpark and they climbed off to join a fair sized crowd of other sightseers, some already licking their Walls ice creams from the Refreshments counter in the concrete bunker called the Visitors Centre. The henge itself had already been glimpsed, astonishingly close to the road, before they turned off into the carpark which, like the centre, was set below ground level.

Despite Richard's cautioning Jessica did feel disappointed as she emerged from the tunnel that went under the road and jostled along the thronged, tarmac path that interlinked in a wide crescent with the outer circle of the monument. At the crescent's furthest point, it allowed a reasonably close but unsatisfying view of the famous sarsen and bluestone rings. Unlike Avebury's oddly pleasing counterpart of English village and neolithic stones, the proximity of Stonehenge to major roads seemed only shocking; the presence of the army base close by, an oddity, a violation.

Jessica found it difficult to know what her own first impressions of the stones were because their image was already so familiar to her.

'I'm afraid Richard was right,' she said to Suzanne who was walking next to her. Now that Suzanne had shared her secret, and Jessica had laid hers to rest, the connection between them had opened up again.

'Ooh I don't know,' said Suzanne.

'Oh come on, it isn't anything like the photos of it.'

'I haven't seen that many pictures, so I suppose I don't have as much to be disappointed about.'

'Still, it's awful – all these people, barbed wire, the road –'

'But the stones are still here, aren't they?'

'What do you mean?'

'Well, it's like – all these other things are sort of peripheral, aren't they. The beauty of the stones is there, it can't be changed.'

Jessica looked at Suzanne. It was an oddly mystical comment for her to make. 'Are they beautiful?' she asked.

'Yes, they're incredible.'

Jessica stared at the archetypal image of the huge linked stones, provoking the urge always to find the other pieces and snap it all together again like giant lego. 'You know beautiful is just not a word I would use to describe them. I think I find them a bit brutish.'

They were standing at the closest point to the monument and therefore the most crowded part of the path. As they turned to move on round, their viewing spot was immediately filled.

'Are we going to be here long?' asked Jessica.

'I don't think so. Richard's going to talk about the place a little bit, after everyone's seen it, and then we move on to Glastonbury.'

'Good.'

Richard gathered people together at a spot just removed from the tunnel entrance. 'Stonehenge is probably the most well-known and impressive ancient megalithic site in the world, but as you can see, it has become a monument under siege and in my opinion has virtually lost whatever presence of power it might once have had. There is, however, much to impress about its construction.' Some of the other tourists, curious at this megalithic tour guide approach, started to attach themselves to the outer circle of their group. Richard took no notice: 'The gaps between the inner sarsen stones align with the spaces between the uprights in the outer lintel ring to give sighting windows to key sun and moon rising and setting positions. Originally four so-called "station stones" formed a rectangle in the main outer circle of the henge which encoded all the main sun and moon rising and setting points. Some theorists claim Stonehenge was a temple dedicated to the marriage of the sun god with the earth goddess. Professor Meaden in his book *The Stonehenge Solution* even proposes that the shadow cast by the Heel Stone at the summer solstice symbolizes the phallus of the sun god penetrating the womb of the mother goddess – the inner horseshoe of trilithons, eventually falling on the altar stone, or as he calls it, the Egg or Goddess stone. Thus, the re-fertilization of the earth was re-enacted each year and watched as a grand spectacle of the gods by the populace.' Suzanne poked Jessica in the ribs and giggled.

'One or two dramatic accounts of light phenomena are associated with Stonehenge, in particular a light ball that fell into the ground with a clap of thunder just before the solstice and a partial solar eclipse. However, we have found no unusual emissions of radioactivity and no magnetic anomalies. Hopefully this is not a sign that the earth goddess is dead!' Richard smiled and paused. 'As always there is much more to say, let's cover some more ground, if you want to, one to one, or later today. I have a bibliography if you'd like to do some further reading on this – but now let's move on to lunch and a more leisurely afternoon in Glastonbury.'

'Have you ever had a tarot reading?' asked Suzanne, hesitating by a sandwich board that glowed with rainbow colours and advertised readings by Adina in glossy red letters.

'No,' said Jessica. They hovered aimlessly in front of the shop, its windows full of the by now familiar paraphernalia of crystals, incense, mystical books and silver jewellery. They had climbed up the Tor, visited the Chalice Well and the Abbey ruins, drunk tea in a pretty but hectically busy teashop and perused Richard's notes. The afternoon was hot, everywhere was crowded.

'Do you want to have a go?'

'Not really,' said Suzanne.

'I don't want to see or do anything more myself.'

'No,' agreed Suzanne, 'but where can we go, it's ages till supper, and anyway I'm not hungry.'

'There's a church a bit further down, let's just go and sit in the churchyard.'

The church was large and set back from the street. On its other side the churchyard was quiet, looking out onto school buildings and the orchards of Butt Close.

'Oh God, this is great,' said Jessica as they sat down on the grass. The sound of traffic was muted. They could hear birdsong. 'I don't think much of this place, do you?'

'You just said it was great.'

'No, I mean Glastonbury.'

'Don't you?'

'No, it's like Stonehenge, it's become a theme park of itself.'

'I should think it's very different when there's not so many tourists here.'

'I suppose that's what happens when too many people come to look, to take something rather than actually renew the mysteries in themselves.'

'Mm.' Suzanne lay back and closed her eyes. 'You know, you should get pregnant too, Jessica.'

'Huh, oh yeah.'

'No really, you should.' Suzanne sat up. 'Then we could have our babies together – wouldn't that be fun?'

'Oh come on Suzanne – I don't even know if I'm still together with Paul, let alone about to have a baby with him.'

'You really think you might split up?'

'I don't know. Probably. I've been feeling today that I've almost had enough of this tour – but then I think about going back and I don't know where I'd be going to.'

'Mm – that would make it more difficult, but you can get all kinds of allowances, you know. As a single mother, you go to the top of the list for housing –'

'Suzanne! Having a baby is about the last thing on my mind.'

Suzanne smiled and lay back again. 'Pity,' she said, 'but Jessica, don't give up on the tour – if you go I'd want to go, and I can't. It's only today you haven't liked. Just think, we'll be in Cornwall tomorrow.'

'Yes, I know, and we'll also be meeting up with the film crew – is Paul still coming?'

'I think so, Steve hasn't said otherwise when I've talked to him.'

'It's going to be so weird to see him – I feel as if I've been away for a hundred years.'

'He must care for you though, Jessie, if he's coming down.'

'He's probably just coming on a jaunt with Steve.'

'It's going to be a long day today, everybody.'

Richard held on to the tops of the two front seats and hunched forward, his body swaying as the coach pulled and heaved itself out of the small hotel carpark and into the narrow streets. His voice was crackly and difficult to hear over the PA system. 'That was why we had a leisurely time yesterday afternoon and evening in Glastonbury. We're going to head straight down the motorway to the wilds of Cornwall, first stop at Trethevy Quoit, near Liskeard; from there to Bodmin Moor and a brief look at the Altarnun or Nine Stones Circle. That will be our exercise for the day!' There was a groan. 'And then on to St Ives which will be our base for the next few days. A reminder too that a film crew will be joining us when we reach St Ives.'

Terence, who had been listening with his usual dutiful attention, wrinkled his forehead and asked: 'What will that mean Richard?' At the same time a frown came over Uta's kindly face.

'I realize you have already told about the filming Richard, but for some reason I feel like I'm only now registering the information – I don't want to sound awkward at all, but won't this be a little intrusive?'

'Will we be filmed?' called out Jonathan.

A sense of alarm spread among the group. Richard waved his hand and shook his head.

'As I understand it, no one will be filmed against their wishes. If you do consent to be filmed, you will be asked to sign release forms – but you will be background only –'

Someone laughed.

'Will we be paid as extras?' asked Simon.

Richard smiled and shook his head again. 'Myself and the megaliths will obviously be the main focus.'

'But –' Bill began.

'I think the way to look at this is as an opportunity to assist in spreading the word about the importance of these sites to our modern civilization – I look at it that way, and I really appreciate your support as well.'

Jessica and Suzanne watched impassively as Richard, who seemed to have accepted that their ranks were inexplicably closed to him, swung obediently round into his seat, next to Bahira, who had been nodding in emphatic agreement.

The coach surged out into open countryside again where it joined the M4.

The motorway was dense with holiday traffic, its six lanes curving their way through the rolling countryside of Somerset and Devon, green and lovely and kind, like a promise that is always fulfilled. Suzanne sat, hand on belly, and flipped the pages of magazines, leaving Jessica free to stare out at the faint projection of her face upon the moving landscape. She was grateful for the journey and the busy schedule ahead, which seemed to grant more time for her to adjust to seeing Paul again. She also felt relieved to be out of the narrow Glastonbury streets and on their way again.

Suzanne scraped shut her magazine over her stomach and chucked it on the floor with the others.

'I need a pee,' she said. 'I think I'll see if we're going to stop for a loobreak.' She got up and went forward. The voice of Simon Greaves in the seat behind broke in on Jessica's thoughts. 'It depends on what kind of film the guy's intending to make – I don't want to be associated with a lot of inflated possibilities … What channel is it, do you know? I mean it's obviously not the BBC, right?'

Jessica looked out of the window attempting to shake off the voices. Clouds were moving in from the west, the traffic had grown even thicker. Were her perceptions based in anything real? Or was it just fantasy, chasing elusive patterns, like a gossamer web placed over random emotional upheavals to force a coherence that did not exist? A web that Paul's relentless realism would quickly tear down. But she was not the same – that was definite. Some part of her had been reclaimed. Suzanne was making her way carefully back down the aisle of the coach, holding on to the seat tops to keep her balance.

'Yep, we'll be stopping soon,' she announced as she lowered herself into her seat. Jessica sighed. 'Good,' she said.

An hour or so later the group were trekking out into the eerie, open spaces of Bodmin Moor, and found themselves once more in the presence of a ring of stones: the Altarnun circle. There were nine stones, including one in the centre. Two stones facing each other across the circle leaned over in opposite directions, like stiff limbo dancers. Fingering their old, lichen-covered surface, watching while Richard spoke to the group about their magnetic anomalies, Jessica realized that the old glimmer of excitement she always felt on returning to Cornwall was mingled with a keener-edged anticipation.

Some in the group needed to rest after the hike across the moor. Jessica sat against one of the leaning stones. The two red-haired American women, overweight and unused to walking, were collapsed on the grass inside the circle, perspiring and pale from exertion. Simon and Peter were examining one of the stones on the western side. The wind flickered through the close cropped rough grass and gorse, clouds in dark and light shades of grey ranged slowly, slowly across a low sky. The others in the tour, subdued after their walk, and by now familiar to her, no longer intruded on Jessica's awareness. Richard had said there were ways to tune others out, she must have learnt them. Stuart and Hazel walked past with their divining rods. Measuring energy lines. How did you measure the presence of the stones, as strong now, or stronger than the humans walking around them? She blinked, letting the mesh of grey and light in the sky and on the stones go out of focus, and for a moment slipped into time's negative. From the stones' viewpoint, the tour group were like butterflies, richly coloured and transient, fluttering giddily about them for a few microseconds; or like rowdy children, invading their council, hooting and running round then disappearing as noisily as they came, finding their company too uneventful.

Richard had stood up, and was signalling that it was time to leave. Now the stones can return to their deliberations. The last to leave, Jessica looked back at the circle from the rear of the group. She saw august elders, sighing as they gathered themselves back together again, a little impatient at the interruption, but weren't they also secretly wistful that they could no longer run off and play themselves?

'Come on Jessie, let's go round the shops.'

'What about Steve and everyone – when are they due?'

Suzanne shook her head. 'It could be any time, late, I 'spect, anyway, we don't have to put on a reception committee do we?'

'No, OK.'

Their hotel was one of the many that lined the steep winding hill which led down the cliff to the small harbour town below. Luckily it was at the bottom of the hill, a short walk from the town centre, but still affording a wide view out across the silvery bay to the green tumbling Atlantic beyond. Gulls called and arched across the sky, the traffic was non-stop.

'What a pretty place!'

'Yes, I love St Ives.'

'It's so great to be in a *town* again.'

'We were just in one.'

'Yes, but a real town, not a new age bazaar. And by the sea.'

'Very touristy though.'

The narrow cobble-stoned alleyways slotted behind the main quayside were closed to cars and lined with souvenir shops. Bright hats, flickering windmills, and plastic buckets and spades were strung from their doorways.

'I feel like I've been away at sea, on one of those fantastical journeys that people in legends go on, and now I'm back on solid ground.'

Not too solid, I hope, thought Jessica, apprehensive at the imminent arrival of Paul. 'You're getting very mystical Suzanne.'

They meandered all around the main hub of shops and out along the harbour wall. When they got back Steve was in the hallway, talking to Richard.

'Well hallo there, how are you?' He gave Suzanne a kiss and Jessica a brief hug. 'Are you having fun?'

'Yes, it's been great.'

'Paul's around somewhere, Jessica.'

'Right. Are you all staying here?'

'No, we're up the street, there weren't any rooms free here. Listen, Richard and I need to talk some more – I'll see you at dinner OK, we'll all eat here.'

Suzanne smiled and turned to Richard. 'OK,' she said.

Richard smiled sunnily back. Jessica had to hand it to him, there was no shadow of awkwardness or guilt as he talked eagerly with Steve.

'Hey Dave,' Steve gestured to a man in leather jacket, jeans and white trainers who had appeared in the hallway. 'Dave, I want you to meet Suzanne, my girlfriend, Jessica, a good friend, and Richard who's heading up the tour.'

Dave's eyes were slightly downturned, making his face look as if it was slowly melting. He smiled sadly and said hallo.

'Dave is our cameraman, and a very good one at that. Oh, by the way, have you seen Paul anywhere?'

'Er, yeah, well no – he's gone for a walk round.'

Steve raised his eyebrows at Jessica who smiled and nodded.

'We'll see you later.' Steve had already turned back to Richard. 'So we'll need to get together with you later Richard ...'

'Come on Jessica, let's leave them to their plotting and go get a drink.'

'But you shouldn't –'

'No, don't worry, mineral water for me.'

In the cosy bar, Suzanne came over tired, and took her drink upstairs. Jessica sipped her lager and studied the model ships and black and white photos of lifeboats on surging seas which adorned the walls. She looked up and with a pang of tenderness saw Paul's face at the door. He came over.

'Hi, can I get you another drink?'

She nodded, and watched his elegant figure lean easily against the bar. The shock of seeing him was matched by an odd sense of relief. Now, finally, the two halves of her life were coming together, to do battle, to split apart, to blend, she did not know which.

'How are you?' To Jessica's disappointment, Paul's tone seemed to twist the solicitude into an interrogation.

'I'm fine, very well,' she said, unable to neutralize her note of self-justification.

'There's no need to be so defensive.'

'I'm not being defensive.'

'Good. You look well.'

'Thank you.'

'Oh for God's sake, Jessica, loosen up – I've come all this way to see you.'

'Have you?'

'Well I'm here aren't I?'

'Have you come to see me?'

'Of course I have.'

'How's Caroline?'

'She's fine too I think.'

This was not how Jessica had envisioned their meeting. She knew her sulkiness played right into Paul's slightly patronizing view of her. She started to feel all her newly claimed territory undermined by Paul's presence, just as she had feared. Now she felt stupid at her attempts to have an affair with Richard. Had her motivation really only been to get back at Paul? She wasn't even sure that he had slept with Caroline: she'd been too proud to ask.

'So how's it been? Are you enjoying the tour? Has it lived up to your expectations?'

'Yeah, it's been great.'

'What have you been doing, have you learnt anything?'

Again, the hint of interrogation inhibited her. She wasn't going to blurt out that she'd slept with Richard, although she'd quite like him to know. She couldn't tell him about the goddess, her fear, the dance, her dream. It was all evanescent, it wouldn't mean anything to him, and in the telling, it might evaporate completely.

'Oh, there's been so much – we've visited loads of sites, some of them the really well known ones, you know, like Stonehenge, or, or Avebury ... and then lots of smaller, less well known ones. It's amazing just how many there are.'

Paul nodded, his hands cupped over his mouth.

'And we've learnt a huge amount about them – magnetic anomalies – there's a hill in Wales where the magnetics are the same as when the poles reversed millions of years ago!'

'Really? And how's Cora?'

'She's wonderful – she did this beautiful dance ...'

'Dance?'

'Yes, with Helen ...'

'Where?'

'Oh, one night we stayed at this community, and had a kind of group ceremony.'

'Ahuh. So, anyway, you're enjoying it.'

She nodded.

'Well, that's good.'

Jessica lapsed into lonely silence. Why was it so difficult to talk to Paul? It was always the same. She should know better by now than to even try.

'What's the weather been like?'

'Em, it's been good, on the whole.' Jessica felt her stomach drop, yes, he would really rather talk about the weather. Steve looked into the bar. Dinner was ready, and he wanted Paul to eat with the film crew.

'If that's OK, Jess.'

'Of course.'

After dinner Paul asked Jessica if she wanted to go for a stroll round.

'I think Richard's going to do some kind of presentation.'

'Yeah, but it's going to take a while to set up the lights and everything – we've got a bit of time.'

'OK.'

Although the day had been cloudy, the evening was warm and balmy. They walked along the quayside, past gift shops and Cornish ice-cream vendors on one side, moored fishing boats on the other.

'Well – here we are in Cornwall.'

'Mm, yes.'

'We can still make it a bit of a holiday – go and visit your beloved beach …'

'But you'll be busy won't you?'

'No, there's not that much for me to do, I'm just tagging along really, carrying a few boxes, taking some pictures.'

'I suppose it depends how full our schedule's going to be – I think there's a lot of sites to cover.'

'But you can miss a few, can't you?'

'I'm not sure I want to – I mean,' Jessica sighed with frustration, 'I'm not just going to go scampering off because you're here. I'm *interested* in this tour.'

Paul did not reply. Putting his hands in his pockets, he leant against the harbour wall, his face frowning against the wind and the bright sheen of the sea. He was beginning to wonder whether Jessica wasn't more trouble than she was worth. He had wanted to get away, have some fun, find relief from his depression. Now he felt a fool: he had come all this way, and she was in a sulk. Nothing unusual about that either. Above all, he couldn't believe how she could make such a fuss about nothing – or be so uninterested in his work. She hadn't asked him anything about the oil spill. The ecological plight of the earth clamoured all around, and she was only interested in a load of old stones.

They walked back to the hotel where their icy silence was dissolved into the bustle of the tour group arranging themselves around the camera, lights, cables and Steve's directions in the spacious front lounge of the hotel. Uta and Terence watched grave-faced as Dave held the white half globe of the light meter to Richard's face. Jonathan looked on warily while the camera angle was checked and double checked. Stuart, Hazel and Bahira had already perfected the studied indifference of celebrities. The powerful white lights turned the ordinary room into a magical, glamorous setting. The intense focus which the camera brought was a kind of enchantment – suddenly everything was special, heightened.

Richard was not slow to catch the mood: 'The Land's End area, a district known as West Penwith, is a hard, high granite plateau, joined to the rest of Cornwall by a strip of marshland only four miles wide, like a fragile gateway to the otherworld. This bare moorland contains more ancient stones and alignments than any other area of comparable size. Cromlechs, circles, single monoliths, tumuli and holy wells all abound, as well as other rarer features: the strange underground passages or fougous whose ritualistic purposes are lost in the mists of time.'

Outside, in a sudden soft rush, the clouds had started to empty out their rain. Curtains flapped at the open window. 'Cut,' said Steve, as the softness swelled into a downpour drumming on window pane and pavement. Paul closed up the windows and Steve motioned Richard to continue.

'Many of the megalithic sites we have visited on this tour were constructed of granite. Granite, you will remember, is a crystalline rock that gives off high levels of radiation, which, combined with other factors at the sites, such as the presence of underground water, or a close by fault line, can induce altered states of consciousness.' Slowly, unobtrusively, the camera swung round and moved across the listening faces. 'It is my surmise that the unusually high numbers of ancient sites in this area is due to the presence of the granite. Not only was it in plentiful supply, but there was already a background field of resonant energy which could help amplify whatever effects the builders sought to achieve. Granite in fact predominates throughout Cornwall, and may also help to explain the fascination this little part of the world has for so many holiday makers – because it certainly can't be the weather!' Everyone laughed. Steve nodded at Dave and drew his finger across his neck. The camera was switched off, the lights dowsed. People blinked and looked around in surprise at the dimly lit room.

'God it's stuffy in here,' someone said. Others yawned. Most were tired and the room emptied out quickly, leaving the film crew to pack away their boxes and wind up their extension cords.

Suzanne sat in one corner, not even making a show of helping. Jessica hovered uncertainly.

'Have you told Steve?' she half-whispered.

'Mmhm.'

'So – what did he say. Is he pleased?'

'He was OK. You know, he's so distracted, I'm not sure it's really registered yet.' Suzanne yawned. Steve was having a final consultation with Paul, Dave and Tony the sound man.

'No, we'll load up in the morning, we can keep the gear here overnight. All right – thanks lads, good night.'

Suzanne went over and took his arm. 'Come on Steve.'

'Good night,' he said again, and Paul and Jessica were left alone.

'So – what do you want to do, Jess? You want to stay here – or come back to the other hotel?'

'Oh –' Jessica felt a jolt. 'Oh Paul – no, I – want to stay here, on my own.'

'Yeah?'

'I'm sorry – I feel so confused – it feels like everything's crowding in on me – I don't – I can't sleep with you at the moment.'

'Don't you even want to try?'

She shook her head. 'I can't, I just can't – I need to be on my own.'

'I've come all this way and you're giving me the cold shoulder.'

'It's not that simple –'

'I mean, is this what you want, do you want to split up? I mean if that's want you want, it's fine, just say so.'

'Oh God, I'm not sure, I don't think it's just a matter of what I want. Anyway, I don't *know* what I want – except, right now, I want to be on my own. It's like I'm in something, and it's not finished yet, and I have to let it finish.'

Paul looked at her with cool blue eyes. He shrugged. 'I'll see you in the morning.'

Back in his room, Paul took out his camera and blow brush and cleaned the inside of the camera body. When he'd finished, he opened his window and looked out at the sea, just visible above rooftops below. He felt restless, uneasy. Jessica was acting very strangely. Maybe it had been a mistake to come. Still, it was only a couple of days. West Penwith was an area that interested him visually. The place and the megaliths might even make a good subject for an exhibition.

## CHAPTER ELEVEN

'And she wants to keep it?'

'Yep.'

'What do you feel about that?'

Steve rubbed sleep from the corner of his eye and wrinkled his forehead. 'I'm not overjoyed. But I mean at the moment I can hardly take it in – I've got too much else to think about.'

Paul nodded. 'Does she want to make it legal, splice the knot and all that?'

'She says she doesn't care. She'll have it either way. It's the last thing I expected of her.' But even as he spoke, Steve found himself picturing the piles of soft animals in Suzanne's tiny flat. He'd always felt uneasy about them.

'It's this tour, mate, I told you – it's Richard the Pied Piper. Jessica's acting really weird too.'

'Oh yeah?' Steve said, without much interest.

'Didn't want to stay last night.'

'She getting it on with the Pied Piper then?'

'Christ knows,' but Paul felt a shock of recognition at the thought. She'd talked about being in the middle of something – was that what she meant?

'Complicated isn't it?' Steve drained his coffee cup. 'Women – can't live with them, can't live without them.'

Paul smiled at the cliché. Dave put his head round the door of the dining room. 'Ready when you are.'

'Right. Come on Paul.'

'Coming, coming.'

'We've become a convoy,' remarked Adam, looking out of the back window at Steve's black Volvo estate and the rented navy blue Ford Sierra estate that now trailed the coach as it wound its way along the narrow north coast road towards Zennor.

'Or a travelling circus,' said Jonathan.

'It feels very different now,' said Uta to Cora, a few seats further forward, 'our little tour. I don't know whether it's the film crew or the magical granite background of the area. But now everything feels kind of intensified.' Cora nodded.

'Maybe it's both,' suggested Suzanne from across the aisle.

Jessica, next to Suzanne, said nothing. She had woken up that morning with fear coiled solid and tight in her stomach, as if she had swallowed something indigestible, like a lump of metal or a stone. The feeling had puzzled her, because it seemed to have arisen out of nowhere and from no traceable cause. She had talked herself through all her current worries in an attempt to break the feeling up and dissolve it. Was this buried insecurity over leaving Paul? Anxiety about what the future held: her job, where she would live? None of these problems had matched the charge of the feeling. Indeed none had even seemed particularly relevant, as if the future were still a pale outline, barely discernible yet. The fear had remained heavily inside her when she went down for breakfast, banishing her appetite. For her the presence of the two cars behind them brought only added pressure, certainly no relief. Frowning, she stared out at the land and seascape moving past and around them.

A solitary stone farmhouse perched on the cliff, surrounded by a few green fields reclaimed from the moor, which, on the other side of the road, rose in treeless purple waves, echoing the ever-moving sea below. She tried to recall the deep sense of well-being from her dream the night before – why should she feel so different now? The land's beauty was due in part to its fearsomeness: hawthorn trees bent double by winter storms, jagged rocks, foaming seas. Now, Jessica found that the wildness she loved so much frightened, even saddened her. In the small, close-packed villages, the cottages and villas, windows dark as if deserted, seemed melancholy and tired, imbued with the hard lives of all their occupants past and present. It was an insight she was reluctant to accept: that great beauty often demanded a great price. This land had made people's lives very harsh: the farmers, the miners, the mothers with no pretty comforts in their homes. Many did not value the beauty of their surroundings, no longer even saw it. The human factor in ecology was not simple. It was not just greed, but desperation, the desire for an easier life, the longing to fulfil childhood dreams of well-being that sometimes drove people to poison fields, cut down trees. This was the inherited conditioning that motivated Mr Pascoe to build his supermarket. For him, putting the welfare of some ancient oak trees first was a luxury he had never even thought to afford. The site in question was close by, she remembered, just outside Penzance. She must check with Bill and find out the exact location. Maybe she could ask Paul to drive her there one evening.

They were standing on moorland, at the last site of the day.

'As you can see, this monument is unlike any megaliths we have seen before: a testimony to the great variety of dolmens in West Penwith. Mên-an-Tol, the holed stone, has a long association in folklore and custom with healing.' Jessica remembered the doughnut shaped stone, with the two upright pillars on either side of it, from Richard's talk. It had been one of the slides he'd shown.

'Children suffering from rickets would be passed three or nine times through the stone's hole, and adults with rheumatism would also climb through the hole. This is fascinating because research shows that the radiation level of the inside of the holed stone is double that of the environment, and nowadays some radical new treatments of arthritis include short, repeated exposures to sources of radiation.'

Jessica found it difficult to concentrate. The fear in her stomach which had waxed and waned throughout the day now grew acute. She felt jumpy, with little rivulets of panic running through her.

'I'd like to get some shots of people going through the stone – yeah?' Steve smiled. 'Come on Suzanne.'

'I'll go.' Adam launched himself through the hole. Edwina followed, smiling self-consciously, then Suzanne.

Steve looked at Tony, who nodded.

'OK, that's great, thank you,' said Steve. Tony moved the camera around one of the uprights and right through the holed stone as if following the people through. Then he panned out across the wavy moorland horizon. High on one of the dark curves of the moor, to the south-west, Jessica could make out a dark, mushroom shape, silhouetted against the sky. She recognized it as the dolmen whose image she had seen so often.

'All right, everyone, it's been a long day. Let's head back to the hotel. If you remember, the plan is for everyone to eat out tonight where and with whom they choose, so it should be a very relaxed evening.'

Steve was consulting with Tony and checking the sound through headphones. Their clear-up procedure had become well-rehearsed and speedy, and Paul took the opportunity of the hiatus to take some photos of the site now that it was more or less deserted. Jessica hesitated, then walked up behind him.

'Paul?'

'Yeah?' he kept on clicking while she spoke to him.

'Would you like – shall we have dinner together this evening?'

'Sure.'

'Will you come to our hotel?'

'OK.'

They opted for baked potatoes and salad at a hotel/restaurant quite close to the harbour.

'So how are you finding it?' asked Jessica, feeling rather formal.

'What?' asked Paul.

'Being here, the tour, the sites –'

'Oh yeah, it's fine. Beautiful scenery, and er, what Richard has to say is all very interesting. It's great, a nice break.'

Jessica nodded.

'I notice you've been taking some photos.'

'Yes – I'm taking some for Steve anyway of the shoot, and some publicity stills. But there's no doubt these sites, especially in this setting, are spectacular, and they might make an exhibition.'

'A landscape exhibition, not ecology.'

'Yeah. I don't make the connection that you do, or that Richard does, between the ancient sites and the well-being of the planet. And I certainly don't see how a photographic exhibition could. But if Richard's work – or Richard – I mean if that's what turns you on, great, go for it. It's a free world.'

'Actually Paul I wanted to ask you a favour.'

Paul looked at her.

'I wondered if you would drive me over to Penzance. There's a site I want to visit there.'

'Another one? What, isn't it included in the tour?'

'No, no, nothing to do with the tour. It's a proposed development I've been keeping an eye on through FOE. A plot of land with ancient oak trees that a local businessman wants to clear to build a supermarket.'

'Oh –' Paul was surprised.

'Would you?'

'OK –'

'Great.' Jessica began pulling on her jacket.

'What now?'

'Yes – well, when else?'

The ungainly Sierra estate curved stiffly round the small roads. The site lay just outside Newlyn, one of the smaller villages that flanked Penzance. They wedged the car into the grassy verge, and set off down a gravelly track that became muddier and more overgrown as they walked along it.

'This lane would become a road,' Jessica spoke in a half whisper. Paul nodded and frowned. They heard an owl calling out of the dense foliage. Here on the south coast, away from the westerly storms, the trees and undergrowth were thick and luxuriant. The lane led to an old gate set in crumbling stone walls. Beyond this the land opened out a little, and in the moonlight they could see, amid the thinner, younger silver birches and larches, a large, widely spaced circle of thick-trunked oaks.

'So this guy wants to bulldoze all this?' asked Paul rhetorically.

Jessica nodded. A cold leap of fear swept through her as she spoke:

'But they've refused him permission. Or delayed it. They've requested he consider other sites.'

'Well at least that's something.'

It was very quiet. The oaks stood still, holding the night in their branches. In the dark it was difficult to see how large the area was. They heard the owl again, this time further away.

'How many oaks are there?'

'I think there's about twenty of them.'

'And they're very old?'

'They've been here for about three hundred years.'

'Not as old as the stones, eh?'

'No. Come on, let's go.'

'Do you think we're just yuppies Paul?' Jessica asked as he started the ignition.

'Someone could say that but we're trying to redeem ourselves, aren't we?'

'But when we protest at settlers burning down the rainforest, we're telling them not to do something that we've already done.'

'That's a bit of an old chestnut. Two wrongs don't make a right. Yes of course our morality in the west can be questioned, but none of those arguments should prevent the attempt to save the forests.'

'People long to be happy and comfortable. That's why Mr Pascoe wants his supermarket. You wouldn't really want to be in the middle of a big, wild dark forest would you?'

'I've just *been* there – but you haven't asked me one thing about it.'

'But you wouldn't want to *live* there. You'd want to clear it.'

'You've lost me darling.'

'I mean all this protest from the comfort of our urban jungles is a luxury – we want the option of the wild to make us feel it exists somewhere, but we don't really want to go there.'

'So what are you saying – you want to accelerate the destruction of the rainforest?'

'No, no. I think I'm just asking whether we are any more in touch with the planet, the wild places than Mr Pascoe is. And if we really want to change things, we have to change ourselves as well, open ourselves somehow.' Jessica had to concentrate to stay coherent as clouds of apprehension swarmed through her thoughts.

'Is this Richard's philosophy?'

'Erm, I'm not sure. I've never heard him say that, although I think he'd agree with me.'

'Are you having an affair with him?'

'Am I having an affair with him – no.'

'I wondered if that's why you didn't want to stay over with me.'

'No, that's not why. I did sleep with him – God it seems like ages ago, it was only a few days ago.'

'Oh?'

'Yes, and then I realized that it wasn't about him – it was about me.'

'What was?'

'My compulsion, my attraction.'

'So what did he think?'

'He was – confused.'

'Christ, I'm not surprised.'

'But there were others …'

'Other groupies –'

'Yes, in a way.'

'So is that it now, have you got your own back?'

'What do you mean Paul?' Jessica's voice had a high rippling edge to it.

'Well why else did you storm off? You thought I'd been sleeping with Caroline –'

'Oh god – if you remember Paul it was because you took off after an oil slick.'

'But that's not rational – I was only gone a couple of days, not even that.'

'Good, *good!*' Jessica screamed at Paul. 'I'm *glad* that's not rational. That's what I want to get away from, that relentless, meticulous rationalism: censoring everything, controlling everything – you still don't have a clue do you? I was being stifled. And now you're here patronizing me, talking about bloody Caroline –'

They'd reached the hotel. Jessica opened the car door and slammed it behind her.

Half way up the stairs to her room she thought she heard sobbing. Cora appeared on the landing. 'Jessica,' she said, as if she'd been expecting her.

'What?' Jessica's eyes were wide with alarm. Cora's face wore its masked, compassionate look.

'Suzanne –'

'What's wrong with her?'

'She's miscarrying.'

'Oh no!'

'And she's *very* upset –'

A door opened, and the sound of sobbing grew louder. Steve stepped out. He looked haggard.

157

'I think she's a bit hysterical – I can't …' he shrugged. 'Could you, I mean I think she'd – I've just got to get some sleep.'

'We'll go in,' Cora put her hand on his shoulder.

Suzanne's face was pink and swollen, her mouth turned down like a little girl's.

'He can't cope,' she sniffed. 'I think he's probably relieved anyway.' Her voice rose into a wail. 'Oh Jessie, my baby's going! And, and the *feeling's* going – I felt so happy –' deep sobs interspersed her words. Jessica held her hand, and Cora gently rubbed her back.

'Does it hurt Suzanne?' asked Jessica.

Suzanne shook her head. 'It's like a bad period pain.'

There was a gentle knock at the door. Uta put her head round. Cora motioned her to come in.

'What is wrong?' she asked, concern on her kind face.

'I'm bleeding – I'm losing my baby.'

'Ah!' Uta drew in her breath.

'It was that stone – I shouldn't have gone through it. It was Steve's fault – he made me.'

Jessica glanced at Cora, but she kept her face neutral.

'But Suzanne,' said Uta softly, 'how far along were you?'

'Six weeks,' squeaked Suzanne.

'Ah, my love, you know, miscarriage at this early stage is very common. It's nothing to worry about. Sometimes mother nature has a practice run.'

'It's not your baby you're losing,' Cora said. 'The spirit does not incarnate until around three months. She'll come again. It's just the preparations, that's all.'

'How do you know it's a she?'

'What else could it be?' asked Cora.

Suzanne allowed herself a sad-eyed smile. The four women sat for a while in silence, broken only by Suzanne's sniffs and shuddering sighs. Cora closed her eyes. Uta rubbed Suzanne's feet. Then Cora took Suzanne's and Uta's hands, and smiled at Jessica to do the same. As they held hands, Cora began to chant in a deep voice; at first just sound, long vowels that burrowed deep into the room and penetrated the bed and energized their circle. The sounds changed to words: 'Great Mother of the deep and Good Father of the heights, of nights and tides, of sun, of soft spring grass, of recession and return, bless this bloodflow, bless the spirit who is seeking to build its being here, let the cycle come again in its right time, bless the womb and the heart of this would-be mother – bless us all.'

Tears pricked at Jessica's eyes. A cloud of sweetness welled up in the room. Suzanne had stopped crying.

Back at the Ship and Anchor, Paul was finishing a beer in the bar when he was surprised to see Steve come in.

'Hi!'

Steve nodded. 'Am I too late?' he asked the barmaid.

'Well, it's right on the line, but go on, I'll let you this time.'

Steve ordered a whisky and brought it over to Paul.

'Is everything OK?'

Steve shook his head.

'It's Suzanne, she's miscarrying.'

'Oh wow, will she be all right?'

'Yeah, yeah, it's at an early stage apparently – it's still a lot of blood though, pretty messy process.'

'Who's with her – Jessica?'

'Jessica, Cora, there's a whole clan of women – they didn't need me, thank God. Suzanne's gone hysterical – I don't understand why.'

'Oh come on Steve, of course she's upset –'

'She's more than upset. It's like it's a calamity, the end of the world. The woman's unbalanced, first she says it's the stones that did it –'

'The stones?'

'Yeah, going through Mên-an-Tol, and it's my fault because I asked her to. Then she says it's all her fault, a punishment for something she's done which she won't tell me about. I mean, it's just not rational.'

'Well for God's sake don't tell her that. I got my head bitten off by Jessica for using that word.'

'Yeah?' said Steve, cupping his face in his hands and rubbing his eyebrows. He shook his head. 'I'm just worried she's going to hold it over me somehow, try and sabotage the film or something.'

'I don't think Suzanne would do that, Steve. Anyway, how could she?'

'I dunno, I think I'm growing irrational myself.'

Paul smiled, but his eyes were thoughtful. He was quite glad Steve was so preoccupied for the uncomfortable thought had struck him that perhaps Suzanne had also slept with Richard, and that it was this which she did not want to tell Steve. Jessica had been defensive, had mentioned groupies. If Suzanne – and others – had been, what, vying over Richard, that might put another gloss on what happened. Jessica's apparent loss of interest in Richard had modified the sting Paul felt over her action, which seemed so uncharacteristic of her. But maybe it was Richard who was ambivalent, besieged as it were, by other options, and Jessica's account a smokescreen for hurt pride.

'Listen, I'm sorry if it's been awkward for you Paul, I mean I was the one who persuaded you to come ...' Paul understood that Steve needed to re-assert control over the situation.

'Don't be, Steve, Jessica is working something out and that's fine. I needed to get away, from London, from work. I'm actually feeling more relaxed than I have for a long time. I've got no responsibilities; I'm taking photos just for the hell of it again – hey – I'm enjoying myself, the craziness of it all, the sea air – it's great!'

If Paul protested a little too much, Steve didn't notice, or didn't want to notice. In the present situation he preferred to know that Paul was fine and he didn't have to be concerned about him.

The next day Suzanne stayed at the hotel with kind Uta, while Steve forged on with his film and Richard with his tour. The group headed first south to visit an underground stone-lined passage known as a 'fogou', part of an Iron Age settlement near the small hamlet of Brane, southwest of Penzance. From there, their caravan zig-zagged back to the north coast through the small backroads and lanes that meshed through the countryside to the grey-stone, storm beaten village of Morvah where they were to stop for a pub lunch.

They clattered into the dark quiet of the pub which was empty save for an old man in tweed cap and dark jacket nursing his beer at the glittering bar. He turned to look at them as they swiftly populated all the waiting tables and corners. The barman called to his wife for help as they thronged the bar. Lunch had been ordered in advance and was a standard Cornish pasty, meat or vegetarian, but drinks were to be ordered separately. Adam was stood next to the old man, waiting to be served. He had taken off his jumper revealing a neon pink T-shirt which bore the message 'Out of Body – back in 5 minutes' in bold lettering.

'I've heard the scrumpy's good round here,' he said to the old man, who raised his eyebrows and nodded imperceptibly. 'It's *strong*, if that's what you want.'

Adam had to lean close to hear his frail voice. 'Yep, that's what I want – don't have to drive so why not.'

The old man blinked and nodded again. 'You on one of these coach tours?'

'Ahuh.'

'What, you going to the Land's End, I s'pose.'

'Er, no, I don't think so – we're touring the megaliths of the area, you know, stone circles and so on.'

'Oh yes?' The old man half-turned in surprise. 'You're all here specially to visit the old stones and that?'

It was Adam's turn to nod.

'Well I never.' The old man sipped his beer, blinking in concentration. Adam finally caught the eye of the barman's wife and he placed his order.

'I knew a farmer once, he had one of them stones in his field, right in the middle it was. There are stories, you know, about how you shouldn't be moving them, but he didn't take no notice, he wanted it out of his field. Greedy I s'pose 'e was really, couldn't get his tractor close enough around it, wanted to use every scrap of his land – mind you though, it was his land wasn't it?'

Adam frowned as he bent to catch the old man's words amid the hubbub.

'Anyway, he got that stone out, took some doing, about two days worth of digging and wrenching and pulling, made you wonder if it was worth all the effort.' The old man took another sip of beer. 'Said he was going to break up the stone and use it to repair his walls.'

Adam's scrumpy came. He quickly paid and turned back to the old man.

'That very night there was a massive thunderstorm, just like out of a fairy tale, and in the morning they found the ground had collapsed in around where the stone used to be – so he couldn't farm it anyway. It had all been a waste of time!'

'Crickey!' said Adam.

'And people say, although, you never really know these things for sure, that the land was never as good after, you know? The grass not so lush, the crops didn't do so well, and the animals wouldn't go near that hole!'

'Wow! And did anything happen to the farmer – I mean was it like he was cursed or something?'

The old man gave a dry chuckle. 'No more than anyone else, I don't think – well, he rowed with his son, got bad arthritis, farming got harder, less money – but that happens to a lot of folks, don't it?'

'Mm,' Adam nodded. 'Well, actually I don't really know – I suppose I'm not old enough yet.'

The man chuckled again and sipped his beer. 'Anyhow, young man, you enjoy your tour, and your youth – while it lasts.'

'Thanks,' said Adam, and drained some more cider. 'Thanks for telling me about that farmer. I'm going to go and eat my lunch now.'

Adam told Richard and Peter the old man's story. Steve listened in.

'Oh yes, there's a lot of stories like that,' said Richard.

'It might make a nice touch, cutting between his story and some of the tour scenes,' suggested Steve.

But the old man shook his head. 'I've told my story, once is enough I think. Filming? No thanks, I'm too old to be on the telly now, when I was younger, maybe, when I still had me looks –' He chuckled again, briefly raising faded eyes to them then looking away.

The next stop was a few minutes drive south of Morvah. The farmer whose lands adjoined the site had obviously taken a different approach towards the ancient remains than the one in the old man's tale. On the side of a small stone building a sign read: 'To Chûn Castle and the Quoit' in neat black lettering on a white painted board. 'The path is marked with a white stone,' it went on. And there was a hole in which people were asked to put 10p for parking in the farmer's field. Richard put in about £5 in 50p pieces and the coins clattered down a pipe into the inside of the wall. Sure enough, by a large, white-washed stone, a thin but clearly worn path led through the prickly heather, fern and brown grass scrub up the slope, one of the rounded, treeless hillocks of the coastal moorland.

At the top of the hill, to their right, a mound began to form, and the path branched towards it. Chûn Castle revealed itself in silence, a large circle of dressed granite blocks, still visible amid the perennial undergrowth. In its centre a pile of stones obscured any former design. Richard gathered them around within the circle:

'Chûn Castle is thought to be an Iron Age enclosure. Within its walls and around it are the foundations of numerous ancient settlements, including many small barrows, evidence of former high population in country now desolate.'

The gateway into the circle was formed by two tall granite posts, and in the middle, a few yards further out, stood another, taller stone. Richard strode up to it and gestured to the group.

'If you stand in front of this stone you can see that it is exactly in line with the Quoit which lies a little further southwest and lower down the other side of this hill.'

And sure enough there crouched the rounded mushroom shape of the Quoit, and beyond it the shining flat of the Atlantic. Jessica stared down at the Quoit. All the images she had seen of it had been close-ups; at this distance its miniature seemed innocuous enough, she thought. Steve conferred briefly with Richard who cleared his throat.

'Erm, the film crew want to do a few re-takes with me. Can I suggest that you wander down to the Quoit and around the area for the few minutes that this will take, and I'll pick it up from there.'

The tour participants obeyed, ambling somewhat sullenly down the slope. They were used to this kind of step-printed approach to things now, but resentment was growing towards the camera and crew. The feeling was common in differing degrees to many, but stemmed from different causes. Some merely found the film crew's presence a nuisance, an additional extra they had not bargained for. Stuart and Hazel murmured that the intrusion of technology disturbed the delicate process of dowsing energy lines at the sites; Bahira expressed the modulated opinion that the filming did tend to interfere with one's ability to commune with the spirit of place. However, their attitudes may have been influenced by the disappointment they felt at being very minor if not completely unnoticed extras in the process. Jonathan fiercely objected to the profanation of the sites by the instruments of mass communication; even Helen couldn't help thinking that the camera equipment and lights all represented a very masculine objectivity, not conducive to the presence of the goddess.

'It's all about observing, isn't it?' Terence had said to Jessica. 'Pretending the old Newtonian paradigm exists, that you can look at something without affecting it. The question is, what *is* the effect of the camera upon us, upon the sites?'

In the absence of Suzanne, Jessica felt herself to be the sole emotional pivot around whom the tensions of the situation revolved. The sentiments of some of the tour participants echoed those self-same accusations she had aimed at Paul: that merely to take pictures of the Earth, whether moving or still, wasn't enough, and even worse, rendered one a parasite upon her ills and her mysteries. At the same time though, she had a loyalty to both Paul and Steve. Paul after all was or had been her boyfriend, Steve her friend. She knew how much the film meant to Steve, and also how Richard hoped it would further his work. Richard himself seemed unfazed by the undercurrents, but Jessica understood by now that Richard's sensitivity was so acutely attuned to his own needs that it made him strangely insensitive to the predicament of others.

Cora had sat down on a boulder at the bottom of the slope and was gazing out to sea. Gabriel was sitting next to her. Jessica knelt down beside them.

'Cora, do you think the film and all that is really spoiling things?'

Cora shook her head.

'No. Firstly I want to support Richard and he wants it to happen, so I'm OK about it. But I am also learning that filming is a kind of magic. Whatever is happening, the camera will intensify it, it's like an atmospheric magnifying glass. So we get to see what is going on.'

'But everyone's sort of wretched about it.'

'I'm not,' smiled Gabriel in his insincere way which she knew to be sincere.

Jessica suspected Gabriel never allowed himself to be wretched.

'You see? And nor am I. So it's not everyone – anyway, it is just a peg to hang their feelings on. It's not about the filming at all really.'

'What is it about then?'

Richard and the film crew had re-joined the group, most of whom were clustered in twos and threes around the Quoit. Steve arranged for Richard to stand next to the monument.

Cora shook her head. 'It's the land, the Earth is beginning to speak. She speaks through us, through our subconscious, our dreams. But we rarely hear her.'

Jessica felt the cramp of fear inside her. She turned to look at Richard who was now outlined dramatically against the sea and beside the megalith. He smiled.

'OK guys, here we go.'

People began to shuffle forwards and re-group around him. Tony worked fast to set up the camera. Jessica found she had a reluctance to approach the stones; without realizing it, she had been keeping her distance.

'Chûn Quoit is one of the best preserved and most complete cromlechs in the district of West Penwith. As I'm sure you can see for yourselves, it is the most impressive example of these structures that we have visited. The rather odd word "quoit" derives from a Middle English word meaning a round flat stone like the discus, thrown for exercise or sport, after of course the look of the rounded capstone. The term "dolmen", probably a mispronunciation of the old Cornish *tolmen* meaning "hole of stone" is really misapplied to these megaliths; cromlech is in fact the most accurate term, from the Middle English "crom" meaning "arched" or "bowed" and "lech" meaning "flat stone". This word also focuses on the distinctive feature of the capstone.' Richard was a tall man, six foot plus, but the Quoit was taller by another foot. He patted the massive granite stone:

'This is a discus that only a giant could throw. Roughly circular, with a diameter of about 12 feet, it weights approximately 30 tons. Like most of the places we have visited, no one knows why or how they were built; no bones or artifacts have been found inside the chamber.'

There was no question, thought Jessica, that these stones were emanating a distinct atmosphere. Unlike her first experience at Castlerigg, when she could not tell whether the circle held a presence other than what she might imagine. Then, the group had been distracting, now she found it a comfort.

'Last summer, an archaeologist and the photographer he was working with had a remarkable experience inside the Quoit. They were engaged in a survey of the Cornish monuments and had spent weeks in the field, literally camping out. The two men surveyed the site during the afternoon and then set up camp for the night a little distance away. After supper, it being a fine clear night, they returned to the Quoit to have another look round and generally relax. They both took a turn at crawling through this gap –' Richard pointed to a narrow black triangle that was an opening formed by the lean of two of the uprights. 'Much to their surprise, each witnessed an inexplicable light phenomenon. Periodic short bursts of rainbow-coloured lights flashed in short bands across the surface of the underside of the capstone. They saw this happen intermittently for about 30 minutes.'

The group were unusually still, fascinated by the story. Jessica noticed that even Paul was listening with real interest.

'By now, perhaps you will not be surprised to know that the granite these slabs are made of had yielded particularly high radiation counts.' Richard paused.

'Has anyone else seen the lights?' asked Adam.

'Not to my knowledge. What's more, there's nothing in the folk record that associates any such phenomena specifically with this site.'

Steve nodded to Tony to cut.

'Could it have been car headlights bouncing off the stones?' asked Simon Greaves.

'Well, you can see, we're pretty remote here from any roads, and anyway, the lights were rainbow coloured.'

'Do you think the lights would only have shown up at night, would they be noticed by day?' asked Peter March.

Richard shrugged. 'Your guess is as good as mine. Certainly that seems to be the implication of the incident. Many more people visit here by day than at night, and yet this is the first report, so one assumes this phenomenon may only show up when it's dark.'

'Can we go inside – I mean, is there time?' asked Edwina.

'Yes, of course, I think one or two at a time. We'll hang around for a bit longer, then it's on to Tregeseal stone circle, our last stop for the day. We are ending a little earlier than usual to give people a chance to hang out for a bit, go to the beach, do some shopping ...'

Edwina crouched down by the black entranceway, then hesitated. Richard smiled down at her. 'You know I think feet first might be the easiest way.' Others were beginning to queue up to go inside. Edwina wrapped her long skirt around her knees, and lowered her legs in, then she corkscrewed her body awkwardly into the hole, her head being the last part of her to disappear inside.

'See anything?' called Adam.

'Not really. Just a few small boulders on the floor. No lights. I think I'll come out now.' She scrambled out again with Gabriel's help, and he went in next. Adam followed, joined by Jonathan.

Jessica watched as singly or in pairs different members of the tour party squeezed in and out of the Quoit's narrow opening. She felt no compulsion to go inside; there wouldn't be time for everyone anyway, she told herself. Dave filmed some of them climbing in and out, and Paul took pictures of him taking pictures. Then Steve gestured to Dave to cut and they started packing up the gear. Paul smiled and joked with them as he helped. He did look very relaxed. His self-sufficiency was maddening. Now he was taking more pictures: of the Quoit, the sea view, the people. He stopped, and ran fine fingers through his dark hair. If only she didn't know him so well! Jessica realized they hadn't spoken since last night, when she had slammed out of the car and into the hotel, only to find Suzanne bleeding and in tears. It was as if events had become frozen in time.

Jessica fingered the green pendant round her neck. The sea, the sea! She hadn't even see the sea yet, except in the view from monuments. She hadn't sat close to the green waves and been soothed by their churning sound and motion. This was what she'd longed to do in the first place, when she and Paul had planned a holiday here. Why had it taken Richard scheduling it into the tour to remind her? A sense of urgency filled her, as if it might not be possible to get back to where she longed to be. Part of the problem was tactical: she could walk to the St Ives beaches, but without a car she would not be able to visit her favourite beach, her place of pilgrimage and renewal, which lay further up the coast towards Perranporth. And how could she ask Paul to take her? She had spurned his initial suggestion to go there, already asked him one favour and then rowed with him, and now he was more content to be without her. It was out of the question to ask Steve, he was too busy and there was Suzanne to take care of as well. Ought she to stay with Suzanne? Was she being selfish in wanting to go to the beach?

But it turned out that Suzanne had no particular need for her company. Most of the bleeding had passed with the night. Uta had gone out to buy more sanitary towels. They had spent a quiet day, breakfasting at their leisure, talking, going for a walk round the town, sitting on the beach. Suzanne was resigned and calm. 'I can't remember what it felt like anymore,' she said sadly. 'The feeling goes with the baby.'

So Jessica went to change into her swimming costume and beach clothes. Coming back down she met Paul on the stairs.

'Hallo,' she said, startled.

'Hi, I was coming to find you. I've got the use of the car, do you want to go over to Glasporth?'

Jessica paused transfixed on the stairs. 'Oh, I do,' she said.

'Come on then.'

'Paul this is really kind of you ...'

'I like the place too, you know. I'm just surprised you haven't already been.'

A single track road, clinging to the cliff, dropped steeply down to the National Trust car park that nestled in between the cliffs at the head of the bay. The tide had turned but was still low, and they could walk out past the cliff heads to the broad band of gold sand that stretched for miles up and down the coast. They walked the length of the beach. The wind and surf crashed into the gaps between them, and blew away any requirement to talk.

Jessica went for a dip while Paul went off with his camera. She waded out through the knee high, then thigh high water, each swift-approaching lacy step of collapsed wave taking her a little deeper. Now the first of the inner waves was rearing up in front of her, she dived into its base and emerged the other side fully initiated into salty wetness and the rhythm and force of the waves. The exhilaration she had always known at bobbing amid the green and silver water returned. She felt a part of the whole land and seascape. Every detail filled her with joy: the faint typing of gulls in the far sky, the different ply of the sea as it condensed into the horizon: blue green, navy blue, white flecks where the wind hit; the fierce cliffs and rocky outlets, the tin mine sat like a pointing fist up on the cliff top; the toppling sheen of the waves; the pale crystal water in the shallows, showing the gold sand beneath tinted a pale green. She couldn't help but smile at Paul when he came back and shouted at her from the beach. He was pointing to where the tide was starting to cut them off from the main bay. The tide moved fast, and they had to pick their way through the lace edge of the surf, back around into the bay, where gradually each rocky outcrop and rockpool, each piece of patterned sand was reclaimed by the waves.

Jessica changed back into her clothes and sat up on the rocks to the north of the bay, watching the endless green bars advance and spill into foam over the rocks and sand. She had found some tar on her towel; the rocks were spotted from a spill further to the south some months back. As the tide grew higher, the waves picked up the tar again, so that when the water curved upwards, she could see the black dots suspended in its green transparency. Watching this, Jessica experienced a curious sensation: she could feel all the old emotions of helplessness, distress and outrage lining up to kick in, but it was as if something said wait, and calmed their reaction. The waves crashed down into a mass of silver, and the oil could no longer be seen. As the next arc of beautiful liquid glass arose, Jessica saw something different, or the same thing differently. She could see that the oil was there, and yet it was not there: the oil was in the ocean but not of it. She was looking through two concentric worlds: one where matter existed in its purity, close to its invisible source; and the other, more familiar and at times grubby world which included the pollution. Even though the pollution was there in the water, it could not blend with it, the oil could not become the water. She breathed deeply, an old tension left her body and blew away on the wind. It was the same for people, she thought, the shadows are suspended in our psyches, but are not the deepest part of us.

Paul had come over. He shouted up to her.

'I think we'd better move again – you'll be stranded here soon.' She nodded. Paul held out his arm to help her down. 'Have you seen, there's oil in the water.'

'Yes I know, it's on the rocks, I got some on my towel.'

'It's the last vestiges of a spill, fortunately, it won't do much harm now.' Jessica realized that in his own way Paul was trying to reassure her.

'That's something,' she said.

'Are you ready to go back?'

'Yes – are you? I'm quite hungry.'

They headed up the beach. At the rim of the car park Jessica turned to look back. The bay was almost full now, just a small crescent of sand was still being churned over by the waves. Soon even that would be covered over, and only the rocky outcrops and pebbly slope at the very top of the beach be left exposed. The lifeguards were locking up their little wooden hut, and had raised the red flag to signify that swimming alone was dangerous. Most of the other cars had gone. Paul turned the ignition, and began to manoeuvre the car round. She walked up to meet it and got in. At the crest of the hill she looked back for one last glimpse of the now small green horseshoe, and then they had rounded the corner and it was gone.

'Did you enjoy that?' asked Paul.

'Yes, it's always great coming here.'

'Not too disappointed then, by the oil?'

'Well – yes, a bit.' Jessica believed by now that Paul lived too completely in the secondary reality for her insight to make sense to him. If she attempted to explain, it would merely upset the fragile balance between them. He would think her crazy, she would feel put down, and the two worlds would collide again.

'I'm planning to go back to Chûn Quoit tonight,' Paul said, as he turned out of the narrow lane that led to Glasporth and onto the coastal road.

'What!' Jessica stared at him, horrorstruck.

'Yeah, I was rather intrigued by Richard's account of the lights there. Those guys who saw them would have been there around the same time of year as this apparently …'

'How do you know?' asked Jessica sharply.

'I talked with Richard about it.'

Jessica was silent.

'D'you want to come?'

She gazed out at the road in front, winding a route familiar to her: past a white pebbledash Victorian villa, a garish new petrol station, tall, lush hedgerows. She knew they were driving south, back to supper and evening and the Quoit at night. She was looking down a tunnel, where darkness converged and she couldn't escape.

'I thought you'd like to come along. You never know, we might see something. Richard's quite keen on the idea – and even if nothing happens, it'll still be a great time and place to take some photos.'

'Yes, OK.'

'You don't sound very enthusiastic – you don't have to come.'

Jessica nodded. 'No, I'll come.' She pictured the green bay again, waves flicking up in the wind, sea birds gliding in long curves over the cliff heads.

# CHAPTER TWELVE

B Y the time dinner was over and they were back in the car headed south again along the coast road, Jessica felt unexpectedly calm and even-keeled. The mellow gold light of evening was wrapped around the bottom of the sky, aiming warm shafts into the car even as it faded.

'So Suzanne's all right now, is she?' Paul asked.

'Mm.'

'Is she?' he turned his head towards her.

'Yes, yes, she's much better.'

Jessica did not feel like talking. She wanted to be empty. The movement of the car, the declensions of its engine were meditative to her. She wanted to keep driving, without having to arrive. Perhaps they could drive all around the coast, as far as Penzance, find a nice little pub and have a beer.

'Because I know Steve's going to be a bit preoccupied tonight.'

'Oh, that's all right, there's lots of other people to look after her, Uta, Cora –'

'She'll be out gallivanting won't she, with her fancy man?'

Jessica didn't answer.

'He's young enough to be her son, isn't he?'

'Well sometimes men go out with women that are young enough to be their daughters, but that's seen as pretty normal, isn't it?' Jessica spoke as if explaining something to a small child.

'It's a bit weird, though, the way she seems besotted with him –'

Paul's amused tone grated on Jessica who did not like to admit even to herself that she was uncomfortable about Cora's relationship with Adam. At first it had seemed a bold and eccentric expression of Cora's liberated femininity, but latterly, it seemed clear that Cora was infatuated with Adam, who in his turn was taken over by the strength of her presence, and was even talking of returning with her to the States. Jessica found it difficult to accept weaknesses in people she had set up as inspirational models. She would overlook or rationalize any human flaws until something hit her in the face, when she tended to ice over and cut out the person entirely, as she had with Richard. Paul's line of attack, which is how she saw it, threatened to corrode further her new found world, and she decided to change the subject.

'Paul –'

'Yeah?'

'Couldn't we go on right round the coast, to Penzance or somewhere, and find a nice little cosy pub and have a beer –'

'No!' said Paul, with frustration in his voice. 'We're going to the Quoit.'

Jessica always assumed that Paul would intuit her moods and the plans that stemmed from them, and then felt irritated and put upon when he objected to her ideas as veering away from the course originally agreed upon.

'Yes, but we could go on the way back, it would be darker then.' If they delayed, there would also be a good chance of Paul being to tired to bother.

'No – if you like, we can try and have a beer afterwards, if there's still time.'

'Well there won't be time to drive –'

'There's places nearby.'

Jessica gave up.

'So does Suzanne want to try again?'

Why does he always have to pry into other people's business, thought Jessica.

'I haven't asked her – I suppose she does, you saw how upset she was. But then, Steve's reluctant. I don't know, it's difficult.'

'Does she care who the father is? She seemed pretty keen to have the baby, regardless of Steve.'

'Gosh, I don't think just anyone would do. She'd probably like it to be Steve.' Jessica winced at what she deemed Paul's brutal insensibility towards other people's problems.

'She slept with Richard, didn't she?'

Jessica was jolted into anger. 'Paul, what business is it of yours anyway?'

'I think it's my business, to a point. Was that why you dropped out of the race? Too much competition?'

'Oh God Paul,' Jessica shouted in a rage of impatience. 'Is this why you asked me to come with you, so that you could cross-examine me?'

'I'm not cross-examining you.'

'You *are*. That's *exactly* what you're doing.'

'I think you owe me an explanation –'

'I don't owe you anything actually. I've already told you why I didn't go on with him.'

'So she didn't sleep with him as well?'

'Yes, she did, but we both decided to stop for different reasons. Me, because as I told you, I had realized that I was sort of deluding myself, that my interest in Richard was a projection of my own need to grow, and Suzanne because she found out she was pregnant.'

'You talked about it then?'

'Partly yes. When she found out she was pregnant she told me, and said she was worried at having slept with Richard while she was pregnant with Steve's baby.'

'But you never told her –'

'No.'

'Why not?'

Jessica shrugged. 'There was no need.'

Paul chuckled. Jessica's mouth tightened with anger, she wished she hadn't come.

'I suppose you're going to sulk now?'

But Jessica had gone into the realm of silence. There was very little left that she wanted to communicate to Paul.

When they had climbed up to the top of the slope, near to Chûn Castle, the sea wind hit them and Jessica shivered, dismayed to realize how inadequately she was dressed. 'Oh God,' she said gloomily, 'it's freezing.'

Paul ignored her and walked on down to the Quoit. They wouldn't be able to stay long, that was all. She'd freeze to death otherwise, standing around, watching Paul take photographs. Paul began to set up his tripod in front of the Quoit, facing the sea. Jessica pulled her thin cotton jacket around her. It was already damp from the sea-laden air, and she shivered again.

'There's a blanket in the car,' said Paul without looking up.

'Is there?'

'Yeah, do you want me to get it?'

'OK,' Jessica said flatly, reluctant to lose her excuse for an early departure, but desperate to get warm. 'I'll come with you.' The thought of heading off into the night to get the blanket herself was almost as alarming as the prospect of waiting on her own while Paul went.

'No – you stay here with the gear – I won't be a minute.'

'No one's going to take it!' Jessica objected irritably, but Paul was gone.

Jessica watched his dark figure and the small 'o' of torchlight disappear up the hill. Shivering almost uncontrollably, she moved back a little from the Quoit, and looked out at the view. The sky was still quite light, the sea a silky silver and gold reflection, tinged with blue, and turning milky at its edges. No light came from the moon, which was hidden in its dark phase. Nestled into the cliff below was a single stone farm house, its windows black. Jessica pictured the warm quiet lounge back at the hotel. When they got back she'd order cocoa and have a long hot bath. Her eyes returned to the massive Quoit. The capstone was shaped like a giant granite hand, curved over the four vertical slabs that supported it. It looked like it was moving ever so slightly. Jessica blinked, and refocused her eyes. The stone gave the impression of flickering every now and then, as if blown by the wind. That was impossible, the stone weighed over 30 tons. Was it balanced so precisely on the other stones that the wind could move it? Or did the background gorse and ferns shaking in the wind give it the appearance of moving? Or was it simply her imagination?

The crackling sound of heather breaking behind her told of Paul's return. He handed her a thick wool blanket, which she gratefully wrapped around her. Now she had something else to look at. Paul screwed a lens on the camera, checked the slowly ebbing light, and pressed the trigger. A brief white splash lit up the stones and a circle of night.

Now she heard a clicking sound. But it wasn't Paul, he was wiping the lens. It wasn't a sound that one associated with large stones.

'You been inside yet?' Paul asked.

'No.'

The small crevice that formed the only entrance showed no evidence of the light which must be entering through the other gaps in the stones. It was black as if opening directly into the depths of the earth; an entrance to the underworld, curiously still and silent, as though condensed with age into a heavier mass from its surroundings, looking as though one might cross the threshold of ordinary matter by going through it. If she stared at it long enough she would never be able to go in, or it would never lead into the small space inside the Quoit, but would give way beneath her and leave her falling into blackness, into a kind of frozen inertia, pressured as if by prehistoric earth shifts and lava bubbles.

'Can you hold the flash for me a minute?' Paul was moving his gear round to the seaward side of the Quoit, which still had a slight glow to the stones from the fading light in the sky.

'Do you think it's dark enough now?' Jessica asked.

'Dunno. Go inside and see if there's anything happening.'

The light of the flash bounced on and off the stones, as Jessica forced herself to climb in. A hard earth floor, some smaller boulders in a cramped space. Four triangles of blue evening sky where the uprights met the roof. It was anti-climactic, but not comforting. Jessica stared intently at the walls and ceiling, bracing herself lest something happen.

'See anything?' called Paul from outside.

'No.'

Or was the top stone rippling? Was it rippling because she was staring at it for so long, or was there some kind of objective rippling effect? What was it, what *was* it? Something almost sub-sensory seemed to be rising up out of the stones and through her whole body and consciousness, a tidal rise that could very easily turn in her to panic. One was simply unused to sensing this much age, this much time passed, it took over the senses.

Jessica pictured the first time she had used a scuba mask, it was in the Mediterranean, at first along the beautiful pale turquoise edges of the beach, gold sand in rippled patterns underneath her, and then out in the waters of a small cove where the blue waters gave way to darker blue depths, funnelling down to inky black. She had been unable to stop the feeling of terror which paralyzed her, and forced her back to the paddleboat on the surface. It was the same kind of sensation now: the bottom falling out of the world, revealing unmanageable fathoms. She wished Cora were here, she wanted someone she could talk to about these things. How difficult to reconcile this breathing out of something so ancient, a cold draft blowing into the present, blending here in the present with flashgun and blanket and her own thoughts. How old were the stones – no one knew. It was surprising, when one started to look into almost anything, how little was known. A long time, the stones had been standing for millennia, and yet they seemed to flicker and move. She had seen several collapsed cromlechs. No matter how long they had stood, when they fell, it happened instantly. There was nothing to say they would not choose this moment to collapse. What was holding them up? They looked so precariously balanced. And there was the power of thought; the more she looked at the great wedges of rock above and beside her, the more she envisioned them collapsing, like a heavy house of cards. The images played and replayed through her mind. She scrambled out.

'How much longer are we going to be here?' Paul didn't answer.

'I don't think it's going to get dark enough, Paul.'

'It was this time of year when those guys saw the lights before.'

'Yes, but maybe it was a cloudy night.'

'No, I remember Richard saying it was a fine night.'

'But it could have related to almost anything: the phase of the moon, the sun, the temperatures ...'

'You're always moaning, aren't you? There's always something wrong, eh?'

'I'm not moaning, but I'm cold and tired and I don't think anything's going to happen and I'd just like to get back in time to have a hot drink –'

'Before it was a beer.'

'Yes, well, it's obviously too late for that now – and it's cold.'

'Isn't the blanket keeping you warm?' Worried about the salt air on his equipment, Paul tasted the tripod with his tongue.

'Christ, the tripod's damp and salty.'

To Jessica's relief, he started to pack up his equipment. The damp sea air had become her ally, a stronger lever than her nagging to get them out of there. Slowly, agonizingly slowly, Paul began to wipe down the lenses, the camera body, the flash, before packing them away in the grey foam-lined box.

Jessica's relief flashed into frustration. 'For God's sake, Paul, can't you hurry up?'

Paul stopped altogether and looked at her. 'Why did you come Jessica?'

She didn't reply. Tears began to prick at her eyes.

'I thought this was meant to be your bliss – stones, lights, Cornish wildness. I thought you wanted to experience the earth, to contact the goddess, or whatever you call it. This is your chance, love, isn't it? To commune with the planet, to become a true disciple of Richard. You talk about shamen, but all you want to do is find a pub and have a beer, or go back to the hotel. It's not that nice a hotel. Here we are in the arms of Mother Nature and ancient man's sacred sites, and all you can do is whine.'

'I'm not whining! You're just oblivious, that's all, as always. You never understand my feelings – you're so insensitive, not just to me, to everyone –'

'Oh yeah, I'm insensitive, that's an original thought, isn't it?'

'Because you have no feelings, you suppress everything, you're only interested in your bloody tripod and your stupid pictures and – your car!'

'Feelings! Jesus, I don't think you know what feelings are. You're too damned self-centred to have any feelings. You're the one who's insensitive. You don't have a clue what it means to connect with the planet. You haven't seen what I've seen, you've never felt what I've felt – it's all just imagination to you. What's more, you still haven't asked me anything about my trip!'

Jessica was leaning back into the Quoit, blanket wrapped around her Indian-style. Paul was shouting at her, it was almost a relief. The surface pattern of her behaviour had catalyzed this outburst, but his anger was not really about her, and her behaviour was not really about selfishness. She was surprised at how strong her desire was to return to the ordinary world. She felt ashamed at herself, but she knew that underneath the shame was fear.

'I've seen smoke billowing 100 foot above the forest, while screaming animals stampede from the flames; I've seen acre upon acre of burnt tree stumps that can never be replaced, I've seen land turned to useless wilderness after it's been stripped and over-grazed –' Paul stood upon the small grass apron before the Quoit as if upon a stage, a Shakespearean actor against a dark backdrop, summoning up, by the force of his words alone, huge images from far away. Unconsciously Jessica inclined her head to the rhythm of his litany. She saw the places, lit up bright as a slide show, right there in the night.

'I've seen cracks that reached six foot down in land that used to be fertile. I've seen seals and seabirds choking on crude oil, and what's more I earn my living from it, and there's nothing I can do about it, and then I have to listen to you wittering on about some nutcase who thinks he's going to heal the planet by having a conversation with it, and when we come to a place like this, you whine and go on at me about returning to suburbia –'

Paul's face was ugly with misery. Jessica was still nodding her head a little, the images had gone. She knew she had never seen Paul like this before, but this realization, like all others, was subsumed in the outbreath of the stones which filled her head. Paul seemed to be shouting a long way away, so that she could barely hear him.

'Thank God,' she said.

'Thank God what?' Paul was brought up short.

'That … that this is you – this is your passion, your vision, *not* mine. You're right, in some ways I'm not engaged any more, in the same way. I'm … I'm too exhausted by it. It's endless, don't you see, at this level of things?'

'But – but this is why we're together, isn't it? This is what gives our relationship meaning, makes it – worthwhile!'

'Is it?' Jessica said, suddenly tired and disinterested.

Paul finished wiping the tripod and packed it away. Then he looked at Jessica with angry, puzzled eyes. 'What's wrong?'

She didn't answer. Paul hesitated a moment.

'I'm going to go inside – all right?' His fury had abated, as if drawn up to heaven and dissipated like the short, fierce trail of a typhoon.

Jessica sat down on the camera case, her back against the Quoit. She stared out across the moor, suddenly quiet and empty again. It was darker by now, and colder. She drew the blanket closer around her. In the distance, car headlights turned the corner on the zig-zagging coast road. Further up the hill she could just make out the standing stones of Chûn Castle. Was there something shining out on the moor? Everything was thinning around her. A longing to be anchored came over her.

'I think I'll come back in, Paul.'

Inside she reached for his hand. It was warm, a little roughened. They held each other, Paul wiped her cheeks where tears brimmed out of her eyes. Jessica wrapped the blanket around them both, forming a cocoon of body heat, a warm flesh heart within the stone. She buried her face in Paul's neck. He stroked her hair, and a sigh shuddered gently out of his body. They were still enough that energy formed a pattern between them almost of its own accord and their love-making followed the same still beginning, echoing the heart beat of the intensity between and around them. The cramped interior of the Quoit required that each movement be tentative, precise, as if the limitations of their physical space delineated exactly the delicate nature of their connection. There were no images, no quick rush to smudge over the odd familiarity, the sense of being strangers. Jessica grasped hold of Paul as though she would fall if she let go. And she fell anyway, as at last the well opened up, and Paul became the archetype, the point of access through which to surrender.

Afterwards Paul could not tell how long they had stayed there, it could have been minutes or hours, it had seemed timeless. Crouched with his arm around Jessica, her face still hidden, he watched the lights playing across the underside of the capstone. He realized later too, that it had been odd not to have remarked on the lights to Jessica. They came in bands, just like Richard's description, intermittent, rainbow-coloured. Every now and then, erratically, it seemed, they broke into a more random pattern, scattering across the stone like a screen-saver. The second or third time this happened, Paul saw or thought he saw images begin to form themselves within the mesh. The lights became flames, plumes of smoke, tree stumps, bulldozers. He blinked and refocused his eyes, but then the lights disappeared altogether, and gradually he came to realize they must have been crouched together inside the Quoit for a long time.

If Paul's arm had not been round her, she might not have stayed. She seemed to have become fluid enough not to break now, she could perhaps bear the weight of the stones. Her dread was still present, gurgling fiercely, a black spring disappearing through a narrow opening in the rock, sucking her down, in utter dark, where no light had ever been. The strong current would carry her down, there was no other way, she would have to go with it. Fear burnt and crackled like lightning, shorting off against the stones; there was a malignancy in it. Then she was gone, pressed down, falling, she would never be able to get back, she could never return – the old world, her old self – she was pouring away from them, driven by massive forces. Falling as if exploded out of an aeroplane, hurtling towards earth where the ocean waited like concrete; dropping between massive cliff heads, sheer and black as the sides of titanic battleships; tumbling round and round into black waters, through the layers where balloon-shaped fish glow with phosphorescence, to the substrata where only bacteria survive, and disappearing through a fissure in the ocean floor; falling as if floating away into the unending black hole of space, a fragment of ash whirling and whirling forever.

And then she was still, lying in the damp cramped darkness; and after a very long time, the darkness slowly turned into presence. Silvered outlines appeared and disappeared as if torchlight flitted across different corners of a tomb: massive stone pediments, folded wings and glimpses of features – great lidded oval eyes, a smooth, closed mouth – forming a face that was not a face, that darkened and changed like the moon, that turned still like stone. Jessica could not stop looking, and into its circle and out of its eyes the dead weight of past time, of millennia, ages upon ages poured heavily through her mind and body, as if some artery in the subconscious archives had suddenly ruptured, spewing out information from a bottomless pit that overwhelmed the fragile arena of consciousness. A foment of water and dust, fathoms spinning with shafts of blue echoed in the misty air above; the first moist running of waters, the rich swarm of oceans; rocks grinding slowly into shapes; cold stars patterning an empty sky. An endless, obscure development and subdivision of cells, the warming and cooling, slow, aeons of adjustment until the long wait began to flower into plants and creatures and humanoids and people, who helped to sew the web of inner and outer more definitely together, ordering and evolving pattern and design. The simple beginnings in lushness, the light clear and resonant: the turning wheel, clay pots, the turning of the soil, white pillars to symbolize the echo, the reflection of the high sky in its mirror. Everywhere the light in foliage, water, rolling like clouds over landscapes, breaking out of rock, flaring in the dark places.

And then, without warning, she was dropped into pain, a red river, twisting tendons, ribbons of muscle, contortions, volcanoes, lava burning across the land, boiling oceans, then the spreading ice-caps. White stones lay fractured and broken, a blade lay stained with blood, a man's face stared up at the sky where the light rises up in balls and ribbons, seeping out of eyes, out of rock, leaving. The images quickened, scenes flashed past like film whipping out of control through the gate. And then the images blurred and slowed: long piles of emaciated bodies, a mushroom cloud, white smoke clouds billowing up above the canopy of a forest. The images stopped: she saw a familiar circle of night held by thick ancient oaks trees, heard the hoot of an owl. The foliage rustled, there were men coming. She saw the outline of their weapons, and then the drilling whine of the chainsaw start up. As everything was ripped apart, she screamed: no meaning, no kindness, no coherence, and her scream was sucked into the black stream, its noise carried away into the abyss and she lay inert as if dead upon hard ground, earth that had not yet known age. As she stared out through the spaces between the stones, she saw the primordial world outside, and she knew it had always been there. It existed shining like the pure green waves, pollution suspended in it but not of it. She could go there if she wished. The landscape was the same but a little different. There was a silvery gleam over everything, yet there was no moon. She knew that if she went outside she would not see the farmhouse, or the roads, or Paul's camera case. The Sierra Estate would not be parked at the bottom of the hill. And she realized how fond she was of the eccentric details of the secondary world, and that she was not ready to leave. She wanted to stay and do her bit to join the worlds – and there was at least one urgent matter that required her presence. And then she saw the lights; they were flashing a signal – if she did not want to cross over, she must now leave.

Jessica stirred and blinked her eyes. Gripping Paul's arm, she pulled herself more upright, thus undoing the intricate knot that they had woven together. Paul, who had been staring thoughtfully at the granite capstone, turned to look at her.

'You OK Jess?' he asked.

Jessica nodded, frowning slightly. A sense of urgency overrode the stiff exhaustion that drenched her emotionally and physically. The interior of the Quoit looked as it had before: a few small boulders scattered on the hard mud floor, the uneven triangles of night sky at its corners, but the whole of its granite massiveness seemed to vibrate with the silent command to leave.

'Paul, we've got to get out of here.'

'Yes, we've been here a long time.'

'We don't want to be here any longer,' Jessica said, disentangling herself from him and crawling out of the entrance hole. Paul followed immediately behind. Outside, the night was as dark as it was going to get and they realized it was colder, the sea sighing beyond the cliffs with a new, chill wind.

They wanted only to go, to walk replete with enormous experience along the track up the small hill and down the other side. The night no longer held any fear, everything around them, the bracken and heather, the stone gate posts of Chûn Castle, the whispering sea, the farm outbuildings, even the waiting car had taken on that stark, simple wonder that is seen by people who've passed through great change. The car door clicked open, the yellow electric light went on and they got in. Paul spread his arm along the seat behind her and turned his head to reverse, and as the car wobbled its way back along the track Jessica hugged herself and shivered. Staring out into the night as they wound along the narrow roads, she searched out a word in her head, *shriven*, or *cleansed*, was what this was, how she felt; it wouldn't last, as they headed back to the rounds of daily life, but that was all right too, and anyway, there were the oak trees to rescue.

'Paul,' she said.

'Yeah,' Paul spoke in a soft monotone, staring out at the cat's eyes lighting up the curve of the road ahead.

'We've got to save the oaks – I think we've got to do it tonight.'

After a few moments Paul said, 'Mm, it's funny, but somehow that sounds more – I don't know, I'm not sure I could just go back to the hotel and try to go to sleep right now.' He paused. 'How are we going to do it?'

Steve was not pleased to be woken up at 2 am with an invitation to stake out an ancient oak grove, but Paul managed to persuade him it would make great television.

'But it's trees, not stones – how can I use it?'

'You don't use it in the film, you make it a news item. Local news for sure, it might even make Channel 4 News, you know, tarted up with interviews, an account of this guy's business empire and all that.'

Dave and Tony were cynical but resigned, hopeful as well of claiming overtime. Jessica woke up Cora and Adam, Jonathan, Uta, Helen, and, deciding to give him a chance to redeem himself, Bill. Soon they were all gathered in the hall, sleepiness turning to suppressed excitement.

They managed to pack everyone and the necessary gear into the two estate cars, with people sat on one another's laps, and Jonathan and Adam squeezed into the luggage compartment. They parked the cars in a turning a little distance away from the lane that led to the oaks. Jonathan was posted as watch. The others were distributed among the circle of oaks, while lights, camera and sound were set ready. Then they all waited.

'How did you find out about this?' Steve asked Paul in an undertone.

'Jessica had a premonition.'

Steve stared at Paul open-mouthed, then he smiled. 'Oh yeah.'

'No, I'm serious, that's how we know.'

'Christ, Paul, you of all people!'

Paul said nothing.

'But if it's a bloody premonition how do we know when it's going to happen? I mean, it could be tonight, it could be a few days from now – or it could be never.'

Jessica was standing a little way off. She could hear Steve remonstrating with Paul. At first, she had felt only relief that they had arrived before the attack. No damage had been done, the trees rustled in the darkness in all their glory. Now she felt an edge of panic bite into her as she thought through the implications if nothing happened. It would be difficult to bring everyone back the next night, they might miss them. She overheard Steve's indignant voice again and caught the words 'the crew' and 'overtime'. Suddenly she turned her head away and strained to listen above their voices. She thought she heard the noise of engines turning over and then cutting out.

'Ssssh!' she motioned to Paul and Steve. The invisible circle of people tensed, Dave readied the camera on his shoulder. The slight crackling and breaking of undergrowth signalled Jonathan's approach. 'They're here,' he hissed.

Then more and louder crackling and breaking, torchlights – Paul nudged Steve. 'Start the film rolling.'

Steve nodded, but waited two seconds more, before speaking quietly the magic words, 'Lights, action.' The cobalt lights exploded into white, flooding the dappled night with bright light. At the same instant the silence was filled with the whining drill of chainsaws, and the shouts of the intruders as they were blinded by the lights and stunned at the spectacle of various long-haired divas of the land with their arms tightly embracing the wide girth of the threatened oaks.